To Mike & MaryKay Stay out of the Triangle !

Ty Jodouin

Voyage to Oblivion

By

Ty Jodouin

authorHOUSE™

1663 LIBERTY DRIVE, SUITE 200
BLOOMINGTON, INDIANA 47403
(800) 839-8640
WWW.AUTHORHOUSE.COM

First published by AuthorHouse 11/02/04

ISBN: 1-4208-0130-9 (e)
ISBN: 1-4208-0129-5 (sc)

Library of Congress Control Number: 2004097336

Printed in the United States of America
Bloomington, Indiana

This book is printed on acid-free paper.

ACKNOWLEDGEMENT

To Barb and Bob Wetzel, for their expert technical advice; to Bob Noonan for his excellent editing and sound counsel; and especially to my wife, Helen, for her never-ending support and encouragement throughout my vain attempts to achieve literary stardom.

DEDICATION

Dedicated to a future Captain Richardson, who will dare venture into the mysterious depths of the Bermuda Triangle someday...but never reach their next port o' call.

CHAPTER ONE

*Bermuda Triangle, seven miles east of Puerto Rico
-- 12:55 p.m.*

Tom Blocker's adrenaline was running at fever pitch. It was as if the athletically built 38-year-old from Nevada had taken a dose of speed. He could feel the fiery passion of anticipation mounting with every breath. It all began the moment he had stepped aboard the 45-foot Dominican Republic fishing boat, the *Hispaniola*. After pausing for a brief moment, forcing his body to relax and letting the events of the day catch up to his racing pulse, a twisted grin slowly split his face. All of a sudden it struck him as a piece of irony that the boat took its name from an island originally discovered by Christopher Columbus.

He glanced over the gunwale at the slow moving swells. The old scow probably wasn't going any faster than what the caravel, *Santa Maria*, had managed in the explorer's day either, he reflected wryly. In his mind that didn't matter, as long as the oscillating deck under his feet got him to where he was going.

The boat had a large, patched, sun-washed canopy over the middle deck space, which was barely providing enough shade for the crowd of people laughing, drinking, and generally bent on having a good time. He gazed at them disdainfully. For many of them, this venture was only an excuse to party. To Tom Blocker, their revelry was a mark of disrespect. He came from the old school of business before pleasure. And for someone who had devoted countless hours to the study of Atlantis, learning to appreciate its nuances, its subtleties, diving on the legendary lost continent was like recapturing a glimpse of what was once mankind's golden age. *After all, the opportunity may only come along once or twice in a lifetime.*

True, there were only traces of Atlantis left now, just scattered pieces of collapsed walls and broken stonework languishing on the ocean floor. But that's where the paradox lay. Contrary to archaeological discoveries of recent decades, historians were still challenging the sunken lands' reputation as having been the world's most scientifically advanced civilization. Skeptics would tell you it was only an ancient legend, born from the imagination of a Greek philosopher named Plato. On the flip side, proponents claimed the legitimacy of Atlantis came through the dissertations of Solon, an Athenian lawgiver. He attained this knowledge from Egyptian priests whose temple records antedated those of the Greeks by thousands of years. As a result of this universal tug of war between philosophies, Atlantis became a hotly debated topic that has never been resolved.

Regardless, its controversial standing still demanded a bit more respect, he thought. To the true believer, Atlantis was the original homeland of us all. It was also the focus of a smoldering dream ready to burst anew inside him.

A serendipitous opportunity had presented itself 20 years ago when he was in the Navy attending Officer Candidate School in Pensacola. That chance occasion came at a time when the fabled continent was just starting to arouse public interest again. The first time it exploded on the international scene was back in 1968 when the famous *Bimini Wall* was discovered.

Now, as before, perfectly formed underwater ellipses, circles, and squares were frequently being sighted from the air in several locations of the Bahamas, indicating *man-made* rock formations. These latest discoveries, after years of futile searching, propelled the sunken civilization back on everyone's lips almost overnight. Paleontologists had repeatedly shunned the thought of a prehistoric civilization ever existing in the Atlantic. No more. Not since Ignatius Donnelly's best seller, *"Atlantis: Myths of the Antediluvian World,* published in 1882, was such a renewed awareness being indelibly etched in the human psyche. Divers were finding artifacts and unexplained formations lying at the bottom of the Atlantic's continental shelves that provided irrefutable proof of ancient habitation. Further examination revealed artificially constructed stone buildings and temples of cyclopean proportions. Cyclopean, in archeological terms, meant antediluvian—before the Great Flood. Atlantis definitely fell into that category.

3

Tom's first exposure to Atlantis all began when his Navy buddies had finagled a way out to one of the Berry Islands aboard an instructor's 27-foot cabin cruiser. It was the latest craze site where, as slim as the chances might be, a bona-fide statuette or piece of amphora could bring a handsome reward to the lucky owner.

To Tom, a man born and bred in the desert, it all sounded excitingly new, so he had eagerly decided to tag along. His lifelong curiosity about the underwater world was about to be realized. As luck would have it, these particular ruins rested in relatively shallow water, so mask, snorkel, and fins were the only equipment needed to enter a wonderfully new environment that he had never experienced before. Up until then he couldn't understand why people got so aroused examining a bunch of antiquated stone and mortar buried under tons of water. But that was before the magic and mystique of Atlantis captured his imagination. That was before further traces of the drowned continent started making a dramatic resurgence. Artifacts were continually being discovered further down the Bermuda chain for example, near the Turks and Caicos Islands and into the shallow depths of the Caribbean. Roads, temples, carved pillars, statues, and most baffling, concentric circles of giant dolmens resembling the likes of Stonehenge and Avebury. It all added up to more evidence that a far-flung civilization had once existed in the western Atlantic.

Then, as the years passed, and as a result of seaquakes, violent storms and the development of better locator devices, more ruins eventually shed their cover of sand and sea grass. This time they revealed themselves further afield in such out-of-the-way places as the Azores and Canary Islands, and off the coasts of Yucatan and Venezuela. Not just ordinary ruins, mind you, but pyramids measuring larger dimensions than anything yet found in Egypt, Mexico, or Central America. Some were even bigger than the gigantic pyramids found in China. Their existence proved, beyond a doubt, that there was a common origin of architecture between the Old and the New Worlds—Atlantis.

Tom could feel the flutter in his stomach all over again. A lifetime had passed since his Navy days when he had first splashed beneath the waves in true neophyte fashion, and witnessed the last remaining vestiges of a grand world culture come to life before his very eyes. It had only whetted his appetite for more. Some people that knew him intimately might have described it as the beginning of a burgeoning obsession.

Now he was about to experience it all over again. A shiver of excitement rippled down his spine. Hurricane Minerva had provided him with another such opportunity, and he found himself silently thanking the gods of chance once again. Just a week before, the devastating Category 5 hurricane had ripped through the area like a ripsaw, exposing additional underwater constructions, this time off the coast of Puerto Rico. Again, what appeared to be threadlike lines signifying stone walls, which even looked like clusters of buildings to some, had been spotted from the air, always a red flag to hunters on the lookout for underwater anomalies. But what was even more intriguing was that giant domes had been added to the mix, inexplicably discovered in places previously found empty. These shallow coastal depths of the continental shelf had been scoured repeatedly by countless storms and nothing was ever found by divers before except turtle corrals or beach rock. Tom figured the next storm could easily come along and bury whatever new evidence came to light. This could be his last chance.

It was just by the protective hand of the Almighty that he and Tricia and the two boys, Richey and Tom Jr., went unscathed; the full fury of the hurricane missing them by scant kilometers. They'd been vacationing at a place called Sharky's Beach Resort on Chatter's Cay when the giant storm struck. Chatter's Cay was just west of Tortola, one of those tucked-away Robinson Crusoe hideaways lost within the larger conglomerate of the British Virgin Islands. Instead, Minerva ended her destructive rampage by swinging northeast and battering Puerto Rico mercilessly with 180-mph winds before expending herself out at sea. It had been a close call. Their little island paradise had just escaped with only a toppled palm tree and some roof shingles ripped off one or two bungalows.

Tom squinted out past the guardrail. He was wearing dark shades, but the glare of the sun bouncing off the shimmering blue-green water was still intense. He wiped the sweat off his brow with a towel he had draped around his neck. The Caribbean sun seemed a lot hotter than the desert sun he was used to. Humidity was higher, making it seem as if he were inside a pressure cooker. But the weather was perfect for diving, and to him that was all that mattered — a cloudless blue sky with the sun high, to eliminate shadows and maximize visibility. The sea was as smooth as a millpond, making it appear like glass. It would be excellent for diving — if they ever got to where they were going, a place called Skeleton Reef.

He was starting to get anxious. The ride out was taking longer than he expected. Off to the west he recognized the 113-mile-long island of Puerto Rico as a large dark smudge on the horizon. *It shouldn't be long now*, he thought. Then, in the near distance, not more than a mile away, he spied what Carlos Mendoza, *Hispaniola's* captain, was aiming for; a superannuated 150-foot steel-hulled ketch flying the Haitian flag. The sides were streaked red with rust and were in bad need of scraping and painting.

As they approached to within hailing distance, Tom saw at the stern a large A-frame and winch. There seemed to be a flurry of activity around it as he made out some kind of torpedo-shaped, two-man submersible being lowered into the water.

"Those are the scientists I was tellin' you about," Carlos yelled over his shoulder to anyone listening, pointing a callused finger through a salt-encrusted windshield. He was wearing a yellowed, sweat-stained T-shirt and matching shorts that Tom guessed had once passed for white. Bare-footed and with a yellow straw hat to match the rest of his outfit, Carlos sat propped on a high leather stool inside a small, partially enclosed deckhouse.

The boat was open on both ends, and had been converted to accommodate about a dozen divers with full gear. A bank of 5000-cubic foot air cylinders with fill-hoses attached, were secured inside what had once been fish storage tanks. Twin 250-horse Chrysler diesels rumbled deep below the worn steel deck. The craft wasn't built for speed or comfort, Tom admitted, just convenience. Carlos had made it a point to tell Tom that it was the only dive boat in the islands with large enough gas tanks to take him this far out into the Atlantic and back to Chatter's Cay without refueling.

"Is this where we're diving?" someone hollered.

"No, mon," Carlos answered. "We will follow the reef into a little bit deeper water. Don' worry. There is plenty to see for everyone." He flashed a toothy grin across his black, featureless face. It was a pose that made most people feel he had their best interest at heart. But Tom wasn't so sure that it wasn't more of a condescending sneer.

It somehow reminded him of the cold, calculating stare he had received when brushing past a couple of odd-looking passengers earlier that morning. Although their eyes were shielded by wrap-around Polaroids, he could sense an overpowering malevolence behind them. One of them was quite tall, and could easily have passed for a pro-basketball center. The other character only came up to his partner's waist but displayed the same olive-skin features. Their look had given him such an uncomfortable feeling that Tom couldn't quite erase the sense of foreboding it had ingrained in his mind.

Gazing past the seated Carlos, Tom could see the dark outlines of the two men silhouetted against the brilliant opaline sky. They were sitting by themselves on a small bench at the very bow of the boat, staring fixedly out at sea. Neither had made a move to mix with the crowd. Both were dressed like pallbearers, wearing black pants and black turtlenecks under black sport coats, topped with black fedoras to match their funereal attire. They seemed completely oblivious to the hot sun, or the carnival atmosphere around them. Carlos didn't seem to pay any attention to them. Nor did anyone else, for that matter. *Very strange*, Tom thought.

"Hey honey, stop daydreaming. It's time to get suited up!"

The cry promptly snapped Tom back to the present. It came from his wife, Tricia, as her smiling blond head looked back at him from across the milling throng. She was standing near the stern of the boat where a wide step-down was attached to the outside hull, for easy accessibility to the water. Tom saw that she and the boys already had their wet suits on, and were in the process of strapping on their buoyancy control vests.

While he had been reminiscing, the sounds of merriment had toned down dramatically to an annoying murmur. Only the gentle swishing of water against the hull and the purring of well-tuned motors continued to be a soothing anesthetic to him. It seemed the majority of people around him had broken off into small groups and were in various stages of suiting up also. *I'd better get my ass in gear too*, Tom thought quickly. He wanted to be ready when Carlos dropped anchor.

There was a myriad of dive tanks and scuba equipment scattered about the open deck, clogging every available space. Tom guessed that Carlos had taken on more passengers than what he normally booked, because there wasn't much room to step around as he made his way aft. He had counted 14 divers altogether, including him and his family. They ranged in age from Bobby, the son of a young couple from Toronto, who was the youngest at 12, to Frank and his wife, Alice, both in their 60s. Except for tanks and weight belts, which were usually furnished by a charter boat skipper anyway, the usual paraphernalia of his fellow divers included a rich collection of accessories. They ranged from state-of-the-art, hand-held magnetometers to the latest in underwater flash photography.

Tom briefly glanced over his own equipment. It consisted of just the standard hardware, nothing fancy. He didn't believe in extravagance. High on his list of essentials, however, was what some divers considered optional in the islands — a neoprene wet suit. He and Tricia had dived all over the Caribbean and had learned by long experience that, under prolonged exposure, even the bath-water temperature of a tropical sea can sap one's body heat like a ravenous leech.

He stepped over to where the air bottles were stored, searching for one that registered on the air gauge just a few extra pounds more above the full mark. He knew that a generous supply of compressed air would give him that extra boost he would need to stay down longer.

Tom could see that Carlos was steering the *Hispaniola* past the scientist's boat, following the irregular outline of the reef. Casting a glance over the side of the boat, Tom saw that the brilliant colors of coral were slowly receding. They were definitely heading into deeper water. His gaze involuntarily followed the path of the shallow plateau until it disappeared into the bottomless depths. Diverting his eyes above the transom, toward where sea and sky merged into nothingness, he couldn't help but give a small shudder. Within that enormous expanse of ocean lay the infamous Bermuda Triangle—or its southern fringe, anyway.

Tom had spent a lot of time studying this mysterious body of water. It supposedly extended east from Puerto Rico to about 40 degrees west before angling back north to Bermuda, its most northern terminus. According to Plato, this was where earthquakes had reduced Atlantis into an archipelago of smaller islands.

Tom had read of the debate between geologists that added an addendum to the controversy surrounding Atlantis. Critics sited core samples that revealed rock strata of volcanic basalt too anomalous to support a presupposed landmass in the middle of the Atlantic Ocean. On the flip side, the ocean floor was continually renewing itself through a phenomenon called sea-floor spreading. Earth's seething liquid mantle was continually seeking new avenues of escape by venting itself through a network of weak fissures dotting the globe. Scientists had even proven this through the discovery of hydrothermal vents producing giant smoke chimneys, found mainly in the deepest ocean crevasses and trenches. Some reached as high as 15-story buildings. Once cooled and solidified, the fresh magma constantly kept redefining the earth's crust.

The continents, on the other hand, riding on a patchwork of moving plates, were constantly being spread apart by these geothermal paroxysms. Where

11

two moving plates ground together one had to give, eventually slipping under the other. It was a process called subduction.

Unfortunately the North American Plate, on which Atlantis was riding, fell into that category. What was left of the magnificent civilization was slowly disappearing under the weight of these titanic forces. Tom figured that in the next few thousand years, tectonic changes would erase completely the last traces of the former continent. He was going to make sure he saw as much as he could of it first.

"Carlos!" he yelled. "How deep are you bringing us?"

"Not deep, Senor. Maybe 50 feet." He gave a desultory wave to his assistant, a Panamanian mulatto of tiny stature with darting eyes and a nervous facial tic. Tom saw the native was pandering to a pair of loud, boisterous firemen from Schenectady. They were guzzling an inordinate amount of Cuban whiskey, he thought. Drinking before a dive was asking for trouble. Tom's frown grudgingly softened into a bemused smirk. *What the hell. It was Christmas season.*

"Miguel!" Carlos ordered. "Stand by the anchor. Drop it when I say."

By the time Miguel finally staggered to the bow, Tom had suited up and was assembling his regulator to a tank he had managed to find bulging with 250 pounds of extra air.

Tricia sidled up next to him, giving him a disapproving look. "Time to get wet, don't you think?"

"You got that right sweetheart" he replied in a Bogie accent. As an afterthought he gently gave her a playful smack on the rear. *It won't be long now.*

CHAPTER TWO

Somewhere in the Bermuda Triangle -- 1:43 p.m.

The 6-foot 2-inch detective shimmied his lanky frame down the anchor chain as fast as his muscular arms would take him. He had discovered a long time ago that it was the fastest way to propel oneself down from an anchored boat. He stopped and swiveled effortlessly three feet off the bottom, eyes agape like a preying hawk. He quickly inspected where the anchor had lodged itself into a hunk of coral. Mixed hordes of fish were already swimming around the rusty flukes in a dazzling display of riotous harmony. *Fantastic!* he thought.

The water was crystal clear. Had to be 200 feet in all directions, he figured. All around him was a virtual garden of exotic colors and movement: white and orange striped clownfish darting in and out of crevices filled with spiny lobster, a blue-girdled angelfish hanging motionless next to elegant purple sea fans waving to and fro in the soft current, shafts of golden sunlight dancing in between large clusters of brain and staghorn corals. The detective's body literally quivered with excitement. The weightlessness made his head giddy. He waited with growing impatience for his family to join him.

Something he had spotted earlier from the boat had grabbed his attention, something pushing its way up through the sea floor that he thought, at the time, might prove interesting. He quickly acknowledged the fact that it might be artificial—the first signs of Atlantis! *Mysterious looking spheres had been reported from the air in this general locale,* he reminded himself. While in the process of reconnoitering, however, Tom realized Carlos had landed them in deeper water than originally planned. The boat was sitting atop a small guyot, or seamount. Its crusty backbone was littered with voluminous amounts of black lava globules, strangely mixed with sparse pockets of crushed coral and marine growth. A small volcanic elevation from one of earth's hiccups that never made it to the surface, Tom surmised.

A sudden chill coursed through his body. He glanced around, anticipating something unexpected. It took an extra effort on his part to shrug it off. It seemed odd that he should feel such an overpowering sense of desolation around him. *Maybe that's why they called it Skeleton Reef.*

His gaze gravitated into the distance, toward the infinite blackness of the abyss, where the shelf he was perched on inexplicably ended. There, he knew, the sun stopped shining. The abyssal plain was one of earth's lowest depressions, filled by miles of mysterious, depthless ocean. His body shuddered reflexively at the thought of what sea creatures might lay beyond. He was quite satisfied to just hang onto the anchor chain in the comparative shallows and wait.

Seconds later Tricia and the boys were grouping around him, their eyes bright with wonder. It felt comforting to have company. He motioned quickly for them to follow his lead. Not more than 50 yards away loomed a series of linear formations that reminded him of giant loaves of bread laid out in a straight line. *Nothing in the ocean grows in a straight line,* he silently told himself.

With the natural magnification of the water, the objects seemed tantalizingly within reach. Out of the corner of his eye, under the shadow of the boat, he could see the rest of their merry party thrashing around near the surface. Some were even breaking off from the group and advancing toward them in a lazy, deliberate fashion. *I've got to hurry!*

Tom's powerful jet fins propelled him over the broken coral in a smooth, effortless glide. In between were patches of white beach sand that made him speculate in the back of his mind as to what its presence indicated. Sand meant wave action. Sometime in the remote past this underwater seascape had been on the surface, as part of an island perhaps, he guessed.

He stopped short as the closest of the objects he had zeroed in on suddenly materialized into sharp focus. His heart skipped a beat. Part of what he was gawking at was covered by drifting sand, but there was no mistaking their artificiality—perfectly cut polygonal blocks of flint-hard micrite stone fitted so tightly together that he doubted he could slip a sheet of paper between them. Beach rock, as many geologists would probably claim they were, was out of the question. Each monolith was over 20 feet thick, with rounded edges sheared off to precise measurement. There were dozens of them poking in and out of the sand, and they all seemed to be linked together to form a contiguous barrier. *Shades of the Bimini Wall!*

Narrowing his eyes, Tom warily followed their line of flight until their spectral outlines disappeared like wraiths into the gloom. *Something strange about them*, he thought. There was definitely a purpose for their presence, perhaps as part of a wall or road, but it was hard to determine what.

As he continued to cautiously track their progress, using slow, rhythmic kicks, he realized their magic was acting like a powerful magnet, leading him and his family into deeper water.

It was almost imperceptible at first, but Tom soon began to recognize the first signs of deteriorating conditions around him. The colorlessness of the coral and the abundance of dead flora were the first indicators. And the sunlight was just barely reflecting its warm radiance in what was once an earthy glow. The fine chalk sand had taken on the texture of dark gravel, and the water had definitely gotten colder. Visibility was half the distance of what it had been originally. Strangest of all, the rich variety of fish had suddenly disappeared.

Without warning the wall of stones vanished, leaving a void where there was once continuity. Like bubble-breathing creatures from another world, Tom and his family suddenly were hovering at the brink of a deep, wide crevasse. Peering over the edge, he could only guess what had happened. The seabed had somehow convulsed in a giant cataclysm that was lost in the mists of time, creating a rupture 40 feet deep. The breadth of the crater became lost in an amalgam of shadows, leaving him perplexed as to its true size.

Sitting on the bottom, a half-buried hemisphere gleamed innocuously in the washed-out light, like a burrowing genetically altered scarab beetle. He paused briefly, the adrenaline racing through his veins, his heart pounding with excitement. This was something new, something he had never seen before. Whatever the object was, he had an uncanny feeling there would be more.

As a group, Tom, Tricia, and the boys descended to the bottom of the gorge in lazy spirals. At the base of the cliff they found that the stone blocks surprisingly picked up where they had left off. Their direction led to a scattering of more domes, enigmatically emerging out of the gloom. Tricia and the boys stopped to stare, their eyes the size of owls through their masks. They knew as well as Tom did that a higher intelligence was at work here.

He shot a quick glance over his shoulder. Some of their group was trailing them, but still a good distance away. They didn't seem to be in any hurry. *Good. We still have time to be first on the scene.* Using sign language, Tom hastily motioned everyone to stay together. When he was sure everyone understood, the big Nevadan wheeled impatiently toward the nearest dome.

The closer he got, the more Tom was convinced his first hunch was right—the domes were part of a larger complex. *Maybe a storage facility*, he speculated. The one he was approaching was as big as a house. It didn't take much imagination to wonder what its overall dimensions must be beneath the sand. It had to be enormous. His pulse quickened. He sensed what treasure hunters must have felt when diving on sunken 16th-century galleons for the first time. Atlantis promised even greater rewards. His mind's eye kept conjuring up visions of ornate temples and glittering palaces filled with gold. In reality, he had to admit that whatever remained of the ancient island continent still lay hidden under tons of sediment. Its true value would never be realized, except in the minds of archeologists and dreamers like him. But sometimes the sea revealed its secrets, if ever so fleetingly.

Like this innocuous salmon-colored circular anomaly looming over him, for instance. It had a strange aura. As he approached, the ghostly orb filled his field of vision like an onrushing truck. He stuck out his hand and braked by touching it gently. He rubbed his gloved fingers over the smooth surface. His suspicion that the dome was metallic was immediately confirmed.

He slowly began inching his way forward, examining it with the eagle eye of a brain surgeon doing a pre-op diagnostic. He followed the curvature of the mysterious object like a fruit fly cruising over a giant orange. He marveled at its polished exterior. There didn't appear to be a crack or seam of any kind to mar its symmetry.

He surmised there had to be an entrance, some kind of opening into the structure, which he wasn't able to detect right away. As he crossed to the other side he discovered that more of the sphere was protruding above the sand, although its overall dimensions remained frustratingly hidden. He really had no idea what the object was, although he thought he had initially felt a small tingling sensation when he first touched it.

If only another storm would come along and finish the job, he silently entreated. On second thought, a hurricane as powerful as the one that had uncovered the objects could very well have the opposite effect and cover them again for all time.

He had a sudden crazy idea. Now was the time to act, before it was too late. He could rent an airlift, the kind commercial divers used to remove sand from around buried treasure. With the boys to assist him, he could have one of these babies uncovered in no time. But he would have to hurry, before the authorities declared the area an archeological site. Maybe his business partner, Matt, would like to get in on the act. It was hard to imagine that the phlegmatic detective wouldn't be at least a little interested. It wasn't everyday one had the chance to capture the thrill of discovering something built by his predawn ancestors.

He was ready to renew his inspection when something subtle nudged the back of his brain. Call it a feeling, a presentiment if you will, but whatever it was, it honed his sense of awareness like a fine tuning fork. His instincts immediately told him something was wrong. Long frigid icicles slithered down his backside as a strange vibration suddenly rippled over his body. *What in the hell was that?*

Simultaneously, a low rumbling penetrated the sound of his pounding heartbeat. Suspended vertically, he whirled around in panic. *Where were Tricia and the boys?* He realized with a start that they weren't with him. Lost in his reverie, he had completely forgotten about them.

Suddenly, out of the corner of his eye, he caught movement. He turned, hoping it was his wife or one of the boys, but it was several stragglers from their group instead. Some had already reached the drop-off and were beginning to clamber over the edge, heading his way. *No! No!* He wanted them to stop. They must turn back!

His head began to spin out of control. His grasp of what was happening around him was suddenly relegated to a series of speeded-up images, tumbling over each other in a chain of confused patterns. It was as if he was a spectator watching a Stephen King movie being played in fast-forward. Somehow he knew something terrible was about to happen, and he could do nothing to stop it. He could sense it as surely as if a gun was pointed at his back. The hairs prickled at the back of his neck. Instinctively cringing, he slowly pivoted in the direction of the unseen threat.

From 60 feet away Tom saw it -- the black, gaping maw of an open dome. Tricia and the boys were hovering over it like fixed statues. "Don't just stand there!" he screamed into his mouthpiece. "Move! Move away!"

He started toward them in a burst of panic, his legs pumping like pistons. But it was as if he was swimming against a powerful current persistently pushing him back. He kicked as hard as he could, until his legs ached. His breath came in short gasps. Finally, excruciating seconds later, he reached Richey, the closest of the trio. Tom grabbed the boy's shoulder and swung him around, shaking him.

But there was no reaction. His young son's eyes were locked in morbid fascination at something he was seeing inside the dome.

Tom's guts tightened into a hard knot. He forced himself to follow the direction of his son's gaze. What he saw made his blood freeze. At the same time, its beauty mesmerized him.

His brain could only describe it as a magnificent, whirling kaleidoscope of light. It was emanating from inside a brilliant, cylindrical crystal radiating with pure energy. At its narrowed apex burned a white-hot capstone that glowed with the incandescence of a thousand suns. The entire assembly was mounted on a telescopic device that was slowly unraveling itself. *That's where the rumbling was coming from,* he realized. Then the rumbling stopped, and the big Nevadan's mind and body ceased to exist.

It all happened too quickly for Tom to fully understand. His whole being was instantaneously ripped apart by livid pain; his senses were frozen in eternity. Something inexplicably occurred that only a fraction of the neuro-centers in his brain were able to conceptualize before becoming extinct. The water around him had suddenly become energized with voluminous concentrations of radiation, which literally baked his insides alive within nanoseconds. The exterior of his torso was the first to incinerate, as large layers of skin inside his wet suit instantaneously peeled away like rotten flesh. His blood boiled briefly at a million degrees before evaporating inside shriveling, blackened cords of viscera that were once life-pumping vessels. Super-heated air vaporized his lungs, frying his throat and tongue into charred strips of desiccated sinew. His face became a bug-eyed caricature of inhumanity, a grotesque death mask of melted flesh and bone. The last lucid image his cooked brain was able to envisage from a pair of cauterized retinas was the grisly skeletal remains of his family, floating in a blazing arena of light.

CHAPTER THREE

Green Valley, Nevada -- 4:07 a.m.

A shrill cry of terror stabbed the blackness of deep sleep. Matt Benner's eyes popped open as though they had been traumatized. He had been in the middle of an erotic dream before being brutally yanked back to wakefulness.

Again, an ear-piercing scream filled the air.

"Wha ... " Matt's body tensed and became instantly alert. Not waiting for his thoughts to collect, he catapulted out of bed. The sounds were coming from the downstairs bedroom, he realized. His daughter, Stacey, was down there.

Taking the stairs two steps at a time, he reached the bottom landing in record time. He was sucking in air as if he had just run a 40-yard dash. "Damn, I gotta lose some weight," he cursed softly. To beat all, he ended up stepping barefoot on one of the dog's knurled bones, with sharp edges. The pain shooting up his leg caused another bout of expletives to tumble out of his mouth. Then came the clincher, silently and without warning; a blazing ball of light the size of a grapefruit barreling out of the darkness toward him.

He had just enough time to duck before it disappeared around the corner of the living room wall. *What the hell* ..

While his brain censors were trying to analyze what was happening, another bloodcurdling scream let loose from behind the bedroom door next to him. Blindly he threw it open. By now his nervous system had released enough adrenaline in his body to overpower a sumo wrestler. His heart was pumping pure octane.

There was just enough moonlight slicing through the venetian blinds to make out shadowy outlines in the darkened room. His 15-year-old daughter was sitting up in bed, head pressed against a pillow next to the headboard, the covers drawn up tightly to her chin. Her face was contorted with fear, her eyes as big as saucers.

"What's wrong, honey? Having a nightmare?"

At first she just stared at him with disbelieving eyes, as if he were some kind of monster. Normally Stacey's big brown eyes reminded him of a Shirley Temple doll, but that was not the case now. For the moment, they had the crazed look of a trapped animal.

"Th ... tho ... those men," she stammered. "They were standing at the foot of my bed." Her voice was almost hysterical.

Matt's wife, Barbara, came bursting into the room. Trailing behind her was their 13-year-old son, Terry, rubbing the sleep out of his eyes.

"What happened?" Barb interjected, her eyes darting from Stacey back to her husband.

"What men?" Matt pressed, as he edged closer to the bed. "What did they look like?"

Barb sat next to Stacey on the bed and put his arm around the trembling girl's shoulders. Her whole body was making the bed vibrate.

"They … they were giants. They wore robes and their heads were covered with hoods. Two of them. They were just standing there, staring at me. I could see their eyes … horrible eyes. They were red … and glowing. I asked them what they wanted but they wouldn't answer. Instead … my head started to feel funny … like something was trying to enter my thoughts. And then, when I screamed, they just turned around and walked through that wall," she said, pointing toward the outside wall with a shaking finger.

Matt glanced in that direction. The wall separated the room from the pool deck … and on the other side of that, open desert.

"When you say giants, how tall are we talking about?" Matt insisted. People often mistook their assailant's height, especially under stress.

"Their heads almost touched the ceiling, Dad," Stacey replied emphatically. "They were really tall." Matt knew they would have to be, to reach the bedroom's 9-foot ceiling.

It was when his wife turned on the bedside lamp that he noticed a red splotch on the sheet, near where Stacey's head was scrunched against the pillow. It appeared to be blood.

Barb saw it too. "Honey, your nose is bleeding."

Stacey's trembling hand instinctively went to her nose, leaving a small smear of red on her finger. She looked at it inquisitively.

"I ... I have no idea why," she answered haltingly. But she had the strange look of someone trying to sort out some unimaginable dilemma in her mind. Matt had seen that same look on victims who had just suffered some traumatic event in their lives.

His eyes made a quick turn around the room before focusing back on Stacey. Everything appeared normal. "Are you sure you weren't just having a nightmare?"

"I'm sure, Dad. I was wide-awake. I kept asking them what they were doing in my room. They ... they just kept staring at me with those awful eyes," she said, sobbing.

"Okay, I believe you. Barb, you and the kids stay put while I look around outside."

He stepped back in to the hallway, glancing furtively from left to right, hunching his shoulders like a fullback in case he ran into any more of those flying lights. He wanted to be ready this time. But nothing occurred out of the ordinary as he made his way back upstairs to the bedroom. He managed to avoid any more bones as he flipped on every light switch he could find. On the upper shelf of the closet he found, after a long arm's reach, what he was looking for. It was his .38 Colt Python Revolver, which he kept loaded and ready for emergencies such as this.

Compared to today's small arms weaponry, it was an antique. But it was good enough for what he had in mind. Burglars breaking into houses were his specialty. An ex-cop turned detective, he hated punks who wore robes and hoods and thought they could intimidate people. The fact that they were tall punks with glowing eyes didn't make a hangman's difference to him. They could have been basketball players wearing masks. Slipping on a robe and slippers, he walked back downstairs, his mind mulling the situation. The one thing that bothered Matt's sense of logic, however, was Stacey's insistence that the intruders walked through the bedroom wall. *And that flying ball of light. What the hell was that all about?*

At the entrance to the patio by the sliding doors he almost bowled over Basher, their 5-year-old German Shepherd. The dog normally slept outside on the patio, but since the nights had turned unseasonably cold lately, Barb had allowed him to sleep inside. A small whine could be heard as the dog struggled to its feet. *He doesn't seem to be in any hurry to greet the new day*, Matt thought. It was almost as though the dog was drugged. With all the commotion going on, Matt would have thought the overgrown mutt would have been barking its head off.

Outside, the desert night air felt invigorating. Matt shivered slightly. *Should have put my jacket on.* No matter what anybody said, deserts can get abysmally cold at night.

He stopped to look around. Even from a distance of 20 miles the lights of Las Vegas could be seen, the flashy neon reflecting a pink glow against the surrounding Spring Mountains and the Sierra Nevada. He and his family lived right at the edge of the Comstock District, one of the last reserves of arid wasteland that made up the Great Basin Desert. Matt liked the openness and privacy it provided, although he knew that was changing rapidly. There would be more mega-hotels, more casinos that would rival the Taj Mahal, until the entire valley was overflowing with people to service them. Once that happened, he would find a deserted island in the middle of the ocean somewhere.

His eyes adjusted quickly to the shadowy moonlight. He felt vulnerable and exposed to attack. He shrugged it off. There was no way anybody could jump him out here in the open like this. Nevertheless, he kept his gun at the ready, just in case. If there were somebody out there, he would let them know directly he wasn't taking any prisoners.

Walking boldly to the edge of the concrete, he tried to ferret out any movement among the cactus and mesquite that bordered his one-acre lot. Six-foot privacy fences separated him from his neighbors on either side, ending where the desert began. The only trees big enough to hide somebody were the Joshuas scattered in clumps like crouching sentinels. Barb had planted them when they had first moved there 15 years ago, to break up the monotony of sagebrush and creosote bushes. Their stucco split-level was one of hundreds similarly built and landscaped on a 500-acre plot. Matt always figured their exact likeness was some grand scheme that the builder fiendishly devised to drive a drunk bonkers when trying to find his way home. Otherwise, the dark terrain remained bleak and empty.

As he stepped out onto the desert's hard-packed sand, the soles of his slippers made ridges that reminded him of the astronaut's footprints on the moon. Matt stared at the ground with a wary eye. It was not unheard of for diamondbacks, sidewinders, scorpions, and tarantulas to greet unsuspecting trespassers. He cautiously slipped from one shadow to the next, the .38 handy. A brilliant gibbous moon hung low on the horizon, etching the shadows deeply on the desert floor. The millions of stars dotting the heavens gave the added touch, enough pale light to provide him an unobstructed view of a surrealistic moonscape.

There was no telltale sign of anything that resembled footprints. Whoever had been there had long vanished into the night.

Just as he convinced himself it was time to go back and resume that dream, he saw something that could only be described as odd—a blotch of shadows with a distinct pattern. Thinking they were only a peculiar configuration of shallow depressions, he had almost overlooked them. But something red-flagged his alert centers. In his profession, it was always wise to pay attention to your body's subliminal signals. In other words, play your hunches.

He studied the markings closely. Sure enough, there was an unmistakable artificiality to them. These were not shallow traces made by some sage grouse or coyote, he was certain. They were deeply set, made by something big and heavy.

His eyes scanned three symmetrically shaped indentations, 10 to 12 feet apart, forming a perfect triangle. *A machine?* He bent closer. They reminded him of landing pads that had flattened the soil five to six inches deep, under tremendous pressure.

Matt's eyes took on a thoughtful look. UFOs? A whole rash of them had been reported buzzing the desert skies lately. Could one of them have landed in his back yard? *Nonsense!* He didn't believe in such rubbish. Some animal he hadn't come across yet probably made the markings.

Matt widened his search area to include anything within 100 yards of the house. Frustration began to set in. *If a UFO had landed, why hadn't any of the neighbors seen it?* He mentally kicked himself. The fact that it was 4 o'clock in the morning might have something to do with it. He spread his arms in a display of mock despair. *Where are those Peeping Toms when you need them?*

Suddenly, a cold sweat gripped him. A grim scenario flashed into his brain. Everything he had read about UFOs implied abductions. Missing time, bloody noses, amnesia, all were part of the MO. Stacey's bloody nose made him stop and think. The aliens also liked to tag their victims with some kind of monitoring device. He clenched his fist in anger. *Stop it!* He was letting his imagination run away from him.

Releasing a long sigh, he finally shrugged his shoulders in resignation. Perhaps in the daylight he would be able to find more clues. For now, it was time to get back to a warm bed.

Just then he heard the faint ringing of the telephone coming from the house. *Who the hell would be calling at this hour?*

A moment later, Barb's shrill cry calling him to the telephone pierced the distance. Giving one last look around, Matt was reasonably certain he had left no stone unturned, or in this case, no shadow uncovered. But a persistent feeling of uneasiness followed him back to the house, making him glance over his shoulder more than once. Gratefully he walked briskly back into the light.

CHAPTER FOUR

McCarren International Airport, Las Vegas, Nevada -- 11:25 a.m.

The temperature outside the Boeing 777 Airbus was hot and dry, typical of a desert temperature in mid-July. *Except this isn't July*, Matt Benner fumed under his breath as he stepped aboard the airplane. It was December. *And almost Christmas at that.* Perspiring heavily, he was finding it hard to believe that dry heat was good for your health. Ironically, that's exactly what he had come to Vegas for.

People kept jostling him as he made his way down the aisle, looking for his seat number. He was trying his best not to start using his elbows as weapons. *This is no way to spend the holidays, joyriding in a friggin' flying circus,* he told himself. Besides having a deathly fear of flying, he hated crowds.

Thankfully finding his seat by the window before coming to blows with someone, he quickly eased his bulk into the soft cushions and let out a sigh of relief. The cool manufactured air blowing from the tiny nozzle above his head was just what the doctor ordered. He settled in his seat, even slipping on his seatbelt before being asked. Detachedly, he watched the other passengers embark. Most were tourists who had shot their wad in the casinos and were not in the best of moods. He resigned himself to the fact that it would be a while yet before everyone was boarded. It was a big airplane.

He began to fidget. It had been a long night, and he was anxious to get off the ground. He had never liked air travel. It nauseated him. Even the thought of it made him queasy. Luckily for everybody around him, the Dramamine that Barb had given him was keeping his stomach in check.

The detective's destination was Miami, then on to Chatter's Cay via a small air taxi. Chatter's Cay was a little island, he was told, just a few leagues away from Puerto Rico, in the British Virgin Islands. It wasn't even marked on the sea charts. The first time Matt had heard of the place was a postcard he had received three days ago from his long-time friend and partner, Tom Blocker. Tom and his family were spending their vacation there, at a resort called Club Maine. Matt recalled that they always made the pilgrimage to the Caribbean when the boys got out of school for Christmas. Besides the traditional "Wish you were here" and "Having a great time," Matt remembered Tricia writing how they had narrowly escaped a hurricane a week before. *Doesn't sound like the best spot to get some R&R*, he mused. What sounded even less appealing was hopscotching across a bunch of islands to get to this remote tropical oasis. Unfortunately, Matt hadn't been able to get a direct flight. Because of Christmas, everything was heavily booked. *Maybe if I'd been notified sooner.* With a big sigh, he resigned himself to the torture he was about to endure.

Idly he glanced over at the empty seat next to him and picked up a day-old copy of *U.S.A. Today,* which was stuck in between the cushions. While scanning the headlines, something caught his attention. Almost as if the editor wanted to downplay the incident, the article was tucked away on the next to last page.

ATLANTIS RUINS FOUND

Further evidence of the famous lost continent of Atlantis came to light a week ago, when local divers discovered scores of underwater artifacts near the island of Puerto Rico. In waters less than 100 feet deep, vast structures resembling walls, roadways, and giant domes were uncovered by the recent passage of Hurricane Minerva. Professor Vail, renowned epigrapher and Atlanteologist from New Delhi's Institute for Linguistic & Historical Research, has been sent to investigate the find. Several disappearances of boats and airplanes has also been attributed to this late seasonal storm, which left 57 dead, 15,000 people homeless and claimed over $18 million in property damage.

Matt laid his head back against the headrest and closed his eyes. The article brought home with startling clarity the reason why he was there—the telephone call in the middle of the night from a cockney who introduced himself as Stu Barrett. He claimed to be Tom's old Navy buddy from the Gulf War. He also operated an inter-island air taxi service, which had happened to ferry Tom and his family to the resort isle.

It seemed strange to Matt that his partner had never mentioned this British fellow before. But Tom never talked about the war much, let alone any acquaintances he'd made during it. What he did talk about, on more than one occasion, was the lost continent of Atlantis. He was overwhelmed by it. Ever since he dove on what were reported to be Atlantis artifacts in the Bahamas, the big Nevadan always made the pilgrimage back whenever he could, looking for more.

But, according to Stu Barrett, something had gone wrong on this trip. Tom had supposedly hooked up with a diving expedition to those same Atlantis ruins featured in the paper. To have another opportunity like that fall in Tom's lap, Matt realized, must have been like Bob Ballard personally handing him an invitation to visit the Titanic.

Except the boat and everyone aboard never returned. Barrett had managed to exchange a few war stories with his comrade in arms just before he went dashing off with his family into, as the Englishman so eloquently put it, the devil's lair, i.e. the Bermuda Triangle. That was three days ago. It was the last the sky jockey had seen of them.

The final passengers were beginning to seat themselves as Matt broke from his reverie. He couldn't get out of his mind his daughter's reaction when he had laughingly told her he was going to be traveling inside the Bermuda Triangle. It was almost as if he'd said he was going to the other side of the moon. She had the oddest look on her face, as though she wanted to say something but at the last minute, changed her mind. *Oh well*, he thought. *Teenagers are prone to mood swings*.

He looked up just in time to see two strange-looking characters sauntering up the aisle. They looked like a Mutt & Jeff duo, definitely out of touch with the latest fashion. Dressed in black alpaca suits with black shirts, black ties and black fedoras, sporting dark Polaroids, they looked like the comic edition of the Blues Brothers. Dark complexioned, Matt felt they could have passed for Latino or even Middle-eastern. He had to stifle a laugh. It was as though they were part of a cabaret act and hadn't had time to change before the flight.

But something else about them disturbed him. As they shuffled past his seat, a sharp pinprick sensation instantaneously pierced his skull. It left him momentarily stunned, and somewhat bewildered. His brain felt as if a pair of cold, calculating probes had just scanned it. He turned to follow their progress, but lost sight of them as they disappeared to the rear of the plane.

Suddenly the huge jumbo jet began to tremble, its mammoth engines churning the air with an indescribable whine. His heart began palpitating like a trip hammer. Beads of perspiration magically appeared on his forehead. All thoughts of the strange pair were erased from his mind as a visceral fear gripped him. It was a curse every time he flew. *If man were meant to fly, he would have been bred with wings*.

A tinkle of chimes and the blinking of a "fasten your seat belt" sign overhead suddenly commanded his attention. Matt peered out of the window at the moving landscape. In spite of the Dramamine, his stomach was beginning to flip-flop like a butter churn. He could almost hear the agonizing groan of the wheel struts beneath his seat, the rubber tires screeching under the tremendous weight. The aircraft slowly rolled past the terminal and onto the main runway. Once they were past a row of parked private jets and a series of utility sheds, Matt was able to gain an unobstructed view of tall hotels and glittering casinos shimmering like mirages in the desert heat.

At the end of the runway the pilot slowed his charge down, made a 90-degree turn, and pointed the nose of the giant carrier toward the late morning sun. Clutching the armrests with a white-knuckled death grip, Matt braced himself for the takeoff. This was the part he hated most. He locked his eyes open in a dead man's gaze and he held his breath, wondering in the back of his mind how such monstrous machines could get off the ground.

A high-pitched whine filled the air as the aircraft lurched forward, gaining speed with every rising decibel. As his body compressed against the seat, his subconscious instantly became attuned to the sound of the engines, waiting for the inevitable silence before the crash, the screams of his fellow passengers before impact—including his own. His mind's eye witnessed the horrifying scene of metal and flesh being consumed in a pyre of smoke and flame. He stared transfixed out the window. Everything was rushing past in a nightmarish blur. He closed his eyes and dug his fingertips even deeper into the armrests. An instant later, his body tilting at a 52-degree angle, the compression of G-forces pressing him down against the seat made him forget why he was even there.

CHAPTER FIVE

Miami International Airport -- 1:35 p.m.

Matt recognized Stu Barrett from 50 yards. The shock of red facial hair gave him away. He was lolling in the shade under the wing of a blue and white single-engine, six-seated Cessna Centurion 210. Although Matt wasn't that familiar with small aircraft, he could tell the machine was kept in superb condition.

Heat waves bounced off the smooth metal finish, making the plane's aluminum surface shimmer like a hot skillet. "It's got to be over 100 degrees," Matt gasped under his breath. Walking the short distance from the main terminal to where the private aircraft were parked, he was already soaked with sweat. He could actually feel the blistering heat from the concrete apron radiating through his loafers.

He wondered how much longer his 40-year-old legs could carry him and the bulging Tourister that Barb had packed. He was only supposed to be gone a couple days, but he was carrying enough clothes to last a month. Transferring the load from one aching shoulder to the other, he stepped up the pace. His only hope was that the airplane cabin was air-conditioned. If it wasn't, he was surely going to melt like the wicked witch in *The Wizard of Oz*. Matt sighed. *Being doused with water wouldn't be a bad alternative.*

As he approached, the red hair quickly advanced toward him. "You looked bushed, old chap," a husky voice announced as a solidly built man of medium height stepped out of the shadows. "Here, let me help you." With fluid grace he grabbed Matt's suitcase with one hand and pumped Matt's hand with the other. "I'm Stu Barrett."

He looked like he'd just stepped out of a misplaced advertisement in *Suave* Magazine, with his bushman short-sleeve khaki shirt, matching knee-length shorts, a rattan-colored baseball cap with a Disney World logo on the front, and a tan and white bandana tied around his neck. The only deviation to his safari getup was his canvas deck shoes—with no socks.

When they got out in the sunlight, Matt noticed that the Englishman's clipped beard and mustache seemed two shades redder than the patch of shoulder-length hair he had tied in back in a tight ponytail. He could have passed for a hippie throwback from the 60s. And yet, Matt instinctively knew it would be a mistake to stereotype this man. He guessed him to be in his mid to late 40s.

"Yeah, I've had better days," Matt replied. "This heat is ready to do me in. I must be getting old."

Barrett laughed. It was sort of a carefree guffaw; a certain spontaneity from someone who seemed to enjoy his position in life.

"Well, I hated to call you on such short notice," Barrett said. "But I thought it only right to let you know as soon as possible. I'd forgotten about the time difference, though," he said, looking a little chagrined. "The Coast Guard and a bunch of my pilot friends have been out looking for Tom and his group since last week, but so far, no luck. After tomorrow, the Coast Guard is calling off the search. I thought you might want to be in on the last day. Maybe you'll have better luck knowing where to look for them than the bloody lot of us do." He glanced at his watch. "It's best we not waste any more time getting started. I'd like to be back before dark." Matt sensed a trace of uneasiness in his voice.

As Barrett opened the plane's cabin door, the pungent aroma of new leather assailed Matt's nostrils.

"Just got it reupholstered," the pilot announced proudly. "Old Bertha here needed a new facelift. Jump in."

Matt looked at him skeptically and then at the narrow opening. For him, it was tantamount to jumping into a coffin.

Soaring into the wild blue yonder in what seemed to Matt a motorized kite was sheer terror. As the ground gave way beneath him he closed his eyes, clenched his teeth, and gripped the armrests again as if his life depended on it, praying he had enough strength to keep his dinner down. *It won't be a good start to a new friendship if I heave all over the man's new Moroccan interior.*

When Matt reopened his eyes Barrett had leveled out the airplane at 8,000 feet, engaged the automatic pilot, and had the nose pointed in a generally southeast direction. The engine sounded muted in the air-conditioned, pressurized cabin. A splash of yellow-orange from the blazing sun glinted off the right wing tip, like the edge of a golden razorblade. Far below, Matt saw the unruffled crystal-clear waters of the South Atlantic splotched with various shades of blue-green glass. Off in the distance, a string of large and small islands dotted the horizon. With their tops of sun-ripened colors of greens and turquoise mixed with strands of bleached coral sand, they looked strangely illusory. *As a matter of fact, the entire panorama has a touch of surrealism*, Matt mused.

"Atmospheric effect is all, my boy," Barrett explained, as though reading the detective's mind. "Right now we're approaching the Great Bahama Bank. Those islands you see there are the Bahamas. Nearly 700 of them altogether. Stretching almost all the way down to the Caribbean. Most of them uninhabited. And beyond is the Greater Antilles. That's where we're headin.'"

"How long to get where we're going?"

"About five hours—give or take. Latest weather forecast checks out okay. No advisories. We should be on schedule. You'll be staying at my place tonight. I have a small cabana on Culebra, a small island off the east coast of Puerto Rico. That's where I stay when I visit my sister. By air, Roosevelt Roads isn't too far away."

"Didn't they close that Navy base a while back?" Matt inquired.

"They did, but they still use it for emergencies."

Matt remembered Barrett mentioning the fact that his sister was serving aboard a U.S. Coast Guard cutter. She was supposed to make the arrangements to have them billeted aboard when the vessel resumed its patrol. *Somehow that seems a little bit too easy,* the detective mused.

"Aren't we flying over the Bermuda Triangle right now?" he asked.

Barrett gave Matt a sidelong glance before cracking a smile. "Sure are. But you're not afraid of its big bad reputation, are you?" Matt could read a slight derisiveness in his voice.

"No, I'm not afraid. Just a little concerned is all. I've heard stories about too many disappearances in the area to take it lightly. I remember on the *Discovery* channel a while back, they had a documentary about the Bermuda Triangle. They said that an average of one private plane and two boats, along with their passengers, have vanished without a trace every week for the past 40 years."

"Probably true, my good man," Barrett replied in a more deferential tone. "But for the most part, storms and human error are the biggest killers out here. Currents can also scatter wreckage far from their initial sinking so it only looks like they vanished. But they're really still around. You just have to know where to find 'em."

"They also mentioned the lack of distress calls sent. It seems to me people who know they're in trouble would have time to send out an SOS."

"Not necessarily. People underestimate the speed of flash storms. Some call them small hurricanes, or neutercanes. They can overwhelm a craft in virtually seconds. And then there's pirates to consider."

"Pirates! I thought they went out in the 17th Century."

"Modern-day pirates are even more notorious—and deadly. They roam these islands like vermin, looking for rich Yankees with their million dollar yachts. They can finagle their way on board without the owners even suspecting it. The other way they go about it is, of course, less sophisticated but just as effective. They run them down on the high sea and kill whoever's aboard. Then they use the boat for smuggling drugs or even refugees. They usually keep the boats for one or two trips, then scuttle them."

"Do you think that's what happened to Tom and his group? Either a flash storm, or highjackers got 'em?"

Barrett screwed his face into a thoughtful expression, then said with sincerity, "As much as storms, especially hurricanes, furnish me with a lively business, I can't say either one is responsible for our friend's disappearance, mate. Tom chartered a boat with a bunch of divers from a local who knows what to look for out here. As a matter of fact, I know the bastard—Carlos Mendoza. He's a sleazy character, but he knows his business."

"If I'm not getting too personal, Mr. Barrett, how do you manage a flying business in U.S. territorial waters? You sound British to me."

Barrett turned his head and flashed the detective a toothy grin. "Please call me Stu. And I don't mind you askin'. I sound British because I am. Make my home in Durham, a little town in northeastern England, whenever I'm there. But I carry a dual citizenship. So does my sister. Our father was stationed in Bermuda during the war. Flew PBMs. Liked the islands so much, he decided to stay." He gave a quick smile. "I kinda carry on the tradition."

"I didn't think flying people around the islands were that much in demand," Matt confessed.

"It keeps me hoppin'. During season mostly, I fly divers out to the more remote wreck sites. There's a lot of good shipwrecks around, and you have to know where to look. Storms keep shifting the bottom so one day you see one, the next day you don't. I also dive. Mostly salvage, you know, with the hard hat and canvas suit. Picked it up in the Navy. Comes in handy sometimes whenever I come across a boat that has been listed missing and I have to stay down for any length of time. Most of the newer boats are made of fiberglass and hold up extremely well in salt water. I find out through the registration number what rich bloke owned it, and I get a pretty penny from the insurance company to raise it. If the claim is already settled, the insurance company turns around and sells it at auction." He chuckled. "In the end, everybody's happy."

Matt didn't think there was anything funny about it, but he kept his mouth shut. It was going to be a long flight, and he wanted to keep the conversation light. Besides, lack of sleep and the enervating heat had done a job on him. The cool atmosphere and soft leather were starting to make him sleepy. His head began to droop. His eyelids felt like lead shutters. Nervous exhaustion was starting to set in, and his back and shoulders still ached from carrying that damn luggage. He laid his head back against the headrest and closed his eyes. *It won't be rude if I just shut my eyes for a second.*

The purring of the engine in the background was like a soothing lullaby. Before he knew it, his mind had slipped into a blissful state of unawareness.

CHAPTER SIX

Somewhere over the Bermuda Triangle -- 3:40 p.m.

Matt slowly opened his eyes, finding his body slumped over like a deflated balloon. He quickly jerked himself upright. The shoulder harness had thankfully prevented him from sliding out of his seat. He felt a little sheepish, but Barrett seemed not to have paid him any attention. *I couldn't have been out for more than a few seconds*, his brain rationalized. Yet he sensed a subtle shade of difference in the cabin lighting. He gazed out past the gently undulating wings as they bucked the air currents.

The world around them had been suddenly cast in shadow. Then he realized that a gigantic anvil-shaped cloud had maneuvered itself between the sun and the aircraft. Nothing to get excited about, he decided, except he could have sworn it wasn't there a minute ago. Far below and to his right, a large mountainous island began to materialize.

"Cuba," the pilot volunteered. "And those mountains you see are the Sierra Maestra, where Castro hung out during the Revolution. And over there is

Andros," he said, nodding toward an elongated island on the opposite horizon.

"Isn't that where the 'tongue of the ocean' is?" Matt queried. "Weren't parts of Atlantis found over there?" *It was just like Tom to keep me abreast of the latest archeological findings.*

"Quite right, old chap. I see you've been well informed," said Barrett, raising an eyebrow. "But many archeologists would beg to differ with you. Most claim that they're only old Carthaginian ruins that sunk in some seismic convulsion ages ago. Others say they're natural bottom formations that just look like large temple platforms and walls. I tend to disagree with them on that one. I've seen them for myself, from the air. They're ruins all right. How bloody old they are is anybody's guess."

"I read that the ones Tom and his group went after were allegedly Atlantean ruins," Matt replied. "It said something about walls and dome-shaped structures."

"Now, that is interesting, isn't it?" Barrett responded airily. "You know, the effects of a hurricane can be a bonanza to some. Sometimes islanders will play on that fact just so they can lure people down to look for artifacts that aren't really there. With all the amateur treasure hunters around, those kind of reports only promote business."

Barrett seemed to take pleasure in playing the devil's advocate, so Matt asked, "You think the reports are false?"

Barrett gave his guest a condescending look. "Put it this way, mate. This planet's been around for four and a half billion years. During that time a thousand civilizations could have come and gone. Who's to say Atlantis wasn't one of them?"

A lull in the conversation followed as Matt pondered the question. He remembered some of the things he learned in school, a lifetime ago. Like the fact that only in the last 300 million years has the earth been able to sustain life. Continental drift, which created the Atlantic Ocean, began during the Paleozoic Era around 200 million years ago. Geologists postulated that the Atlantic Ocean would have been sufficiently wide to accommodate a continent the size of Atlantis by the end of the Mesozoic Era. Sial, the granitic rock of which continents were made, had been found in abundance on the ocean bottom precisely where Atlantis was said to have existed.

Matt allowed his stream of consciousness to push him even further into a meditative mood. He had always liked to study earth history, and had made a point to memorize all the geological periods when in high school. *Why didn't I follow it further in college?*

He unseeingly stared out the window, thinking of those days when he was more interested in girls than in scholastic achievement. That was one of the reasons he ended up being a cop. Girls always liked guys in uniform, although Barb wasn't like that. Maybe that's why he married her. They were both nervous and self-conscious when they went to their first high school prom together. He remembered how appealing she had looked. Her blue eyes matched to a T that beautiful blue chiffon dress she was wearing. Tiny rhinestones highlighted her neckline, like miniature stars. He remembered when they were dancing, the shiny rhinestones giving off a shimmering blue glow under the ballroom lights. *Similar to the blue glow outside the passenger window here.*

Matt blinked once, twice, then suddenly straightened up in his seat, his senses full awake. His brain made a quick mental assessment. There shouldn't be any blue glow out there!

The glow was radiating off the leading edge of the starboard wing, slowly working its way toward the fuselage. The metal appeared to be on fire. Anxiously, he peered past Barrett to the other wing. The same thing was happening there.

The glow seemed to get brighter as its first feelers reached the struts. There soon followed a sputtering and sizzling noise, to Matt like the sound of bacon frying. The air inside the cockpit had suddenly become warmer, with the smell of burned ozone. At the same time the aircraft began to shake, as if caught in some giant's fist.

"Stu, what the hell's going on?"

"I don't rightly know. It looks like Saint Elmo's fire, but I never saw it radiate this much energy before."

Like creeping vines crawling alongside a building, long, slender shoots of light quickly spread to the engine cowling. The sky had turned murky, with a sickly yellowish cast.

"Look at my instruments!" Barrett yelled.

Matt pulled his eyes away long enough to gaze incredulously upon an array of jerking needles, indicators, and crossbars. A couple the small computer screens had suddenly gone blank.

Barrett gripped the yoke firmly and switched off the autopilot. "Brace yourself. I'm going manual."

The Cessna immediately gave a precipitous lurch before beginning a series of seesaw motions and side twists, in a good imitation of a bucking horse. Matt's stomach shot up and lodged in his throat.

A long moment passed before the Englishman could bring the plane back under control. "Believe it or not, I've lost my GPS, and both my flight director and VOR are out too. Look at my bloody gyro and mag compass. They're twirling faster than a couple whores in heat. The only thing I got working are my altitude and heading indicators."

Matt didn't understand the technical jargon, but he was taking the pilot's word that they were in trouble. Then he found bigger things to worry about. "Look outside!" he yelled. "Where'd the damn ocean go?"

Looking down, all Matt could see was a hazy white shroud of stagnant milkiness. There was no more division between sea and sky. The green-capped islands, the sun-kissed ocean, had all but disappeared. An impenetrable curtain of angry black clouds blocked their path instead. It was as if they were suddenly entering a disheveled world of roiling, atmospheric mayhem.

The electrical phenomenon had somehow worked its way into the cockpit, making the instrument panel glow an eerie bluish-white. Matt could feel every hair on his body standing on end. Luminous ionized air containing tiny fireflies of electricity danced, hovered, and spun all around their upper torsos.

55

The aircraft gave another vicious lurch, this time more pronounced and threatening. Matt knew his stomach wasn't going to stand much more of this.

"We're definitely in some kind of electromagnetic force field," Barrett announced off-handedly, as if addressing a physics class. The detective could tell the pilot's voice had gone up an octave, but the man was still reacting as if it was all in a day's work. As though following the next recommended procedure in the *Aviator's Handbook* for *Unscheduled Crashes*, he nonchalantly slipped on his headset and pressed the radio mike button. Matt noticed that the single sideband was already preset on the 125.0 civilian emergency band.

"Andros Tower, this Cessna Seven-Three-Three-Niner Bravo. Am approximately 10 miles west of your location. Am experiencing severe electromagnetic disturbance. My primary navigation, including my GPS, is knocked out. Have basic flight instruments only. Request vectoring instructions for emergency landing. Over."

Static.

"Andros Tower, this is Cessna Seven-Three-Three-Niner Bravo requesting emergency vectoring instructions. Come in please."

Again, more static.

Barrett reached over and adjusted the radio to a different frequency, then repeated his message. This time Matt detected a trace of urgency in the pilot's voice. Once again his renewed attempts were met with silence. *If it were me,* Matt thought, *I'd be screaming into the mike by now, demanding someone to acknowledge.*

"Damn!" Barrett's expletive shot through the enclosed cabin like a rifle shot. "Even my ADF isn't working. It looks like I'm going to have to fly this bucket like I did in the old days, before computers." He readjusted his seat and cinched his shoulder harness tighter. "I suggest you check your harness, old chap. This might be a rough ride."

Meanwhile, the airplane was starting to pitch and yaw as though powerful crosscurrents were trying to pull the ship in opposite directions. Matt could tell his companion had all he could do to keep the machine from plunging out of control.

"Looks like I'm going to have to find that bloody airstrip myself!" Barrett hollered above the increasingly buffeting wind. He indicated with a nod the turbid display raging outside. "I don't like what I'm seein' out there."

There was a growing sound of popping and crackling in the air. The stench of burned ozone was stronger. It left a metallic taste in the detective's mouth. The fireflies were dancing to a frenzied tempo as electricity jumped from their bodies. Matt didn't like what he was seeing outside either. In just a matter of minutes, the sky had turned a dark ugly jaundice. Muddled black clouds with jagged streaks of yellowish-green lightning zigzagged across their path like an electrified fence. It wasn't as if they had flown into the storm; the cumulonimbus clouds seemed to have suddenly materialized out of nowhere.

"It doesn't look like I can climb above 'em," Barrett mumbled under his breath. "And it doesn't look like I can go around 'em. I think it's time to get the bloody hell outta here."

The pilot was fully caught up in his own world now. He banked the Cessna in a steep left turn, jamming the rudder pedal to the floor. The wings went vertical and the G forces against their bodies responded accordingly as the aircraft pivoted on an invisible spit, doing a complete 180. The centrifugal force slammed Matt against his seat like a giant's fist. His body hung in the shoulder harness at a crazy angle, unable to move. His stomach teetered on the brink of regurgitation.

The plane started acting sluggish, as if the 300-horsepower turbo-charged engine was desperately clawing for more air. They had somehow entered a void, where the molecules and gases in the atmosphere had suddenly ceased to exist. For several heart-stopping minutes Barrett struggled to level the aircraft. Then, with agonizing slowness, the other wing finally righted itself.

Once back on a reasonably straight course, both pilot and passenger stared through the windshield with unbelieving eyes. The cumulus clouds had closed ranks on them, transforming themselves into mountainous battlements. Their crests rose to towering heights that formed a solid roadblock in their path. Matt realized there was slim chance of getting through that way.

The energy level was also intensifying. The color of the lightning was changing into white incandescent strips of eye-searing brilliance, leaving ghostly afterimages in his retinas. *It would be like running through hell's gauntlet*, Matt decided. Strangely absent was the sound of thunder, and even the savage pounding of the wind hitting the fuselage had diminished in intensity. A vacuum of silence had suddenly enveloped the aircraft. The scream of the engine was their only link with reality.

"Have you ever seen anything like this before?" Matt gasped.

"No, I can't say that I have. Bloody good thing too, or else I would have given up flying a long time ago. Look on your side and see if you can find the horizon for me, would you, mate? I seem to have lost it."

If it weren't for the icy calmness of the Englishman's voice, Matt would have been experiencing a coronary by now. He knew Barrett's laissez-faire attitude was only a cover, but it was effective. It kept the detective from climbing the walls and beating his head in frustration.

He peered through the side window, trying to pierce the blinding glare that had swamped the cockpit. By now the aircraft was lit up like a Christmas tree, the glowing energy casting a reflective curtain all around them. By cupping his hands around his eyes against the glass, Matt was able to find a small slice of open sky. What he expected to find, but didn't, made his jaw drop. The conditions had worsened considerably since he last looked. What little semblance of earth there had been down below was completely obliterated, replaced by a mass of distended, billowing clouds, churning and twisting in convoluted madness.

An enormous, swirling tunnel of energy loomed menacingly in front of them. The sides were shrinking rapidly, forming what looked like an ever-tightening vortex. Matt could see its dark flanks, ringed with tongues of electricity, narrowing precipitately the closer they advanced. It didn't take a Rhodes scholar to tell him that if they stayed on their present course, they would end up being incinerated inside the whirling mass like an overcooked duck.

"We have to turn around NOW!" shouted Matt emphatically. "We're in some sort of wormhole ... and it's closing fast!"

"Okay, okay, I'm working on it!" Barrett snapped back.

Just then, the Cessna hit another powerful downdraft that sucked Matt's stomach into his throat. He tasted the bile that came with it. *It won't be long now!*

The plane plummeted like a falling elevator. It was taking the pilot longer and longer to regain control, Matt noted. To the detective, it seemed interminable. Even with eyes narrowed to slits and patches of sweat soaking his shirt, the Englishman's face stayed extraordinarily composed and relaxed. His strength to keep the plane under control was a pure display of willpower. It was also a damn good job of staying extremely calm in a crisis, Matt thought.

But even the most stalwart can grow weary of the game after awhile. Barrett finally resigned himself to the fact that he was fighting a losing battle. Almost reluctantly he tripped the radio switch. "Mayday, Mayday. This is Cessna Seven-Three-Three-Niner Bravo declaring an emergency. My flight instruments are inoperative and I have no visual reference. Request vectoring instructions from any station. Does anybody copy?" He repeated the appeal several times, but the airwaves remained deathly silent.

Barrett glanced at Matt. "It looks like we're on our own, dear boy. Let's pray they've got the right type of glue holding this crate together."

He had no time to elaborate further before another hammering blow of agitated air shook the Cessna from nose to tail. Gazing into his corner of the world outside, Matt could see the right wing flapping up and down like a broken tree limb. He could hear sharp crackling sounds of metal flexing and twisting from the tremendous G-forces being exerted on the aircraft's outer surface. He likened it to an aluminum can being slowly crushed.

"This bloody thing isn't going to take much more of this kind of punishment," Barrett declared. "We better head for the deck and see if we can't make a soft splash somewhere before she breaks up completely." Other than the cockney accent having a little less aplomb, the Englishman wasn't showing any signs of panic.

Matt was deeply grateful for the confidence builder, because there was no doubt in his mind that spit was the only thing holding him together. It was as though this battle with the elements was all part of a grand scheme to test his level of tolerance to a myriad of physical tortures. From the time they had hit the first pocket of air turbulence his heart had begun pounding as if trying to exit his chest while his blood raced ice cold through his veins. His stomach had permanently coalesced into a hard knot. If by chance they got out of this alive, he would forever kiss the ground Barrett walked on.

The doughnut-shaped mass of clouds was closing in on them like a bloated whirlpool of roiling mud. Matt felt as if he could almost reach out and touch their sides. Lightning bolts as white as arcs from welder's torches licked out at them hungrily. They were getting closer to the center of the wormhole. The stink of burned ozone was becoming overpowering in the stifling heat. He could feel one rivulet of sweat after another streaming down his backside, like miniature rivers.

"One of them bloody bastards hits us, it'll fry us for sure," Barrett declared through clenched teeth. The pilot was struggling a lot harder to keep the aircraft from pitching and rolling on its back. His neck cords and biceps bulged every time the plane went through a series of violent whiplashes. His face was reduced to hardened cement, his eyes frozen in concentration. Wind shears were coming from every direction, pounding the machine mercilessly. Matt didn't have to be told that the end was near. Skin-crawling sounds of tearing metal could be heard crying out as the overstressed airframe began to pull apart.

"She's breaking up!" Barrett shouted. Desperately he shoved down hard on the yoke, while at the same time cranking up the engine rpms. The airplane literally screamed through a phalanx of perpendicular valleys, seeking some meager pocket of stability.

As the nose dropped, Matt saw a sliver of light. At least, he thought he did through somewhat bleared eyes. It wasn't much, but it was something against the boiling cauldron of black monoliths that had suddenly reared up to intercept them.

"Down below, Stu! I see a break!"

At first Matt thought the pilot hadn't heard. There was no letup to their dizzying rate of descent. Matt's stomach was surprisingly quiescent during this latest maneuver. He knew it was only because his guts had congealed together by centrifugal force.

"Where?" Barrett finally asked.

Matt had lost sight of it for a moment, but spotted it again as the airplane approached the speed of a falling rock. His body was floating in mid-air, restrained only by the harness strap cutting into his thighs.

Matt pointed. "There, five o'clock!"

Barrett saw it then, a faint glimmer of light. He was getting dead tired. Almost by sheer willpower alone he brought the nose of the Cessna up and pointed in that direction. Matt stared mesmerized by the glow, as would a shipwrecked sailor spotting a rescue beacon. It had a strange ephemeral quality to it. It was pulsating, as if a light bulb was being continually turned on and off behind a partly closed door. He had the feeling that once that door closed, their fate would be sealed forever.

Minutes dragged. There seemed to be no letup to Barrett's continuous game of wits with a world gone mad. It was as if some cosmic force was in play, determined to wrench the aircraft out of his grasp. The plane suddenly buckled under another vicious blast of air, the airframe once again groaning in protest. Barrett had the throttles wide open. The light was now only a pinprick of its former self. Their avenue of escape had suddenly diminished to a thin wafer. Within seconds the light seemingly blinked out

"It's gone," Matt said dejectedly. After he spoke, it was as if a pall of doom had descended upon them. He could now smell a heavy odor of burned wiring and overheated hydraulic fluid. He realized they would eventually be overtaken with fumes if Barrett didn't land soon. Already his eyes were watering. Matt guessed they were still inside the wormhole because the darkness was almost complete, although super-charged electrons of white heat, sputtering like a barrage of sparklers, were still flickering perilously close to them.

"Look!"

Barrett's yell shot through Matt like a boost of adrenaline. As if in answer to their prayers, the light suddenly reappeared, changing its shape to that of an open portal the size of a silver dollar held at arm's length. It had moved somewhat south of their position but, unlike before, its renewed brilliance held bright and steady. *Whoever's opening and closing the door is keeping our options open*, Matt thought. It promised a new lease on life, and Barrett wasn't wasting any time thinking about it.

Matt barely had a chance to brace himself before he was being lifted into space again. The blood drained from his face. The plane shuddered as it humped like a submerging whale under another backbreaking nosedive. To Matt, it was as if he was suddenly slammed earthward to a cavernous world of dirty yellows and grays. Seemingly, they had broken free of the wormhole. But that was only an illusion. The clouds were uncannily twisting and convoluting, keeping pace with their advance. *It's almost as if they're being intelligently controlled,* Matt thought.

The Englishman seemed impervious to the acceleration. His jaws were set, and the dead man's look in his eyes gave Matt the impression of a kamikaze pilot. Under the pilot's iron grip, the plane punched through the troubled air at bone-rattling speed. *It's incredible how much punishment this machine's taken,* Matt thought. *In fact, it's incredible how much I've taken.* And it wasn't over yet. Every time he heard a loud popping noise from some structural component of the airplane letting go, he was sure his life span was diminishing exponentially. Every time the plane careened and buckled like a drunken boxer, he was betting 10 additional hairs had just turned white atop his head.

While the battered aircraft stubbornly fought its way toward what promised to be some respite, neither pilot nor passenger spoke. There was no need to. The light had become a symbol of salvation for them both, and neither wanted to break the spell. Matt was mentally drained, and couldn't imagine how his companion felt. The Englishman had kept them in the air far longer than the detective had expected. It was now a matter of waiting, hoping the aircraft would stay in one piece for one last effort.

Matt breathed a sigh of relief when the glow inside the cockpit began to dissipate. It had been getting on his nerves. It seemed that as they were getting closer to their objective, the atmosphere was becoming less electrically charged. It was a hopeful sign, he thought.

They came upon the light in a tumultuous rush. The Cessna's 32-foot wingspan cut through the first wispy tendrils of dark cloud as if surging through a sun-filled tunnel. They had made it! Matt looked back just in time to witness mountainous folds of blackness converge behind them.

Suddenly a dazzling white light was all around them, enveloping them with a pristine brilliance. What Matt thought was open sky turned out to be something totally foreign to his sensibilities. Instantaneously, a welter of strange sensations pervaded his entire being. Heat and pressure inside his body made him feel as if he was getting ready to explode. Deep inside the cortex of his brain, he realized too late that the light he and Barrett had entered was not of this world. It was a world made up of phantasms and disincarnates, caught up in a spirit dimension of indistinct, ephemeral shadows. He could see their fleeting shattered bodies and hear their mournful cries calling out to him. He could have sworn he recognized Tom's voice but it was soon drowned out by a host of others. Their pitch rose in intensity, filling the aircraft with an increasing cacophony of sound, assaulting Matt's eardrums, overwhelming his ability to hear anything but the accompaniment of his own screams. His last fleeting moment of consciousness was capturing the mirrored look of horror in Barrett's eyes, his mouth frozen wide in a grotesque, rictus grin.

CHAPTER SEVEN

Somewhere in the Bermuda Triangle

Matt felt cold and miserable. His 5-foot 10-inch frame was ensconced in a cocoon-shaped vehicle barely big enough for him to move. He was sitting with his knees practically up to his chin, his arms pressed tightly to his sides. The air was too dry for his liking, making his mouth cottony and his throat raw. His lungs hurt if he inhaled too deeply. It was difficult for his brain to conceive the fact that he was still alive— partly alive, anyway. Except for his head, the rest of his body felt dead. It was as though his arms and legs had been put to sleep. Other than being extremely uncomfortable he was in no pain, which was some consolation. The last thing he remembered was his head getting ready to burst. And then, peaceful oblivion.

When he fully regained consciousness, he had the strangest feeling of being underwater. He saw multitudinous pinpoints of light on all sides of him, seemingly floating on a diaphanous liquid carpet. It reminded him of sitting in an airplane four miles up, gazing through a hazy fog at a large metropolitan city far below. The spread of light extended as far as the eye could see.

But he wasn't in an airplane, at least not the kind he was familiar with. He was wedged in a clear, transparent bubble, which seemed to glide effortlessly through a sea of infinite blackness. There was sufficient light reflecting from below to illuminate the interior of the strange craft. There was no instrumentation or control panel present that he could determine. He was cushioned in a small contoured seat seemingly made for a midget. Next to him sat Barrett, with his head lolling to the side, looking as if he was dead drunk. He had the sonorous exhalations of someone sleeping one off. But the Englishman seemed okay, although Matt could tell his companion was having trouble breathing. His chest would jerk in sporadic, fitful spasms. It was like watching an epileptic in seizure.

Even more disturbing was the mysterious bluish-white light suddenly beginning to circle in the distance. It was directly ahead, looming out of the darkness like the maw of a giant whale. As the capsule rapidly approached, it grew in circumference until it looked big enough to drive a freight train through. Seconds later, the light washed over him and Barrett like a spotlight, bathing them in a pale radiance. Matt found it extremely soothing.

They had entered a large, subterranean cavern of some dimension, extending several hundred feet in diameter. The transition was smooth. Matt hardly noticed that the capsule had come to a stop. It was now resting on a cradle inside a cathedral-like room with craggy rock walls that had a crystalline, wet sheen to them. The floor seemed to be the same polished material. Everywhere there was a soft glow that seemed to emanate from the walls themselves. In the background was the muted sound of air being recycled through some kind of ventilating system.

Matt's senses were benumbed by the fact that he and Barrett had just been transported into an alien world, made up of weird looking machinery and instruments, the likes of which he had never seen before. Several table-sized platforms were scattered about the huge chamber. They somehow reminded Matt of sacrificial altars. He looked for any telltale signs of blood and gore, but didn't discern any. Instead, everything about the place implied sterility. He had the distinct impression of being inside a hospital operating room.

The clincher came when he saw four humanoid-type beings wearing silvery gowns, surgical masks, and caps walking toward him. They were oddly reminiscent of a team of surgeons.

But they weren't walking — they were gliding! This should have frightened him, but oddly, his instincts told him he was in no immediate danger. Instead, he had an overwhelming curiosity to learn what was going to happen next.

The figures stopped outside the capsule, staring at Matt and Barrett as though they were specimens, and as if contemplating which one to choose first. The entities were about 3 ½-feet tall and had protruding snouts. They almost looked bug-like. But the most compelling feature about them were their eyes. They were expressionless orbs, peering at him over their masks with an Oriental look of mysticism. Their black pupils effectuated a cold and pitiless stare. *They're definitely not human,* Matt realized.

The top of the capsule suddenly sprang open like a Delorian. Matt could feel no pressure under his arms as two of them effortlessly lifted him out. They left Barrett alone. *Do they think something's wrong with him?* Matt wondered. His friend's chin was resting on his chest, and those horrible sounds still emanated from his throat.

Matt was placed supine on the nearest table and his clothes were adroitly removed, in an almost fastidious manner. The air was chilly and damp. Once Matt was nude, goose bumps layered his entire body. The creatures then proceeded to poke and prod his body in every imaginable place, pausing briefly to minutely examine his moles and scars. During that time Matt didn't hear a sound other than the rustling of his captor's tin-foil-like garments as they moved methodically about the table.

He was unable to open his mouth or even move his facial muscles. Occasionally he would groan whenever one of them pressed too hard in a sensitive area. But although he was uncomfortable, he felt completely relaxed. It was only when one of the beings produced a strange pencil-like device in his scaly hand, with a barbed B-B sized pellet attached, that his blood pressure shot through the roof. A warning bell clamored in the back of his brain. His body suddenly broke out in a cold sweat. The tool suggested to him a dentist's drill. He hated dentist's drills; they came in a close second behind flying.

The creature held the tool briefly over Matt's nose before he felt it infiltrating his right nostril. His throat muscles screamed in silent protest. He managed to squirm and wiggle slightly in a vain effort to escape, but it was useless. Invisible bonds of steel gripped his muscles as if they were anchored in cement blocks. In the end, he just lay there in a pool of sweat and waited for the ordeal to end. He felt the probe puncturing a membrane deep inside his nasal passage. There was no pain, just a sickening sucking sound, then it was all over. He could feel a trickle of blood oozing out.

When the creature removed the instrument from his nostril, to Matt's consternation the ball-like implant was conspicuously missing. *Oh my God!*

He grappled mentally with the significance of what had just happened. Whatever that thing was, it was now inside his head. *A monitoring device?* His thoughts flashed back to the scene in his daughter's bedroom — and the blood on her pillow. *Could she have gone through the same procedure?* If so, these creatures could follow their every movement, read their every thought. But why? It didn't make any sense.

What followed next was something Matt would relive in his nightmares for the rest of his life. He could not believe what his eyes were telling him.

Standing next to him was a hooded figure dressed in a flowing purple robe that characterized him as some kind of a priest or monk. He was a giant of a man, eight or nine feet tall at least, Matt guessed. He wasn't even sure it was human. A cowl hid the stranger's face in shadow. The tall figure leaned over him until the detective could feel its eyes boring into his skull. Cold fingers caressed his brain. Strange impulses invaded the nerve endings of his consciousness—a tingling sensation that felt intensely pleasurable. Matt realized that his mind was being scanned.

A jumble of subliminal thought patterns came rushing to the surface of his cerebral cortex. With it came visions of a land carved with wide canals and gilded covered bridges; docks and wharves filled with strange-looking ships; wide boulevards with towering skyscrapers of exotic designs; assorted peoples of dissimilar dress and style, but all strikingly elegant and graceful. Puzzling red, white and black stone architecture was interspersed throughout the landscape, as well as enormous pyramids that dwarfed everything in sight. On top of a hill stood a beautiful castle, a magnificent edifice with gilded spires and crystalline towers that overlooked the metropolis below. Rising in the background, pasting a black smudge against a cerulean sky, a huge volcano smoked ominously like a wrathful god. Flitting about the sky were aerial cars so unworldly in shapes and colors, he found it difficult to conceive.

The imagery in his head switched abruptly to an underwater environment, where huge dome-shaped structures sat menacingly quiet and still. To Matt they resembled astronomical observatories, but he sensed a more diabolical purpose behind them.

The scenes quickly faded, leaving Matt exhausted. It was as if he had just undergone a mental torture test. He had the most powerful urge to sleep. He rolled his eyes back and nestled in a soft, cottony cushion of fog. But rest wouldn't come. He could hear a voice penetrating the sensory impulses of his brain. The voice was annoying and persistent. It wouldn't leave him alone until he unblocked his mind and acknowledged its presence. Slowly, painstakingly, he opened his consciousness to the intrusion.

"We are the Caretakers," the voice proclaimed. *"Heed our warning. Humankind is not ready for the power of the crystals. All will suffer who come near. Stay away."*

Matt took a deep breath and sighed. Somehow he knew it was important for him to remember the message given him. As quickly as his consciousness assimilated the information into its memory bank, the reason why was suddenly obscured in a whirling cloak of darkness. It was like falling down a long, dark sinkhole.

CHAPTER EIGHT

Club Maine, Chatter's Cay -- 1:37 a.m.

A gentle trade wind wafted through the louvered shutters of the single-storied bungalow window. It settled delicately over Matt's outstretched body with a tender caress reserved only for the tropics. He was lying nude on the top covers of an enormous four-poster bed, in a room lavishly decorated with the latest in bamboo furnishings and tropical plantings. He was wide-awake, gazing vacantly at the ceiling. He had tossed and turned for the better part of an hour before finally giving up on sleep. Even the pungent smells of bougainvillea and heliconia from outside, and the soft whisper of surf on a nearby beach, did little to assuage his uneasiness.

For one thing, he felt uncomfortable lying on a bed that had, just a few short days ago, been slept in by Tom and Tricia. The unit had an attached room, where the boys had stayed. That's where Barrett was now, sleeping it off. The Englishman had not wasted any time tying one on at the Club lounge shortly after they arrived. *And boy, what an arrival!* Luckily, the room was booked and paid for in advance, because there had been no other vacancies. After all, it was tourist season, their host, a lanky Texan from Houston, had politely reminded them. Matt should have been thankful for small favors, but something else was bothering him. His subliminal thoughts were continuously being bandied about in a grab bag of mixed emotions. Hazy and indistinct images kept surfacing around the edges of his subconscious, clamoring for release. But there was a roadblock there he couldn't seem to penetrate.

All Matt could remember for sure was he and Barrett's untimely arrival over a palm-fringed beach in what seemed to be the middle of nowhere. To be jolted wide-awake inside the Cessna, the plane barely 10 feet off the water, skimming the surf of some unknown island, was nerve-wracking enough. But how they arrived was even more mind boggling. The aircraft had literally exploded out of the atmosphere like a meteorite. The pilot soon recognized the island as Chatter's Cay. Matt shook his head in amazement. Uncannily, it was the place where Tom and his family had begun their one-way journey.

Once Barrett found his bearings, it was still a matter of landing in one piece. The machine was rattling like a bag of loose bones, and the engine sounded like a cement mixer. The Englishman proved his skills once more by deftly easing his charge onto the island's only landing strip, a hard-packed ribbon of marl sandwiched between a bracelet of coral and sand. Fortunately, it was located far enough away from the club to avoid answering any embarrassing questions.

On wobbly legs the two of them had walked the two kilometers to the main building, happy they were still alive. Landing impromptu on a remote island with a surplus supply of fuel that should have been long depleted didn't seem to have phased Barrett in the least. As far as the Englishman was concerned, it was simply a matter of their experiencing a time anomaly. It was not an unheard of phenomenon among the airmen and sailors plying the Bermuda Triangle daily, the pilot had muttered conspiratorially after his sixth rum and coke. Even the astronauts were not immune, encountering time fluctuations every time they rode out into space.

Matt involuntarily shuddered at his companion's disquieting addendum. "Normally, old chap, these time anomalies only last a few minutes. In our case, two hours is a bit unusual."

A bit unusual! That was like telling Matt there are no losers in Vegas.

He stared absentmindedly into the darkness, letting his stream of consciousness play out. He kept rehashing in his head the macabre events aboard the Cessna, and the inexplicable memory loss once they entered the blinding white light. He had a strange feeling in his gut that the party was only starting. Barrett had assured him, though, that he would be home by Christmas. *Only if the house rules hadn't changed.*

So far the search for the missing divers had proved unsuccessful, and the prognosis didn't seem encouraging. Hitching a ride aboard a U. S. Coast Guard cutter was the final act before aborting the mission. Matt squeezed his eyes shut and rubbed his temples as a pang of guilt speared into his skull. Was it wrong to want to be with his family at Christmas? As much as he hated to admit it, he was here mainly because he felt obligated, not because he thought there was any chance he could better the odds of finding Tom. Barrett didn't seem to think so.

Matt felt pressure in his bladder. *Must be the lingering effects of all that Jamaican rum*, he mused. After arranging for someone to retrieve their luggage, he and Barrett had tipped a few under the guise of therapeutic medicine. Crediting it to the nerve-shattering strain of time-travel, neither one of them was feeling much pain by the time they staggered back to their rooms.

Rolling out of bed, Matt abstractedly rubbed the back of his hand across his upper lip. It felt wet and sticky. Inspecting his hand in the bathroom light, he discovered a smear of blood. His nose was bleeding. *That's strange*, he thought. He never got nosebleeds.

After relieving himself, he slipped on a pair of shorts and stepped outside onto a flagstone terrace, bordered by palmetto palms on one side and giant blossoms of hibiscus and jacaranda on the other. Framed in between, a magnificent view of white sand and rolling surf pleased the eye for miles in either direction. The tide was out, making the wet sand sparkle under the light of a low-rising full moon. The music of the waves washing against the white beach sand was soothing and relaxing. Yet he had trouble capturing the mood.

He let the fine, smooth sand crunch between his toes as he made his way around a few stunted palm trees. Hurricane Minerva, even around its periphery, had done some collateral damage. It had made short work of the local flora, he noticed. Much of the outlying shrubbery was dead or dying, crusted white with salt. He crossed a wooden walkway that bordered the high-water mark. The path circled the white-stucco cabanas in a wide loop before disappearing in the direction of a cluster of boutiques and shops.

Stopping to admire the view, his gaze took in the all-encompassing immensity of the ocean and the mantle of stars embracing it. The moon seemed fuller and brighter than he had ever seen it before. He thought of Barb and the kids. He knew the same heavenly orb was hovering over their desert home right then, yet it could have been a million miles away.

His mind kept going back to the beginning of his journey. It was more of a voyage rooted in desperation, he felt. If Tom and his family were really out there somewhere, it was hard to believe they hadn't been found yet. It was possible, he admitted, that they were stranded on some deserted island. But as hopeful as that might sound, it seemed a stretch. More than likely Barrett was right. They were hijacked or caught up in a flash storm, either of which had capably disposed of their bodies. Matt was betting on the storm. If they were found, all he could do, assuming their bodies came floating up somewhere, was identify what was left of them before shipping them home. What they would look like after being in the water all this time, wasn't a pleasant thought. He recalled seeing pictures of whale carcasses washed up on shore. Denizens of the deep had torn huge chunks of flesh from their bodies. He couldn't imagine humans faring any better.

He erased the thought from his mind and continued walking, gazing absently at the distant horizon. He and Tom went back a long way. Both befriended each other when going through the LA Police Academy together. Like most young rookies, both had been indoctrinated to uphold the rules of engagement and fair play. But all that went out the window when faced with life and death situations on the streets, and their attitudes changed quickly. Neither could live with such iconoclastic rules that denied a cop the right to defend himself *before* being fired upon first. That was like walking into a lion's cage with only a stick and hoping you weren't going to be their next meal. In shadows or from a distance, paper guns and water pistols looked just as deadly as the real thing. To shoot first and ask questions later always seemed to be the safer alternative. However, the bureaucrats who sat out of harm's way behind their desks didn't see it that way. *They were safe and secure. What the hell did they care?* That's when the both friends decided a career change was healthier. After going through the research and investigative training of a private detective school, Las Vegas presented a promising choice to launch their new careers.

Matt paused in his reflections to look up. A large commercial airliner with its blinking red and white running lights had curiously drawn his attention. His eyes followed the lights as they lazily floated overhead until they disappeared like retreating fireflies amongst the stars. Dropping his gaze to the ocean vista below, his shoulders instinctively sagged at the thought of trying to find someone in its limitless depths. Finding dead-beat dads and runaway teenagers was a picnic compared to the hideouts this place harbored. It was like looking for the proverbial needle in a haystack. He wrinkled his forehead in concentration. Perhaps there were other ways to skin a cat.

One of the techniques they taught him at P.I. School was the 'Escalation to Hypothesis' approach. It was a term used by investigators to reconcile the fact that there might not be a conventional solution to an unconventional problem. In that case, you started with the simplest observations and worked your way toward the more bizarre. From all he had read and heard of the Bermuda Triangle, you couldn't get any more bizarre than that mysterious body of water. Ships and aircraft, along with their passengers and crews, had been disappearing without a trace inside its borders since the days of Columbus, and possibly long before then.

Matt guessed the place to start looking, then, would be where his partner began his journey to the reported Atlantis ruins—here, on a tiny spit of land that belonged to no one, somewhat like an underwater shipwreck. It was an orphan buried within a potpourri of political strife and corruption in the Caribbean.

He pondered the emptiness around him. He knew the larger and more prosperous islands of St. Thomas and St. Croix to the south were where all the tourists fled. All was not lost, though. He had done his homework. Chatter's Cay did have certain attractions, which catered mostly to people who pushed the envelope when it came to thrills and excitement. You needn't bother looking for tennis courts and manicured golf courses here, the brochures expounded. But if you wanted underwater adventure, this was the right place.

Matt smiled. He could see why the spot appealed to Tom. Scuba diving was Club Maine's feature attraction. There was more charter boats for hire to go out to the reefs and shipwrecks, than there were divers to go around. Many of the boats were crewed by local Caribs, Barrett had explained, who drifted from the larger islands to fleece the Yankee dollar. So naturally, the competition was fierce. Perhaps that's where the problem lay. It was not unheard of for a crew to mutiny against the captain, kill everybody on board, and sell the cargo. A boatload of expensive scuba gear and accessories was always worth a few bucks on the black market. This area sported a slew of small, secluded coves and inlets that would make the hijackers and their loot almost impossible to find. They had provided excellent hideaways for such nefarious characters as Captain William Kidd and Sir Henry Morgan in the 16th Century, Matt noted, and virtually nothing had changed since then. For the most part, the smaller islands were still a hodgepodge of uninhabited backwaters conducive to smugglers and pirates.

For some reason, though, Matt didn't think that was the right approach to take. His gut feeling was telling him there was something a lot more peculiar to his partner's disappearance than met the eye.

Matt's introspection was suddenly interrupted when a movement within his peripheral vision caught his attention. He turned just in time to catch a pair of shadows ducking under the drooping fronds of a pineapple palm about 50 yards away. *A couple of late partygoers*, he thought innocently. Yet something about them wasn't quite right. They seemed an odd sort. One was tall, and the other only came up to his waist.

Once they emerged from under the tree and into the moonlight, Matt was able to pick them out clearly. He did a double take. The detective couldn't believe his eyes. It was the same Mutt & Jeff he had seen on the flight to Miami. Amazingly, they were still wearing their crazy outfits.

Matt stood transfixed and watched as the strangers turned in unison and began to walk away. As if on cue, they swiveled their heads together in his direction and studied him with eyes that glowed like yellow moons. *What the hell!* It was like gazing back at two jungle cats studying their prey. His pulse quickened, and cold beads broke out on his forehead. He felt, for a brief second, that same piercing sensation in his brain he had experienced on the plane. It was bizarre.

He quickly decided to follow them. He wanted to ask these characters a few questions—like, how did they beat him here? Chatter's Cay was not known for its easy accessibility. Also, was it just a coincidence, or were they following him?

The duo seemed to sense his intentions and immediately stepped up their pace. Matt followed suit. Soon he was loping at a fast clip behind the fleeing pair, but they were still able to keep their distance. *Obviously not in the mood for conversation*, he thought. They even walked funny, matching each other's footsteps like marching automatons.

"Hey, wait a minute you guys!" Matt yelled. "I want to talk to you." His cries rolled eerily across the empty beach like peals of buckshot.

Mutt & Jeff paid him no heed as they continued their fast retreat, eventually disappearing around a 90-degree bend in the walkway to the boutiques and shops.

"I'll be damned!" Matt mumbled to himself. He lost sight of them as he puffed to a stop at the bend, breathing heavily. *I gotta lose some weight.* Confused, he peered into the distance where the storefront's lighted facades illuminated the surrounding darkness.

There was no sign of them. The buildings were far enough away for his quarry not to have reached them in time to escape detection, and from where he stood to the shopping area, there was virtually no place to hide. Then, where were they? The moonlight, weaving ghostly patterns through a strand of palm trees, only lent an air of growing mystery to the elusive pair's sudden disappearance.

"What the hell's going on around here?" Matt muttered aloud. It was as though the ground had opened up and swallowed them. Were these weird characters somehow linked to all the strange goings-on in the Bermuda Triangle? After all, Chatter's Cay was located close to its mysterious borders.

As he gazed languidly up at several shooting stars leaving long incandescent trails across the night sky, he wondered if they were really the blazing entrails of falling meteors—or something else. Maybe they were the first waves of UFOs to invade earth. *My mind's really going off the deep end now!*

Shrugging his shoulders, he could only speculate at this point. He forced his mind to relax. The gentle murmur of night sounds, the hissing of sand on the beach, and the alluring rustle of palm fronds, should have soothed his troubled soul. Instead, his thoughts kept being pulled back to the ocean like a magnet. Although it looked peaceful and serene, he imagined the blackened depths had its own set of phantoms. His mind cringed at what might lay in wait for him out there. He slowly retraced his steps back to his cabana, all the while trying to erase the lurid images his mind was conjuring.

CHAPTER NINE

Roosevelt Roads U.S. Naval Shipyards, Puerto Rico
-- 06:55 hours

"Isn't she a beaut?" Barrett beamed proudly, as though he were showing off a prize heifer. He and Matt were standing at dockside, watching the U.S.S. Coast Guard Cutter *Proteus* being smartly maneuvered into its berthing space. The Coast Guard insignia, a narrow blue stripe in combination with a wide orange chevron on the bow, with the service shield superimposed on both, caught the glare of the early morning sun like a spotlighted banner. The number 799 along the vessel's hull gave it the lines of a sleek race-boat. Two triple torpedo mounts stood out on each side of the ship, with 76mm guns fore and aft. Silhouetted against the sky were two SPS-64(V)6 air search radar, and an OE-82 SATCOMM antenna with an uplink dish rotating on twin towers 30 feet above the main deck. The ship was impressive all right, Matt admitted. It almost made you feel proud to be an American. It was one of the Coast Guard's FAMOUS Class High-Endurance Cutters. The versatile craft displaced over 3,200 tons, and packed an agglomeration of high-tech ordnance and advanced hardware inside a reinforced titanium-steel alloy hull. A nuclear reactor instead of the traditional diesel and gas turbine engines powered its 378-foot length and 43-foot beam. Its revolutionary power plant could thrust the twin-screwed vessel at an incredible 55 knots through heavy seas at push-button command.

"The *Proteus* was just commissioned six months ago," his companion said. "As a matter of fact, she's the first of her kind. A prototype of the new millenium," he boasted, catching the detective's eye. "Besides having the latest in oceanographic and meteorological facilities, she's faster, stronger, and packs more bloody firepower than anything the Coast Guard has produced yet."

"Why so?" It seemed to Matt a little extravagant for simply homeland security.

"Things have changed. Used to be heavy armament on these cutters was used for combat operations in the Third World. Now the Coast Guard's main focus is chasing drug traffickers and illegal migrants. If her speed can't catch 'em, her guns still make a good deterrent."

"Yes, I can believe it," Matt answered. He couldn't help but notice the vast assembly of ASW weapons and missiles crowding the upper decks. It was an exhibition of sheer power and state-of-the-art technology. An HH-60K Jayhawk Long-range Recovery Helicopter sat squatting on its retractable hangar pad like a lone eagle on the fantail. A female officer in full captain's stripes was leaning over the bulwark, smiling down at them from the bridge.

"That's the captain," Barrett offered.

"I'm a little familiar with chain of command," Matt said. *I haven't watched all those war movies for nothing.* "Isn't a four-striper somewhat of an overkill to command just a Coast Guard cutter?"

"What you see before you isn't just *any* Coast Guard cutter. She was built with the added responsibility of fighting terrorists, plus saving the taxpayers money. You know, quality instead of quantity. Nothing but the best. That includes her officers and crew. All volunteer and hand-picked."

Once the thick mooring lines were tied to iron bollards sticking out of the concrete wharf like petrified tree stumps, the boarding ramp was quickly lowered and they were allowed to come aboard. In the background, the shrill cry of a bosun's pipe cut through the crisp air like a knife. It was immediately followed by an announcement over the PA system to secure the Maneuvering Detail. It lent an official air of finality to the proceedings, Matt thought.

Scampering up the 30-degree incline, he spotted several ships moored across the way. One he recognized as a supply ship lying bow to stern next to a submarine tender. They reminded him of a couple mother hens brooding, waiting for their flock to return. The rest of the harbor was conspicuously empty.

"Where is everybody?" Matt asked off-handedly.

"Still out on search and rescue operations, mate. The bloody storm left a trail of missing people you wouldn't believe. Tom's group only came up later."

After reaching the top of the gangway, Barrett and Matt stepped gingerly across to the steel-gray deck.

The Englishman gave a half-hearted salute to the U.S. Ensign flying at the ship's stern before holding out his hand to a rosy-cheek young Lieutenant, J.G. in gleaming dress whites waiting there to greet them. The name "Fraser" was stenciled prominently on his nametag. A short-statured grisly-faced 1st Class quartermaster in puttees, and with a holstered sidearm strapped to his waist stood discreetly off to the side. Matt recognized a seasoned sailor when he saw one. The veteran had hash marks on his sleeve reaching up to his elbow. A few feet away, a chief bosunmate and two ratings were putting the finishing touches to a white-canvassed awning they had stretched and hung over the quarterdeck, the official welcoming station on all U.S. naval craft in port. Matt didn't have to be reminded that the blistering rays of a tropical sun would soon make any exposed metal surface on board the ship a steaming hotplate in a matter of minutes.

"Permission to come aboard?"

"Permission granted. Welcome aboard, Mr. Barrett," answered the man named Fraser, offering his hand in return. "I didn't expect to see you back so soon."

Barrett smiled, nodding his head toward the detective. "This is Matt Benner, the bloke I was telling you about. Watch your step. He's an ex-cop." Before garnering a response, his eyes drifted toward the work detail. "What's goin' on? I didn't think we were staying long enough for Lou ... I mean, the captain, to grant shore leave."

Barrett's obvious slip of the tongue didn't seem to phase Fraser in the slightest. The officer's demeanor remained in keeping with naval etiquette — stone-faced and magnanimous. "Oh, nobody's going ashore, sir. But it seems we have another visitor coming aboard. Due anytime. Some VIP flying in from Peru."

"Yes, now I remember. A Professor Vail, isn't it?"

"Yes sir."

"Well mate, it might prove to be an interesting trip after all," Barrett replied good-naturedly as he stepped toward the nearest companionway. "I believe the captain is expecting us."

"Yes sir, she is. Would you like some help with your baggage?"

"No, I think we can handle it."

He and Matt had transferred some of their belongings to smaller, more manageable carry-ons. Barrett gave the officer-of-the-deck a truncated wave in farewell as he guided the detective away. Skirting past two four-barrel harpoon canisters and a 40mm grenade launcher, Barrett led Matt up two flights of stairs and several winding passageways before stopping in front of a door marked "Captain." After Barrett tapped gently, a female voice inside told them to enter. The inflection definitely had a 'Don't bother me unless it's damn important' tone to it, Matt thought.

Stooped in front of a chart lying on top of a large battleship-gray metal desk were two officers dressed in khakis. One of the officers was female, her light-auburn hair cropped stylishly over a starched uniform collar which eloquently brandished a set of bronze eagles at the tips. Matt saw she was the same officer he had spotted earlier on the bridge. The other officer was taller by a head and somewhat younger, his eyes staring lugubriously behind wire-rimmed glasses. They both looked up as Matt and Barrett stepped into the beige carpeted stateroom.

"Ahhh Stu, I'm glad to see you," the female officer said, with a flashing white smile as she walked toward them. "I was beginning to worry you might not make it back in time." Turning toward Matt, she proffered her hand in greeting. Her green eyes glittered like flint glass under the florescent lighting. "I'm Captain Louise Richardson, and you must be Matt Benner. Welcome aboard the *Proteus*. I hope my brother hasn't bored you with too many of his war stories."

I'll be damned! Matt spouted inwardly. Now he knew how Barrett had gotten them aboard without going through a bunch of red tape. He smiled and shook her hand, trying to match the captain's hospitality by giving his best "how do you do" in return. One of the ways he could judge a person's mettle was by the grip of their handshake. It was not a good sign if it was limp and lacked sincerity. He was pleased to acknowledge how firm and solid hers was. He immediately got the impression he was in the company of a very determined individual who normally got what she wanted.

Before he could respond to her bantering remark she turned toward the other officer, who was now astutely gazing in their direction.

"This is my Navigation Officer, Lieutenant Grissam. Bob, this is the fella that might give us a clue to where that boatload of divers disappeared. His business partner and his family were among them."

"I'm not too sure I can be of much help," Matt answered as he shook Grissam's hand. Like the captain's, his too had firmness of character. "Tom was always a little compulsive. I think this was just a chance opportunity that came along, and he took it. I didn't know he and his family were even listed as missing until I got a call from Stu here," he said, nodding toward Barrett. Matt felt a little sheepish. It didn't seem to be worth the trouble bringing him here.

"Probably best you're here in case we do find him," the navigator said. "Hopefully, he and his group are just stranded somewhere." Grissom's words sounded genuine, but Matt felt he said it with hardly any conviction.

"We can always use another pair of eyes for the search anyway," the captain interjected. "The search area has been extended to include the southwestern portion of the Sargasso Sea. It seems we have an overdue Belgian cruise ship that hasn't reported in yet. Her name is the *Rainbow* and she's carrying 3,200 passengers and crew. Can't raise her on side-band or HF. She was due in port early this morning at St. Thomas."

"Where was she comin' from?" her brother asked.

"Nassau," cut in Grissom. "Left two days ago."

"We will, however, continue our search for your friends, Mr. Benner," the captain continued, "but I'm afraid it will be just a passing attempt. We've been ordered to a standby status. The disappearance of the *Rainbow* has taken precedence. In any case, we'll be going to the general area where the divers were reportedly last seen. We also have the U.S.S. *Powell,* an aircraft carrier with its complement of war birds to assist us, as well as Bahama Air-Sea Rescue. An advance group is already converging on the *Rainbow's* last reported position as we speak. There are many private civilian boats and planes helping in the search as well, so we have this section of the Atlantic pretty well covered. If they're out there, we'll find them."

Matt noted her emphasis on the word *if.* It seemed to him there was more behind her words than she was letting on. As if on cue, there was a propitious pause while a white-jacketed steward brought in a tray of iced tea. Matt was thankful for the refreshment. Although the stateroom was air-conditioned, his throat felt parched, and his palms and backside were sticky with perspiration. It was a combination of nerves and tiredness, he averred. Something inside his subconscious was crying out for release. It was like water behind a dam, but a safety valve inside his brain was keeping it from spilling over.

The captain invited everyone to sit down. Nearby sat a black leather sofa with matching armchairs that looked somewhat worn, but comfortable. Bright sunlight streamed through a string of portholes overlooking the ensemble. In the near corner, inside a four-foot high wooden cabinet, was a VCR beside a small-screened TV. Atop the cabinet was the only framed photograph Matt could discern in the room. Without making it look obvious he was staring, it featured a handsome airline pilot wearing captain's stripes and a matching smile, standing next to a large passenger jumbo jet. The name *British Airways* inside an intertwining red and white striped logo stood out prominently on his crisp uniform. On the far side of the room was a bunk-sized bed that form-fitted into the wall, a reading lamp, a radiotelephone within easy reach, and a 6-foot metal locker recessed inside an adjoining bulkhead. The bulkhead made up part of a smaller enclosed space, with an attached door, presumably a head. Besides the desk and a swivel chair, in civilian terms the room looked quite sparse. No matter how sophisticated the ship's hardware, it seemed the United States Coast Guard didn't believe in pampering their commanding officers.

The conversation took a more serious note when Barrett launched into his narrative of the storm, and their unexplainable two-hour time loss. Even harder to explain was the reserve fuel remaining. "I never saw anything like it in all my bloody days, Sis. The plane lit up like a neon sign. My instruments were as useless as teats on a boar."

Louise Richardson looked at her brother with a skewed eye. "That's what I love about you Stewart. You have such colorful metaphors." At first glance, she had the look of a chagrined younger sister. But maybe she wasn't so much younger after all, Matt thought. Her trim figure and pert features were misleading. She wore no jewelry except a thin band of gold on her ring finger. On closer examination, he estimated her to be at least five to 10 years older than her brother. The deep wrinkles radiating around the corner's of her eyes gave it away. They betrayed a toughness that had to have crystallized only after many years of command. It probably wasn't easy being a woman in charge of a shipload of men.

She turned to Matt. "Officially I cannot acknowledge any part of my brother's story, Mr. Benner. File Letter

5720 governs the Seventh Coast Guard District, of which the Proteus is currently attached. It states quite clearly that the Bermuda Triangle is nothing more than an imaginary area, and everything unexplainable that occurs within its borders is of natural origin."

"I can vouch for what happened, Captain," Matt said. "I was there too."

"Yes, I know. But the directive does have some validity. Many people misinterpret things they don't understand, yet those things are perfectly natural phenomena. Ball lightning and the Aurora Borealis, for example. However, my personal views of the Triangle are more liberal, as my brother can attest to."

Somehow, the captain was making a point; something he would have to explore later, Matt decided. For the time being he was content just to play along. "Why is that, Captain?" he asked.

"Because I've talked to too many reputable people, including seamen and pilots, who have personally witnessed many peculiar happenings in the Triangle. UFO sightings and geomagnetic anomalies that affect time and space are a given there. Glowing fog banks and mysterious-shaped clouds, when encountered, have produced strange effects on instruments and in some cases, complete disappearances. These fog banks and clouds could be the result of seismic and magnetic faults in the earth, although still considered only theories by many scientists. However, the Bermuda Triangle seems to abound in these kind of phenomena."

"Yes, very true," interrupted Grissam. "That particular region is only one of two places in the world where a magnetic compass points toward true north.

The other is off the East Coast of Japan. That area, by the way, is called the Devil's Triangle. It seems the same kind of anomalies occur over there. Normally a compass points toward magnetic north, but if you're in either place, and you don't compensate for the variation, you could miss your destination by miles."

"You mentioned UFOs, Captain," Matt said. "Are you saying they're also responsible for the disappearances?" He couldn't get out of his mind those strange markings in the desert.

"You be the judge, Mr. Benner. If you ask anybody who lives in the islands, they'll tell you that UFOs are as common as houseflies. By the way, down here the locals call them OVNIs, which translated means 'objects-flying-not-identified.' Mass waves of these craft seen by thousands of people have been occurring for decades. The objects seem to concentrate in known areas of magnetic fault lines. Just a couple weeks ago, a large formation was seen over the hills of San Sebastian, in central Puerto Rico. Dozens of people turned up missing after that sighting. Some theorize that UFOs intensify the magnetic fields with such concentration, the side effects are made intolerable for humans."

"Where do the people go?"

"That's the $64,000 question, ole boy," cut in Barrett. It does seem, though, that what we went through might be a clue."

"Do you think that's what happened to Tom and his group?" Matt persisted. "They were abducted by aliens?"

"It's possible," replied Lieutenant Grissam. "But personally, I don't think so. There were no reports of UFOs in the area at the time. Also, the dive site where they were supposed to have gone, a place called Skeleton Reef, isn't that far from land and in comparatively shallow water. Even without navigation aids, these local charter boat skippers know these waters like the back of their hands."

Matt could tell from the tone of the officer's voice that something far worse might have happened to his friend. With a heavy heart the detective realized he had come to the same conclusion.

"Well, let's not write them off yet, shall we?" soothed the captain. "We're going to get one last shot at finding your friend, Mr. Benner. We have the rest of the day before the search is officially terminated at 2400. If he's alive, there's an excellent chance his family and the rest of the divers are too. But, first things first. I've been ordered to await the arrival of Professor Vail and transport him directly to the *Explorer,* an oceanographic and research vessel owned and operated by the University of Haiti. A team of scientists is waiting for him there. It's anchored at the same coordinates where the Atlantis ruins were found. He should be arriving by 0900."

"Isn't that the bloke who's the leading authority on Atlantis?" asked Barrett. "I remember reading something about him being the original discoverer of those ruins they found off Port-au-Prince."

"Yes, that's right," his sister replied. "And, if you're into Edgar Cayce, he predicted that Atlantis would rise again. So far, the seer's been right. I only wonder if the ... "

The blast of a bosun's whistle being piped over the PA system suddenly cut her words short. It was immediately followed by the announcement of the first duty watch. Captain Richardson glanced over at a small digital clock on her desk and then stood up, signifying the conference was over. Lieutenant Grissam followed her lead.

"Sorry I have to break this up, gentlemen," the captain announced, "but duty calls. I still have a lot of paperwork to do and a ship's inspection to perform before our distinguished visitor arrives."

"Yes, and I have to map out new coordinates in case worse comes to worse with the *Rainbow*," confided Grissam. With a slight stoop to his shoulders he gave a somewhat languid smile to all of them before spinning on his heel and disappearing out the door.

Captain Richardson then turned toward the detective. "Mr. Benner, your watch station will be on the bridge with me. Everybody works aboard my ship," she said while glancing at her brother with a twinkle in her eye. Stu, will you have assigned to our guest a pair of high enhancement binoculars and show him how to use them properly?"

"I've used binoculars before," retorted Matt, bristling at her comment. *What was the big deal?*

"Not these kind you haven't, mate," Barrett interjected. "They're the latest in search and rescue devices. There's definitely a trick to using them. When your eyeballs start swimming in your head after two hours of looking through these high-powered peepers, you'll know what I mean."

Out of the corner of his eye, Matt caught a shadow of a smile playing on the captain's lips. For some reason, he felt he was being duped into something. *I knew I should have never accepted Barrett's invitation.* With a feigned look of self-confidence on his face, he squared his shoulders and dutifully followed the Englishman out the door.

CHAPTER TEN

Bermuda Triangle -- 13:18 hours

Matt stood with legs spread apart in the left wing of the navigation bridge, trying to hold his body steady as the *Proteus* powered her way through a choppy sea. The ship was breezing along at 25 knots, making the deck hum under his feet. He had been assigned the port bridge watch, and was practicing for when they would arrive in their patrol area. Because of his reoccurring bout of nausea and dizziness, better known as seasickness, he could have bowed out gracefully from his assignment. But he still had some pride left, he told himself. The ship was swaying back and forth to the roll of short, broken swells, and it was keeping his stomach in a constant state of flux. He had to miss noon chow and, upon Barrett's advice, force-fed his churning stomach with saltine crackers instead. He had used up the last of the Dramamine earlier that morning, but even that hadn't done much to alleviate his suffering.

The short hop to Roosevelt Roads in the Cessna had been anything but memorable. All the shaking and rattling was an adjunct to his stomach condition. It sounded the whole time they were in the air as though the plane's entire framework was ready to fall apart. The long and short of it was that half the nuts and bolts were missing, the fuselage was buckled, there was a cracked propeller shaft, and most of the wiring was incinerated to blackened spaghetti. Watching Barrett fly the airplane was a lesson in aeronautics. The Englishman had just managed to coax the machine into the repair hangar before the left aileron fell off. Matt had made a vow then and there never to step into an airplane again.

He had his elbows braced on the chest-high windbreak, practicing to focus his eyes through binoculars, and he used the term loosely, that were like nothing he had ever used before. The unit slipped over his head like a virtual reality headset, although its purpose was hardly for entertainment. As was explained to him by an understanding 2nd Class signalman rating, it was that same technology used in spy satellites. For manageability the magnification was greatly reduced, but it could still read a postage stamp a hundred yards away and cut through pitch darkness as if it were broad daylight. It sure facilitated nighttime search and rescue operations, Matt realized. Looking through them was like sitting in the front row of a movie theatre. His eyes were constantly moving and adjusting to any deviation in the changing seascape. If the powerful lens scanned something untoward, a light touch of a finger activated the zoom and the object leapt at you while a sensor triggered an automatic focusing device.

In a tiny corner of the eyepiece was a glowing LCD rangefinder.

The trick was in recognizing what you were looking at. He remembered what the signalman had told him. You weren't searching for anything big enough that radar could identify, such as a lifeboat or raft. That would have been too easy. Instead, you were after bobbing heads, a piece of wreckage, a life preserver, or an oil slick that only a human eye could differentiate from an empty carton or a clump of seaweed.

If you made the mistake of its endless repetition, your eyes got fixated focusing on where ocean and sky melded together. Invariably, your mind became lost in boredom. It became much harder to concentrate on what you were doing. That's where the trick came in. You had to slowly pan the horizon, using peripheral vision only.

Sometimes a person got lucky and the empty sea coughed up a clue as to what had really happened to some hapless ship or crew out there. More often than not, a lookout only got one chance to see what the ocean wanted him to see before it swallowed it up again. You had to be ready when that opportunity came along. Matt was absorbed in that heady thought when a mellow voice laced with a French accent startled him.

"It's the North Equatorial Current."

"Wh ... what was that?" Slipping off his glasses, Matt turned to face an imposing figure of a man—the blackest man he'd ever seen—demonstrating a warm smile and a mouthful of white teeth. He stared at the detective with the scrutiny of someone practiced in the art of discernment. Matt guessed the man to be older than he looked, perhaps in his mid 70s or so. His smooth features supported a robust 6-foot 3-inch frame with hulking shoulders and big chest. *The kind reserved for linebackers*, Matt thought. His hands were unusually large.

"The current, my boy," the giant said. "It scrapes and grinds the continental shelf for thousands of miles before merging into the Gulf Stream. That's why the sea is so choppy. Once we're into deeper water, I'm sure you'll find the trip a bit more enjoyable."

"I appreciate the information," Matt replied. *He must have heard about my seasickness.*

"By the way, I'm Professor Jalmin Vail," the stranger said, sticking out a meaty paw in greeting. "It's really Vailshocki, an Indian name by birth, but I prefer the shortened version. Saves much confusion with my Russian colleague, Professor Valekovsky. And you must be Matt Benner, the private investigator the captain mentioned at lunch. I'm sorry to hear about your comrade-in-arms. I hope he and his family are safe."

Matt took the proffered handshake. He had not seen the professor come aboard, and was somewhat surprised at his sartorial makeup. The old man's noggin was covered in a white turban, while the rest of his outfit could have passed for a bad advertisement in a tennis fashion magazine. It consisted of a beige seersucker shirt with crossed tennis rackets over the pocket, nut-brown and white checked Bermuda shorts, and tan loafers. A large gold medallion draped his thick neck. Argyles of cream and yellow diamonds completed the ill assortment. *Certainly not the scholarly Sigmund*

Freud look-a-like I'd originally imagined, Matt silently confessed.

"I hope so too, Professor," he said. "Tom and I are also close friends. It was quite a shock when I learned he and his family were missing."

"Yes, it seems to be an occupational hazard around here," Professor Vail said, frowning. "Tell me, how did you two decide to go into the investigative field? I understand both of you were policemen at one time."

"Yes, that's true. After five years we became disillusioned with an unwritten code of ethics that kept a monkey on our backs, and not the criminals. By changing the playing rules, we found we could shake off the monkey and parlay the odds more in our favor."

"You seem to be a man of strong convictions, Mr. Benner."

"It's kept me alive so far, Professor."

Just then a metallic voice crackled into life. "Now hear this. Now hear this. Prepare the inflatable for launch."

"Hmmmm. We must be getting close to the *Explorer,*" the professor remarked, as if talking to himself. His statement was confirmed by the *Proteus's* sudden reduced speed.

Matt spotted a small dot beginning to materialize on the horizon. Behind it, as though providing a stage prop, was the same smudge of brown and green that had dogged them since leaving port. Barrett had made passing mention to him that as they were paralleling the island of Puerto Rico, they would be making a close approach to Arecibo before venturing further afield into the Bermuda Triangle. That's where the U.S. government's enormous radio-telescope installation was located. Many UFO sightings had been witnessed near that facility, giving added impetus to the notion that aliens were monitoring earth's signals into space.

Several sailors hurried past while a work detail was breaking out the inflatable on the main deck. Matt sensed a buzz of excitement among the crew. He figured it wouldn't be long before they would be dropping the professor off. Perhaps, in the meantime, he could satisfy his own curiosity.

"Your name intrigues me, Professor. You don't look to be of Indian heritage."

The old man's face split into a wide grin, his ebony skin shining in the mid-day sun. "My father was Pakistani—belonged to the British Queen's Regiment, fought in the Botswana's Insurrection in South Africa. That's where he and my mother met."

"Oh, I see."

"A common mistake people make, my dear boy. Inherited the pigmentation of my mother's skin, the inquisitiveness of my father's brains, and the physique of my African ancestors. Comes in handy sometimes in my line of work."

"Yes, I was told you do a lot of underwater exploring. Your specialty is the lost continent of Atlantis. I thought Atlantis was only a myth, something cultists and die-hards believed in." *Like Tom.*

"Ignorance is bliss," sighed the professor. "Anyone who thinks Atlantis is only a pipe dream isn't aware of how much empirical evidence there is to the contrary.

Besides that, there is a recurring theme of a collective memory throughout the world."

"Collective memory?"

"Yes, a remembrance of a sophisticated knowledge that only through myths and legends have been kept alive. Atlantis fits that description quite well. There are also indications of its past existence around the world by linguistic similarities, as well as a resemblance of prehistoric sites. It had a vast network of colonies, you know. That's what takes me to Tiahuanaco, Bolivia so often. Fascinating, absolutely fascinating finds there." The professor paused briefly while seemingly reviving some recent memory in his mind. "However, discovering old ruins is only the tip of the iceberg. Even Edgar Cayce believed that many of us have and still are, reincarnating from former Atlantean lives."

There was that name again. "Excuse my ignorance, Professor, but who was Edgar Cayce?"

"Who was Edgar Cayce?" The septuagenarian paused, his eyes lighting up to some inner divination. "A basically simple man by birth, a photographer by trade who, through the grace of God, was allowed to help thousands of people through his psychic readings. Cayce tapped into what he called Akashic Records, knowledge possessed by billions of subconscious minds, with which he was able to communicate. He was able to use this knowledge to provide cures for the sick and dying through holistic means that were unthought of in his day. He also, through his life readings, influenced many people to follow their predestined goals in life." He turned to Matt with a gleam in his dark eyes. "I was one of those people. I was only a youngster at the time, but I remember the look of shock on my parents' faces when Cayce told them I had been an architect in Atlantis during one of my previous lives. I was responsible for the design of temples and causeways, and buildings to house their most powerful energy sources. For my present life experience, the reading suggested research as an appropriate career for me."

Energy sources! In a corner of Matt's brain, a chord was struck. "Tell me more about these energy sources, Professor."

"The Atlanteans devised a way to harness large pockets of gas trapped deep inside the earth—the internal energy of Gaea, as Cayce characterized it—and encapsulated the geothermal energy stored there into what he called firestones. As Cayce describes them, these firestones were made up of large cylindrical crystals, cut in such a manner that their energy was only released gradually. A capstone was placed on top to focus that energy or force into whatever suited their purposes. In modern science this form of energy is called a MASER —— Microwave Amplification by Stimulated Emission of Radiation."

Matt was suddenly caught up in the telling of one of Atlantis's fantastic achievements. "How did they apply this force?"

"Oh my, what didn't they do with it is the question. Through induction methods the Atlanteans were able to produce electricity, and by means of beamed energy propulsion they powered their airplanes and ships and submarines quite efficiently. Through the application of rays, they were even able to regenerate healing forces in the bodies of individuals. Diseases were all but eliminated." The professor sighed deeply. "Yes, in the beginning, they did wonderful things to benefit mankind. Who knows what other helpful uses they devised for their magnificent crystals? I would have loved to have been there to see it." Then he chuckled. "In a way I guess I was there, wasn't I? I just don't remember any of it."

"Sounds like the Atlanteans were a highly evolved civilization."

"Yes, very much so. Their technology even went beyond machines. Metaphysical enlightenment such as telepathy, inter-dimensional travel, mind-control, and cybernetics were some of their other achievements. But knowledge alone doesn't insure the wisdom to use it wisely, I'm afraid. They mismanaged their power. It was the Atlantean's disrespect for spiritual and cosmic laws that eventually marked their moral downfall. However, when the end came, not everyone perished. Some managed to escape to new lands."

The story was starting to fascinate Matt. It was obvious the Atlantologist, making a life's study of the legendary continent, had probed deeper into its mysteries than anyone had before. "How did it happen, Professor? The end, I mean."

"No one knows for sure. The leading hypothesis is that the Atlanteans consumed too much, too fast from the earth, and the earth retaliated. They interrupted the natural flow of these gas pockets I spoke of. Over long periods of time these pent-up forces find their own release through the form of volcanoes and earthquakes, you know. But the Atlanteans managed to stopgap these processes. Pressures within the earth became too great."

"Was that how their civilization ended?"

"I'm not so sure their final demise 12,000 years ago was caused by that, Mr. Benner. However, it certainly triggered major earth changes. Once their continent was the size of Europe and Asia Minor combined. Then, in 50,000 BC, the continent was decimated by some cataclysmic event. Five separate islands resulted. The largest was Atlantis, which was then given to Poseidon by the gods. His eldest son was named Atlas, from which the island continent and surrounding ocean took its designation. Then another powerful displacement, probably a series of earthquakes, occurred around 28,000 BC that redistributed landmasses all over the world. But to say, as Plato so poetically put in his writings, *Timeus* and *Critias,* that 'There occurred violent earthquakes and floods, and in a single day and night the mighty continent sank asunder into the sea,' might not be entirely accurate. He did allude to the shifting of bodies in the heavens, which might be closer to the truth."

"Why's that?" Matt was starting to feel like a student in a history class, bugging his teacher for answers before the final exam.

"I don't have any solid evidence to prove it, other than what the ancient Egyptians and Mayans, who were emigrants from Atlantis, left us in the way of glyphs and pictographs on their stele and monuments. It seems they were fascinated with the stars and planetary cycles, especially comets. Remember, it was a comet that crashed into the earth 65 million years ago and ended the dinosaur age."

All very interesting, but for some reason Matt wanted to know more about the Atlantean crystals. Something was telling him that was the key to the mystery behind the Bermuda Triangle disappearances. "You said the Atlantean's misused their power, professor. How so?"

"From their unlimited supply of energy beneath the earth, they created weapons of mass destruction in ways we can only imagine. Edgar Cayce described them as death rays. When antimatter comes in contact with ordinary matter, the entire antimatter mass is transformed into energy. Very similar to our laser technology of today, but much more refined. But, as the Atlanteans delved deeper into the secrets of the universe, their insatiable desire for power grew … and so did their weapons. Instead of pursuing the laws of nature beneficial to mankind's future, they chose the path of destruction. They fought with such weapons as the *Narayana,* which had a vibratory ray that created a mushroom cloud large enough to blot out the sun. And the *Agneyastra,* the 'fire weapon' they called it -- another kind of deadly ray that could encompass all the points of the compass into darkness. The most lethal of all they named *Indra's Dart,* which could disintegrate entire cities."

"How did they attain the knowledge to create such weapons?"

"From the gods."

"Gods?"

"Yes. It was a period of time when the gods walked the earth among mortals. It began as the Golden Age, when early mankind inherited much of their knowledge. No one knows for sure where the gods came from, or when they left. Unfortunately, as time went on, wars followed between the gods and the Atlanteans. The Atlantean's cities were destroyed, and most of their accomplishments with it. It was only later that they rebuilt their cities and their monuments to what we can only find traces of today."

Shades of Von Daniken, thought Matt.

Professor Vail saw the look of disbelief on the detective's face. "It's quite common knowledge, my boy. It's not only written in the Bible, but the Hebrew Book, the Sepher Zohar, the 'Noah Fragments' of the Books of Enoch, the Emerald Tablets of Thoth, and the Sanskrit Book of Dzyan, not to mention the numerous inscriptions found on prehistoric monuments throughout the world."

"It might be common knowledge to you, Professor, but I've never heard of this stuff before."

The sage blinked a few times, as if clearing his head of fog. "Quite right. I apologize for my pretentiousness. I have trouble believing it myself sometimes. Perhaps someday, all this will come to light in a more convincing fashion, once a Hall of Records is found. Then there will be no more doubt. The treasures inside will provide irrefutable proof. People still have a hard time dealing with Atlantis. But I assure you, Mr. Benner, there is scientific basis for its existence."

"Hall of Records?"

"Yes. There were three of them. Just before the final destruction, all their accumulated knowledge was recorded and put in safekeeping in permanently sealed structures or vaults. What we would call time capsules today, but on a larger scale. It is written that many examples of their achievements were saved in these structures as well. Some of their engineering skills were quite remarkable, you know. One of the Hall of Records was located in their oldest colony, Egypt; another in their newest, the Yucatan Peninsula."

The professor cracked a smile. "Sometimes I feel I'm getting close to finding it, but alas, I think it's only wishful thinking. The third Hall of Records was, of course, in Atlantis itself, located where neither wind nor flood would reach it."

Matt had become so enthralled by the professor's account that it took a baby-faced sailor sticking his head out of the pilothouse to bring him back to reality.

"Professor Vail," the sailor announced, "we're within hailing distance of the *Explorer*. Bearing 10 degrees off the port bow. Be there in about 5 minutes."

"Oh, thank you young man. Tell the captain I'll join her shortly." Stealing a quick glance at his watch, he said, "This means I'll be joining my old friend, Professor Valekovsky, sooner than I expected. It will be good to see him again. The last time we worked together was in the lost city of Machu Picchu in Peru. It was one of Atlantis's colonies in the New World, you know. I find it so instructive, I continue my studies there whenever I can."

"I'll be looking forward to hearing more about Atlantis from you again sometime, Professor," Matt said, thinking, *I'll probably never see him again.* "Thanks for the history lesson ... and good hunting."

"The same to you, my boy," replied the Atlantologist as he gave the detective a half-hidden smile before vanishing into the pilothouse.

Matt lifted his binoculars in the direction of the *Explorer.* Yes, there it was, lifting and falling gently in the swells like a floating museum. The scene jumped out at him like a three-dimensional postcard. Strangely enough, he saw no movement on any of the decks. The vessel appeared deserted. He would have thought the scientists, or at least some of the crew, would have been lining the rails by now anticipating their arrival.

Suddenly his attention shifted gears as he felt the first dull feelers of pain creeping along the nerve endings of his brain. *Damn!* First the seasickness, now a migraine. He would be glad getting back on dry land again. Kneading his forehead with his fingertips, he decided to stay out on the bridge. He figured the fresh air would do him more good than being inside one of the air-conditioned steel traps they called compartments.

The breeze had kicked up. Looking toward the sun, Matt saw the first signs of dark threatening clouds beginning to cover the big orange disk.

CHAPTER ELEVEN

Bermuda Triangle -- 14:22 hours

Matt saw several husky sailors scurrying across the *Proteus's* dipping deck, on their way to the fantail where the 18-foot rigid hulled inflatable was being lowered. Low scudding clouds had turned the sky to a dirty gray, heralding a nasty looking squall approaching from the east. Everybody seemed to be hurrying to beat the downpour that always accompanied steamy hot afternoons in this latitude. The sleek white cutter lay idling in the short, shallow troughs, with just enough steerageway to keep her from drifting. Forty yards away, the current was pulling the anchored *Explorer* across the same ragged water, making it yaw and pitch like a bucking horse. Matt stood unobtrusively off to the side, staring curiously at the unfolding drama taking place below. He had to admire the efficiency of the crew. Everyone seemed to know his job, so there was no wasted effort lowering the large rubber raft into the water. Barrett was standing just inside the pilothouse with a bemused expression on his face. Matt decided to join him.

A few feet away, Professor Vail and Captain Richardson were speaking in hushed tones, acting like worried chaperones at a senior prom. The detective could catch bits and pieces of their conversation, and what he was hearing didn't sound good. There had been no response from the *Explorer,* either by radio or loudhailer. The ship appeared lifeless and dead. Matt sensed that whoever had been aboard was long gone. The one conspicuous person missing was Professor Valekovsky. Even if the rest of the scientists and crew were below deck, Professor Vail's longtime friend would have surely been topside to greet him. Yet the ship was completely silent. The only thing the cutter aroused by its arrival was a bunch of raucous seagulls wheeling around the *Explorer's* lone stack.

Six sullen-faced sailors, with sidearms strapped to their sides, sat in stolid silence as the inflatable shoved off. Among them was the Executive Officer, Lieutenant Commander William Cosgrove, whom Matt had met briefly earlier in the day. A congenial sort, Matt reflected, with a smile that made you feel genuinely welcome. About 30ish, he had the build of a fireplug, proportionately built with a barrel chest and short muscular arms. When he shook hands with you, it was like gripping the meat hooks of a wrestler. Besides brandishing a firearm, Cosgrove also carried a walkie-talkie so he could communicate directly with the captain.

In the open sea, away from the lee protection of the cutter, the motorboat's Union Jack flapped violently in the freshening breeze. As the rest of the crew looked on, Matt's gaze fell with detached interest on the *Explorer.*

Right from the start, he could tell it was no creampuff. The research vessel was definitely showing wear and tear around its blistered hull and fittings. Its deck housings and machinery had a worn look. *But then again, Haiti is still a very poor country*, he realized. The ship was probably a hand-me-down from some other backward demagoguery. The 150-foot ketch had been modified to accommodate a research lab facility and berthing spaces for X amount of people. For handling heavy loads, it had the standard power winch and crane under a rusting A-frame. Matt noticed there was also a ramp beneath the A-frame, which could be lowered to provide easy access to the sea. The ship had an almost anachronous appearance. The colorful red and blue of the Haitian flag flying atop the signal mast was the only color in an otherwise drab setting.

A vague uneasiness settled over him as he watched the boarding party scrambling aboard the *Explorer.* His gut instincts told him something was terribly wrong. Whatever had happened on board, happened long before the *Proteus's* arrival.

Matt was within earshot when the first report from Commander Cosgrove crackled over the airwaves. Captain Richardson was carrying an identical walkie-talkie as the XO. As soon as he mouthed the first words of his message, she did an immediate about-face. "What do you mean, nobody's aboard? Did you have somebody check the staterooms?"

"That's an affirmative. There's no one in any of the workspaces, either. The galley looks like the cook was getting ready to serve up some chow. There's a pot of stew on the stove, but nobody's home. Checked the engine room. Looks like there was a tremendous electrical overload. All the wiring's burnt to a crisp."

Captain Richardson gave a perplexed look to the professor, then said back into the mike, "Check the log. Give me their last status report."

"Aye aye, Cap'n."

There followed a dead silence on the bridge as everybody waited anxiously. Nobody dared breathe. It seemed to Matt that everyone knew what had happened, but were afraid to voice it aloud. It was as if they were waiting for the captain to say that there was a logical explanation for all of this. He could have told them they were wasting their time. His gut instincts were never wrong. Instead, he opted to keep his mouth shut. The captain and crew would realize the bad news soon enough.

Soon the XO came back on the air. His voice sounded grim, and he sounded winded. *He must have run all the way*, Matt thought.

In between breaths, the XO's words carried a finality that was not lost on the crew. "It looks like they were getting ready to dive their submersible right after lunch. It was going to be their second dive of the day. I'm going to read right out of their log. Quote: '12:10 p.m. EST, time of proposed dive is 1300 hours. Waiting for other divers to clear the area before commencing.' Unquote. Oh, and here's something else, Cap'n. It's written in a different hand and precedes the last entry. It says, quote: 'Watchman sighted several glowing undersea objects during middle watch. Professor Valekovsky suggests seaman witnessed an exhibition of organic light-emitting protozoan, called *Noctiluca Miliaris,* predominantly found in these waters.' Unquote. The rest in the log appears to be normal routine."

Stealing a glance at Captain Richardson, Matt could tell by her expression that a battle of indecision waged within her. She was trying to come to grips with hard facts that left little room for doubt. Something unexplainable had occurred, something mysterious and totally unpredictable.

"Bill," she said finally, "you and your men get back aboard the *Proteus* on the double. Bring the log with you, and anything else you can carry that might give us a clue as to what happened."

"Aye aye, Skipper." Matt thought he detected a trace of relief in the officer's voice.

Captain Richardson turned toward the officer-of-the-watch, a taciturn-looking individual who appeared to be better suited for a classroom. "I've got to call the admiral on this one," she said. "Have Commander Cosgrove meet me in my stateroom upon his return." Turning toward Professor Vail, she said, "Professor, if you would be so kind as to meet me there also, I will be along shortly." She then retreated to where the radio shack was located, abaft the bridge. There was a telephone satellite linkup directly with the carrier in the small cubbyhole.

Matt agreed with her decision. Following military protocol was the next best step in keeping her butt free of any complications. Having a team of prominent scientists disappear from inside a U.S. protectorate's home waters could have profound repercussions.

Ten minutes later an announcement blared through the ship's PA system: "Attention all officers and guests.

Please meet in the officer's wardroom at 1600 hours for conference."

Matt glanced at his watch. Twenty-two minutes from now. It looked like the moment of truth was about to begin.

CHAPTER TWELVE

Bermuda Triangle -- 1557 hours

Next to the crew's mess, the officer's 20 X 40-foot air-conditioned wardroom was the largest undivided space aboard the *Proteus*. Its deck was covered from end to end with plush wool pile carpet. The ceiling was lined with long panels of recessed fluorescent lighting and overhead fans. Rich oak paneling covered the bulkheads, which were interspersed throughout with plaques and photographs of former commandants and Coast Guard cutters that had served gallantly in the past. A long, linen-covered table stretched almost the entire length of the room. There were enough comfortably padded chairs on each side to accommodate all 17 officers aboard. Matt counted eight on each side and one at the head, presumably the captain's. On the far end of the room were several bookcases, magazine racks, and easy chairs sufficing as a lounge area. A small table-mounted Christmas tree festooned with tiny blinking lights sat in the far corner. A large walled-in TV screen with a built-in VCR and DVD overlooked the assembly.

Next to Matt stood a serving pantry, where there was always an ample supply of coffee and pastries. He helped himself to a steaming cup, hoping the caffeine would stem the tide of building pressure inside his head.

For the moment most of the assembled officers were standing, conversing in small knots, waiting for their captain to arrive. Matt sensed an uneasy mood. The buzz of the conversation was subdued, almost funereal, but at the same time electric. Scuttlebutt had it that the advance group from the carrier to locate the cruise ship had found nothing but empty ocean. To have 3,200 people vanish, on top of the missing scientists, was tantamount to a major disaster.

Matt sauntered over to where he spotted red hair and beard flashing like the color of burnt umber under the bright lighting. The detective had to force a smile. Barrett was wearing a baseball cap with a Cypress Gardens logo this time. The Englishman seemed to be a walking advertisement for Florida tourist attractions. Next to him stood an athletic-looking young ensign with a batch of curly black hair and shiny gold wings prominently displayed over his left breast pocket. The name Bernelli was stenciled on his nametag. After Matt was introduced, he learned that the officer was co-pilot of the ship's HH-60K Jayhawk. *Interesting*, Matt thought. The lad didn't look old enough to fly a kite, let alone a high-tech helicopter. But, like all military pilots, Ensign Bernelli seemed to carry that attitude of false modesty mostly reserved by professionals who knew their jobs and made no pretense about it.

The detective listened in on their discussion about the latest disappearances only abstractedly, contributing to the conversation only when he had to. Learning he was a private investigator working in the sin capitol of the world, Bernelli turned to asking him questions about what many people thought of Vegas as Bugsy Moran's legacy to the world's crime syndicates. Matt tried to set him straight with as few guttural mumbles as possible. He didn't want to seem unsociable, but the pressure in the back of his head was beginning to hamper his best efforts to piece more than a few words together into an intelligible sentence. He had tried taking aspirin, but it was like popping candy. The pain had already started to eat into his sinus cavities. He was content to sip his coffee, listen, and observe.

It was the first time since he came aboard that he was able to see all the officers as a group. He was surprised at their youthfulness. Except for a couple of exceptions, most everyone sported solid chests and flat stomachs inside immaculately trim uniforms. The majority of them were considerably taller than he was, reinforcing the feeling that he was a decrepit old man standing next to a bunch of gladiators.

Suddenly a hush fell over the room as someone in back yelled, "Attention on deck!" Immediately, the assemblage snapped to upright statues as Captain Richardson entered from a side entrance. Lt. Commander Cosgrove and Professor Vail closely followed her. Matt espied the XO carrying a video tightly in his fist. By the somber expressions on their faces, he surmised the news from the admiral hadn't been good.

123

"At ease, gentlemen," the captain said.

As if by some prearranged signal, some of the officers sat down while others stood. Captain Richardson remained standing at her place at the head of table, examining each face in turn as though she wanted to burn their expressions into her memory. Watching her eyes closely, Matt could tell she was visibly worried, although she was managing to hide it well. *The eyes are the windows of the soul.* Once she spoke, however, he had to admit her training and experience made her sound like a consummate toastmaster. Her voice was clear and steady. The four gold half-inch bars on her shoulder boards exuded an air of confidence and authority.

"Excuse my delay, but I have some troubling news from the admiral. It seems our love boat is still missing. She has been officially listed as overdue. Half our fleet, including Bahamian, British, Haitian, and Dominican surface and aircraft, have so far failed to locate her." She paused. "She hasn't been traced on our satellite network either."

There was an instant murmur of voices; the shock of a 120,000 - ton ship disappearing without a trace was hard to reconcile with military logic.

The captain continued. "We have been ordered to join in the search after we tow the *Explorer* back to the nearest facility, which in this case will be Arecibo."

Again, another outbreak of voices before she raised her hand for silence.

"There have been no recent storms in the area the *Rainbow* was last reported in. No distress calls were sent. There is no earthly reason why she shouldn't be berthed and her passengers disembarked by now. She was due in St. Thomas, her home port, at 0700 hours this morning." Matt thought he caught a slight inflection in her voice as she glibly passed by the word 'earthly.'

"Maybe her transmitter's down," someone piped up.

"Always a possibility, Sam," the captain acknowledged to a lean-faced junior officer sitting halfway down the table, "but not likely. The *Rainbow* has the latest in radio telemetry. It would take a freak set of circumstances, such as high-energy solar flares causing an electromagnetic blackout, for that to happen. Nothing of the sort has been reported."

"Didn't the same thing happen to the Queen Mary II a while back?" inquired another officer. "If I remember correctly, she completely disappeared off the radar scope for several hours. Maybe the same thing is happening again."

"One of those freak waves, a 200-foot tsunami we keep hearing about, could have capsized her," another voice quipped.

"Maybe she got hijacked. I saw that in a movie once," came a laconic reply.

"Maybe," spoke a thin-lipped officer. "But my guess is she ran into the same thing that happened to Flight 19."

A hush fell. Some of the officers fidgeted nervously in their seats.

"What happened to Flight 19?" Matt ingenuously blurted out.

There was an immediate swivel of 19 heads in his direction, as if he had just questioned the legitimacy of Noah's Ark. By the tight-lipped smiles cast his way, he guessed he had hit the nerve of a long-standing Bermuda Triangle mystery.

"Flight 19 was the designation given to five TBM Avengers that took off from the U.S. Naval Air Station at Fort Lauderdale on December 5th, 1945, on a training mission," came Captain Richardson's explanation. "The Navy doesn't like to admit it, but they have no clue as to what happened to them. Three hours into the flight, they went off the radar scopes and vanished completely."

"Not only that," intervened the XO, "but a Martin PBM Mariner flying boat was dispatched to search for them, and they also did a vanishing act. We're talking a total of 27 crewmen who were never seen or heard from again."

"That's hard to believe, even for those days," somebody else interjected. "Those rescue planes had sealed radio transmitters and were waterproof. They'd start squawking the moment they hit the water."

"Believe it, mate," said Barrett in a saber-edged voice. "Something unlucky got that Mariner … and those Avengers. My old man was one of those 27 crewmen."

Matt did a mental double take. *That also meant the captain's old man.*

There was stunned silence before someone else barked in a taunting manner, "Now we're talking about UFOs and little green men. I think something quite natural is happening in the Triangle and we just haven't figured out what yet."

"Yeah, well if that's the case, then all those strange objects people keep seeing out there are only hallucinations," came a scurrilous voice from the back of the room."

Before anyone else could put in their two cents, the captain cut in. "Let's move on, shall we, gentlemen?" Her emerald eyes flicked sparks across the room, a poignant signal to end that line of conversation. There was immediate silence.

She continued. "I have a videotape here that was found in one of the scientist's staterooms aboard the *Explorer.* Commander Cosgrove, Professor Vail, and I have examined it already. I want you to do the same, paying careful attention to any details you think might help in our investigation. It has some strange footage that was apparently taken from the nose camera of one of their submersibles. Perhaps one of you can offer a better explanation than what we could come up with." With that, the captain nodded toward the XO who, in turn, slipped the video into the VCR.

The lights went out, darkening the room for a brief instant before ephemeral, watery shapes began materializing on the screen. Matt gathered the submersible was apparently wallowing on the surface of the ocean before getting ready to submerge. It was obviously only one step above William Beebe's bathyscaph from the 1960's, although it had one main advantage, mobility. Its camera was picking up the blurred profile of the mother ship, its radar and radio masts swaying like metronomes in the gentle swells.

Rivulets of water were running down the camera lens, making the scurrying figures on the ship seem distorted and out of focus. Several men could be seen leaning over the vessel's side, staring fixedly at the camera. Except for a slight humming and some distant shouts in the background, the soundtrack gave no clue to the obviously momentous play of events about to happen.

Suddenly the audio picked up the sound of a servomechanism being engaged, followed almost instantaneously by a loud rush of bubbles and foam. The picture immediately steadied, taking on a subdued blue cast as the submersible descended like a living creature beneath the waves. The transition was smooth and pleasing to the senses as the solitude of a subterranean world took over. Almost as if recalling a dream, Matt felt as if he had experienced a similar sight before.

As the seconds ticked away and the underwater vehicle continued its slow descent, new sounds emerged—the whine of an electric motor and the gurgling of air escaping. Matt was beginning to feel as though he was in the tiny capsule with the scientists, experiencing the same sensations they must have felt. The thrill of discovery was paramount to any explorer. To be searching for the lost continent of Atlantis had to be just as exciting as searching for a forgotten Mayan city deep inside an equatorial jungle, he mused.

Suddenly, an explosive gasp escaped from the audience as the first bottom features leaped onto the screen.

Breathtaking scenes of toppled colonnades and crumpled walls began parading in review, as if they were backdrops in a movie set. The picture gradually shifted to a wide causeway, bounded on both sides by partially uprooted buildings that were once the size of modern high-rises. Many of their foundations were still standing, along with open-roofed pavilions lined with life-sized statues that remained remarkably intact. In his mind's eye, Matt visualized spacious palatial gardens that once must have been a part of royal temples or palaces. It was amazing how well preserved everything was. The covering of sand, which had been swept clean as if by a giant vacuum cleaner, had acted as a time capsule over the millennia. The scientists had picked a good day for videotaping underwater. Visibility was almost as good as inside a Florida spring.

The roving eye of the submersible's wide-angled lens was able to capture the death throes of a once-resplendent ancient city in minute detail. As the seconds ticked by, more intriguing stonework emerged, this time highlighting bold hues and shades of granite that only could be described as puzzling. They seemed to be assembled in patterns, as if laid out on a giant checkerboard grid. Red and black pedestals supported elevated platforms the size of baseball diamonds. For some unexplainable reason, Matt's inner eye visualized them as landing pads. *Some looked like they're still being used.*

Further along, scenes like he had seen of the Acropolis in Athens and the Baalbeck Platforms in Lebanon began metamorphosing themselves on the screen. The engineering was characteristic of technology he would have never envisioned in his wildest dreams. They were not ruins in the normal sense, but a compilation of mortar and dressed stone that had somehow escaped the ravages of time simply by the enormity of their size. Everything was big and out of proportion to his normal sense of perspective.

As the scientists ventured into deeper water, variations of blues and violets thickened into a slowly evolving blackness. It was obvious the submersible was not equipped with floodlights. Dark shadows were starting to overpower the last tentacles of sunlight filtering down from the surface.

In the next instant, Matt thought he saw something, a flash of brightness at the left edge of the screen that the camera had accidentally panned in its viewfinder. The scientist who was behind the controls must have spotted it too. The underwater craft suddenly made a sharp 90-degree turn left before zeroing in on the new coordinates. In a space of a few seconds, like a ghost looming out of the mist, the mysterious light began to manifest itself into definite form and substance. In anticipation, Matt unconsciously edged forward in the darkened room.

Once past a jumble of fallen archways and broken pillars, the camera was able to focus its entire attention on what could only be described as extraordinary. A pyramid! Or at least, part of one. What Matt saw erased any doubt in his mind as to its implications. Only Atlantis could have had pyramids this size—40 or 50 feet of its silvery triangular shape still poking through the seabed, as if searching for stars it must have viewed when above water.

A murmur escaped from everyone's lips. The pyramid's limestone facing glistened like a giant polished mirror. Its overall dimensions still lay buried beneath the sand, but laid bare, Matt sensed its actual size would have been incredibly huge, at least twice the size of the Great Pyramid of Giza. He found it hard to imagine that man accomplished such engineering feats. He recalled Professor Vail's words: "The Golden Age, when gods walked the earth among mortals." Could man alone have achieved the knowledge to build such magnificent monuments?

Before the excitement subsided, the picture flickered and a new sequence of videotape began. The visibility had improved, as if the submersible was cruising in shallower water. *Taken at a different time or day perhaps?* Matt wondered.

Mumbling broke out anew in the room, when a strange collection of rounded, lozenge-shaped blocks of stone materialized out of the gloom. Matt likened them to enormous loaves of bread, joined together to form a thick wall or roadway. Each block was at least 20 feet long and half as wide. In his imagination, they seemed to rise out of the abyss like a twisting snake.

As the submersible followed their mysterious path downward, the twilight world of soft shadows and muted colors seemed to take on a different guise. At this point, Matt felt his head was ready to explode. As the camera plunged deeper into the depths, the pain soared in excruciating waves. It was as though somebody had opened the door to his subconscious and was plunging a red-hot poker inside. He broke out in a cold sweat. He had no idea what was happening to him.

131

A subliminal voice was bombarding his very thought processes, not unlike someone screaming into his ears, repeating a message he couldn't begin to fathom. It spoke of deadly forces unleashing an unspeakable power. Whoever approached the forbidden zone would not live to tell about it. It was as if Matt had been chosen to relay the warning aloud.

He stopped himself short as a muffled scream lodged in his throat. In the darkness, Matt was thankful nobody could see the tortuous dilemma waging within him. He clamped his mouth shut, and clenched his teeth until his jaw muscles hurt. He gathered all his mental strength and willed his body to relax. He kept repeating the suggestion in his mind until the overwhelming urge to cry out finally subsided. He looked down. His shirt was soaked in sweat. He was exhausted, and his legs felt rubbery. He had to grip the back of the chair in front of him to keep from collapsing. His heart was palpitating like a runaway locomotive. Gratefully, the pain inside his head subsided to a dull throb. The lingering feeling that he somehow was meant to warn people to stay away seemed to be seared in his subconscious. He shook his head, but the unsettling feeling persisted.

As the submersible crept down the wall, Matt could only watch in horror. It was as if the ancient stonework was a living organism, luring its prey deeper into its lair. He wiped the palms of his hands against the sides of his pants. They felt cold and clammy. *It'll be over soon*, he told himself. How he knew this, he had no idea. But he knew.

Suddenly the wall disappeared. Half the screen had emptied into a black abyss. An eerie nothingness ate away the seconds before Matt realized what had happened. The submersible had unsuspectingly sailed over an immense cavity in the ocean floor. Realizing his mistake, the operator quickly compensated and soon parts of the wall became visible again. It was scattered in several broken sections at the bottom of a steep drop-off. Matt figured that a portion of the seabed had broken away at one time in some prehistoric convulsion, sinking a good 40 feet in the process. A premonition of pending danger was starting to overpower his senses again. This time he was mentally prepared, and was able to cut off another mad impulse to shout out what only could be described as a paranoiac outburst. *Thank God for small favors.*

Then he saw it materializing out of the gloom. It stood silent and pale under the waning light, like a ghostly sentinel. The first impression was that of a giant stone ball lying on the bottom. In the far distance, Matt spotted two more. They appeared ominous, threatening. But as the camera lens focused on the closest one, it soon became evident for all to see that it was not a natural rock formation, nor was it showing its true dimensions. It was the color of a ripened cantaloupe, and it was clearly artificial. Half of it was buried in the sand while the other half stood glaringly unobstructed. Once completely uncovered, Matt estimated it would have been as big as a house.

Immediately he sensed its presence as the sole reason behind his sudden bouts of migraines. His head was pounding again to the beat of an invisible drum. At the same time, the sudden appearance of these domes had to have explained his insatiable desire to shout out a warning.

The next sequence of events showed two divers coming onto the screen. There was no subsequent movement of the camera, signifying the scientists must have exited the submersible. Or perhaps two other divers had entered the picture. There was no way of knowing.

The vehicle was parked about 50 feet from the object, allowing all the following action to be recorded within the camera's viewfinder. Matt could see the scientists running their hands over the dome's surface, apparently attempting to find any seams or openings. One of the scientists then started hammering on the architectural anomaly with the butt of his knife. As the sound echoed eerily across the camera's audio pickup, it sent an icy chill through Matt's veins. Not only was it made of metal, as he had suspected, but its presence suggested a mortal danger to anyone there.

His compulsion to cry out was rapidly ballooning once more inside his head. And again ... that God-awful pain, much worse this time. Words flooded into his brain, overpowering his speech centers, urging him, pleading for him to warn people away before it was too late. He lowered his head and clasped his knuckle to his mouth until skin broke and blood trickled down his hand.

At the last moment, just before his resolve was on the verge of collapsing, the spasm ended as quickly as it began. At the same instant, the TV screen went blank. The videotape had run its course. A long sigh of relief escaped from Matt's lips as his emotions tumbled back to normalcy. He casually took a handkerchief out of his pocket to wipe the blood off his hand, making the pretense of wiping sweat off his brow. His body was still shaking, but he was relieved to find his willpower reestablishing control. He only hoped he hadn't attracted any attention.

As the lights came back on, he discovered his painful attempt at being discreet hadn't escaped the watchful eyes of Barrett. "You okay, old man?" he asked, poking the detective playfully in the ribs. "You look like you just saw a ghost." He had to talk loud to make himself heard above the bedlam of voices swirling around them.

"Huh. Yeah ... I'm fine. Just getting a little warm in here, that's all."

Matt was saved the trouble of explaining further as Captain Richardson called for quiet. As before, once she indicated no more talk, it was like a tap being shut off.

"Notwithstanding the fact that we're anchored over some very old ruins," she said, "if anybody has a legitimate explanation for those round objects down there, let's hear it. The scientists' disappearance could have something to do with them." When everybody kept silent, she turned her gaze toward a square-jawed lieutenant standing a few feet away. Matt later learned that he was her divemaster, in charge of the ship's dive team. "Jeff, you're always good for an erudite point of view. What's your take?"

Jeff looked at the captain with a grudging smile. It seemed to Matt that the officer was reluctant to speak.

He shuffled nervously before answering. "If they were made of stone, I'd say they were just larger versions of what I've seen underwater in Costa Rica, Aruba, and Haiti. Giant spheres lying off their shores, and nobody's figured out what they are yet. I'd guess some sort of ceremonial objects. But these things ... and metal to boot." He shook his head. "Ancient cultures did use iron, but not in this fashion." He paused as if contemplating his next choice of words. "They could range from prehistoric astronomical observatories to nuclear reactors, but somehow those answers seem too banal. I saw no apertures or any seams from where I was standing. One thing for certain, though. By the sound of that knife striking the surface, it was definitely hollow." He shrugged his shoulders in resignation. "Other than a few wild guesses, I really couldn't say for sure what they are, Cap'n."

Those wild guesses are probably closer to the truth, Matt thought.

"Thanks for the input anyway," smiled the captain. "You're not the only one stumped on this one." She then gave a quick glance at Professor Vail, who was standing off to the side, before sweeping her eyes across the room. They seemed to settle on the detective briefly. Matt had the weird feeling she somehow knew what torture he had just endured. She continued her scan as the officers returned her gaze with unbridled confidence showing in their eyes. He could almost read their minds; Captain Richardson was John Paul Jones incarnate, and their resourceful leader would eventually figure it out. Matt seriously had his doubts.

She broke the silence. "Professor Vail has come up with an interesting theory that I'd like you to hear. It's one more piece of the puzzle that might offer a clearer picture of what we're dealing with. Professor ... " she said, indicating the Atlantologist should take over.

"Thank you, Captain." Professor Vail stepped forward as if addressing a student class. His bulk alone demanded undivided attention, Matt thought. Air wheezing through the overhead air-conditioning vents was the only sound infiltrating the hushed room. "This theory of mine comes from the work of Professor LaClare, an electronics expert, who was in charge of magnetism and gravity studies for a French government project. LaClare claimed to have discovered regions of 'reduced binding' in the atmosphere, caused by some unknown power source. These regions, he said, can literally disintegrate anyone or anything in its path. He first thought this power originated from the exhaust of UFOs entering and leaving the earth's atmosphere. However, he has since relegated it to a more terrestrial nature. I do believe, if we're willing to admit that remnants of Atlantis are now resting below us, that a strange coincidence is occurring. It could very well explain why people are disappearing so frequently around here. There is evidence that strong magnetic fields are capable of generating conditions that could induce such reactions."

"Are you saying it has to do with those domes down there, Professor?" an officer asked.

"My theory has to do with what Atlantean technology might have left us with," the scientist replied noncommittally. "They were able to produce powerful electromagnetic fields through devices which they may have utilized as power sources. They may have also used them as defense mechanisms to ward off intruders. They were probably activated by heat or motion sensors, or perhaps even by the electrical field of a person's body. I believe some of those devices are in operation today. They were accidentally uncovered by the storm, and will remain lethal to anyone coming within range."

The professor hit the nail right on the head, thought Matt, with unexpected conviction.

"Sounds like they had their own Star Wars Defense System," someone piped up.

"What happens when someone or something gets in range of one of these devices, Professor?" asked Ensign Bernelli, who was sitting in front of Matt.

"These devices were capable of bringing about complete atomic disintegration, young man," the professor replied. "It would all depend on the strength of the initiating field. Magnetism has long been suspect as an involvement agent to disrupt the balance of atomic structure in matter. In such cases, the attraction between molecules could be temporarily altered, effecting a change of phase. When that occurs, it would in effect cause inter-dimensional release. A person could literally dematerialize, as well as travel into time."

"You mean, being transported into another world?" Bernelli persisted.

"Yes -- an ethereal world, to be sure, but a place where time, as we know it, no longer exists. Ever since Albert Einstein came out with his 'unified field theory,' the concept of dematerialization into other planes of existence has become quite acceptable. He even confessed that he believed man's mind might have once had the ability to disassemble molecules of matter—and reassemble them, voluntarily or involuntarily. Maybe he was referring to Atlanteans."

"Are you still alive when your molecules have been rearranged and reassembled into this other world?" someone queried, chuckling.

"Yes, it's very possible to remain alive," the professor intoned solemnly. "The astronauts prove it all the time when they fly into space. Time for them has slowed down. They are minutes younger than the rest of us on earth by the time they return. That's how we all will be traveling the vast distances between galaxies someday. Some of us think that there are intelligences out there who have already bridged the gap."

"Which means, gentlemen," Captain Richardson cut in, "if Professor Vail's theory is correct, and those domes down there are responsible for the disappearances, we're getting the hell out of here as soon as we secure the *Explorer* for towing. Unless someone has anything else to add, I propose we end this discussion now." There was silence. She nodded. "Meeting dismissed."

As soon as Matt heard those words, it was as though a heavy weight lifted from his shoulders.

There was a loud chorus of voices and the shuffling of feet as many of the officers took leave through the side doors. Captain Richardson, Commander Cosgrove, and Professor Vail huddled together for a brief moment before leaving also. Within 45 seconds the place had cleared, with only the stewards remaining to clean up the empty coffee cups. Barrett looked over at the detective, a mock look of disbelief mirrored on his face. "Well, that's one bloody way to empty a room, eh mate? If your stomach is up to it, let's get some chow."

Matt wasn't sure whether his stomach was rumbling from hunger or some residual side effect from his mental harangue. It was as if the videotape was still playing inside his head. Each individual frame was revealing a little more at a time—scenes from some long-forgotten nightmare, and the accompanying voice burning an indelible soundtrack in his brain. *Humankind is not ready for the power of the crystals. Stay away.* On the back burner of his subconscious, Matt was slowly beginning to interpret its meaning. Without even realizing it, a dawning discovery had suddenly taken root inside him. Professor Vail was closer to the truth than anyone suspected. They were sitting right on top of one of Atlantis's power complexes. *And somehow, I've been programmed to warn people to stay away.*

"Are you sure you're okay?" Barrett asked. "I must say you look a little peaked around the gills."

"Yes … yes, I'm fine. But tell me something. Have you been getting any headaches or bloody noses lately?"

Barrett looked at Matt as if the detective had just uttered a blasphemy. "No, I can't say that I have. Why? Have you?"

Matt grabbed the Englishman by the arm. "Never mind. C'mon, let's go eat." *He probably wouldn't understand anyway,* he thought.

CHAPTER THIRTEEN

Bermuda Triangle -- 1909 hours

The captain always gives me the shit details, the ensign bristled to himself as he gloomily stared at the retreating lights of the *Proteus*. The fact that he was the lowest ranking commissioned officer on the roster might have something to do with it. But maybe that was the price he had to pay to be stationed on board the most high-tech cutter in the world. Under the skilled command of Captain Richardson, with a veteran roster of officers and crew as backup, it was definitely a learning experience. And to top it off, to be riding shotgun with the best chopper pilot in the Coast Guard was nothing short of divine intervention. He had come a long way from the Coast Guard Aviation Training Center in Mobile, Alabama. For a smalltime Wichita Falls, Kansas farm boy, he guessed he shouldn't complain when something not so glamorous came along.

Salvino Bernelli gave a long sigh as he stepped back inside the *Explorer's* pilothouse. The first drops of rain were starting to spatter against the windshield.

He would have liked to have stayed on the *Proteus* a while longer. He remembered his somewhat piecemeal conversation with the detective from Las Vegas. Bernelli had always wanted to go to Vegas, but he wasn't old enough to gamble until his 21st birthday, which was only a month away. It would have been interesting to hear some wild stories the detective could probably have related about his experiences. He did seem a little preoccupied though, as if something was bothering him, Bernelli recalled. He had heard the poor bastard was suffering with bouts of seasickness. Maybe the two-hour trip to Arecebo would settle him down. It wasn't that choppy now that they were finally underway, slow as their pace was.

He couldn't believe what had happened. Nobody could. The *Proteus's* nuclear power plant had inexplicably sprung a leak shortly after the conference had ended. It had something to do with the cooling pump failing, resulting in the reactor tank accidentally draining and exposing the reactor core, and causing dangerous levels of radiation to escape. Apparently, numerous safety valves had all failed at the same time. It all sounded very mysterious. What he knew from scuttlebutt was that until the leak was contained, the ship was a floating Three-Mile-Island. *It could only happen in the Triangle,* he thought.

Scattered rainsqualls had played hide-and-seek with the sun all evening, making matters even worse. Now the rainsqualls were popping up again, making the air heavy and oppressive, and that made him feel uneasy. He could barely see the towline stretched taut over the *Explorer's* bow. The *Proteus's* running lights were barely visible. Besides that, a terrific headwind had kicked up. It was going to be a long two hours. Already the boat, creaking and groaning like an old woman, was starting to give him the willies.

He gave a cursory inventory around the bridge, looking to see if he had missed anything during the first inspection. He had ordered the wheel locked amidships, and any extraneous machinery to be secured. His small detail of men knew what to do, and he didn't have to say much. They had plenty of experience; this wasn't the first time they'd found empty boats in the Bermuda Triangle without any trace of their passengers and crew. That's where his crew was now, he suspected, scouring the darkened passageways and crawlspaces, looking for more clues as to what had happened.

The fact that most of the electrical circuitry on board looked as if a blowtorch had been applied to it was a major inconvenience, although the radio equipment on the bridge seemed intact. He was able to communicate directly over short-wave radio with the captain, which was a big relief. A shiver went suddenly up and down his spine. There was something odd about the research ship that didn't add up. The lifeboat was still secured on its davits, the crew's personal belongings were still aboard, and there was no sign of a struggle anywhere. No distress call had been sent to indicate trouble. It was as though the passengers and crew had been plucked into thin air.

Something else was going on that he couldn't quite put his finger on. Every once in a while, things around him would start fading. It was like watching an old silent reel, where the lighting was of poor quality, and the images kept dimming in and out. The first time it happened he chalked it up to his imagination. The second time, coincidence. The third time he wasn't so sure. Maybe he was just tired. But as the minutes ticked away, it was happening more often.

He felt a rush of wind and a spattering of raindrops on his backside as the pilothouse door was suddenly flung open. Bernelli whirled around expectantly.

"Everything's normal as far as I can tell, Mr. Bernelli," exclaimed a veteran Electrician's Mate 2nd Class as he stepped over the coaming. The name O'Neill was stenciled on his nametag. "Except for the electrical feeds for the boilers, the ship could run herself. The emergency generator is handling the lights and blowers okay, but if we utilize extra systems, we'll need more juice. Probably be a good idea to string an additional power line over from the *Proteus,* just in case."

Just then the remaining three members of the caretaker crew came barging into the pilothouse. Bernelli could tell by their matted hair and wet faces that the rain was coming down harder. He involuntarily shuddered, feeling relieved to have the company.

"If you want music I found some Tchaikovsky and Mozart in one of the passenger staterooms," declared a small missile technician with 3rd Class stripes on his sleeve.

"Who the hell wants classical music?" retorted the last man to enter the enclosed room, a rangy Seaman 1st Class who sported steer's horns on one ring finger and a saddle on the other. "Give me some Shania Twain anytime."

Bernelli smiled as he stepped out from behind the steering control console, taking time to flick on the windshield wipers. All he could see now was a blurry outline of the ship ahead, as the clouds had opened up into a steady downpour. It reminded him of a Kansas summer storm. Sometimes there was even a tornado to go with it. He felt secure there were no tornadoes out here. "Okay men. Let's see if we can't ... "

He stopped in mid-sentence as he saw a mask of horror cross over O'Neill's features. The sailor was looking right at his crotch.

"Mr. Bernelli!" the man screeched, extending a shaking arm toward the officer. "Wh ... where are your legs?"

Bernelli's stomach tightened into a hard knot. At the same time a strange tingling sensation coursed through his body, as if he had just stepped onto a low voltage wire. "Whatta you mean, where's my legs?"

"Your legs, sir. Look at your legs."

There was a loud gasp. "The same thing's happen' to you," exclaimed the Seaman 1st Class as he stared aghast at his shipmate.

Bernelli could see for himself that the man's torso was starting to fade in and out like a light bulb getting ready to fizzle out. "Oh my God!" he gasped, looking down at his own disappearing legs. "What's happenin' to us?" The ensign stepped back in a sudden surge of panic, and the steering control console suddenly appeared in front of him. *Oh my God! I stepped right through it!*

The tingling in his legs was turning into a burning fire of piercing daggers, advancing quickly into his stomach and chest. There was screaming in the background as the missile technician and two seamen bolted out the door. Bernelli reached for the radio mike located in the overhead. A dumbfounded look froze on his face as he saw his outstretched arm beginning to turn transparent. A second later it disappeared completely. Next came his shoulders and chest. Horrified, he watched as his entire body faded into empty space. A strange hazy green mist had suddenly enveloped the bridge.

His crazed mind barely fathomed that O'Neill was doing what every junior officer was trained to do in an emergency: take over command. The electrician's first duty was getting his superior out of there. He tried reaching for the officer, but it was as if his body was mired in molasses. He kept crying out to Bernelli, not knowing the pilot was already beyond hearing anything but the sound of his own blood pounding.

Bernelli couldn't fully comprehend why the electrician kept grappling toward him in pleading, supplicating motions, his movements slow and laborious. He saw that the man's eyes were fixated on the radio mike, trying desperately to reach it. But then he realized it was still clutched in his own invisible hand. It looked weird seemingly floating in space.

It's the officer's responsibility to notify the captain, admonished his befuddled brain. *I must tell her what's happening here*. He raised the mike to his lips and began to speak, but strangely, his larynx was incapable of transmitting sound. Then, almost instantaneously, a mass of colored specks flashed before his eyes. It was the last thing he remembered before his mind, his body, his entire being was catapulted into space, frozen in time.

CHAPTER FOURTEEN

Bermuda Triangle -- 18:32 hours

The crew's mess was brightly lit as the detective and pilot sat under one of its ventilator fans. They had just finished the du jour of the day, roast beef and au gratin potatoes, a side vegetable of green beans, and topped off with lemon meringue pie for dessert. Matt skipped the pie. His stomach was telling him to go easy, but it was managing to hold down the entrée reasonably well. Thankfully, the first decent meal he'd had in two days was starting to make him feel whole again. Just to play it safe, a supply of saltine crackers was still within mouth-stuffing distance. He could feel the deck throb beneath his feet as the *Proteus* sliced effortlessly through the water, towing the research ship back to civilization. Immediately upon stepping ashore, he planned on calling Barb and telling her he was on his way home. The announcement over the PA system had made it quite clear that all civilians were to debark at the next port of call. *I just love that military talk.* Thank God for small favors. He was getting tired of the headaches, the seasickness, and the uncertainty.

Above all, he was tired of his maddening presentiment with death if they stayed any longer over the domes. Supposedly his mission was accomplished, although he didn't feel he had contributed much to the outcome.

Matt had come to the fateful conclusion that Tom and his family had joined a long list of victims in the Bermuda Triangle. The scientists were only the latest casualties. He thought Professor Vail had done a good job of hypothesizing what was happening out here. Matt didn't want any part of the Atlanteans' death-ray machines. Who could tell how many more of them were scattered over the ocean floor? And why did watching that videotape cause such a violent reaction in him? He had yet to explore what deeply buried secret lay dormant in his subconscious. *But he was starting to get a good idea.*

"I dare say, that video was shot in water well over 100 feet," Barrett mouthed in between swallows. "It takes one bloody storm to uncover the bottom at that depth, don't you agree, mate?"

Matt was always amazed at Barrett's range of idioms. He sounded like a cross between Winston Churchill and Crocodile Dundee.

"Could have been sitting there all along," Matt answered. "Perhaps sooner or later someone would have chanced upon the ruins by accident."

"Not likely. I wonder if it was by accident we were supposed to find only one videotape aboard the *Explorer.*"

"What do you mean?"

"It means, my dear fellow, that in a week's time, despite their being scientists who like to record everything for posterity, there was only one tape shot."

"Maybe the others just haven't been found yet."

"Not likely. I think they only had time to shoot one tape before they were abducted. Nothing else adds up."

"Abducted! You mean, by aliens?"

"Yes."

Barrett's answer was so convincingly abrupt, it didn't give the detective time to consider.

"Something to think about, I guess," Matt finally responded. Surprisingly enough, his thoughts had also been heading in that same general direction. "Tell me, Stu. What about that missing PBM your father was in? I thought you said he was stationed in Bermuda."

"He was. But he transferred to the Banana River Naval Air Station in Florida two months before he disappeared."

"Just like what happened to the scientists, huh?"

"Yes, just like the scientists."

"You never told me about your father's disappearance."

"You never asked."

"Is there anything else you haven't told me?"

"Why?"

"Because I'm a private investigator. It's my job to investigate," Matt replied with tongue in cheek.

"Oh … I see," said the Englishman forcing a smile. "Well then, you might want to know about another loss in my family, one that affected my sister mostly."

Matt didn't have to be told it had to do with the photograph in Captain Richardson's stateroom. "You mean, that fellow in the picture in her room?"

"Yes. It happened a long time ago, when she was still living in England. Met this young British Airway pilot chap. Got married—and was very happily married, I may add—until he too disappeared in the Bermuda Triangle less than a year later. Around Christmas time, if I remember correctly. Many disappearances take place around that time of year, did you know that?"

"No, I didn't. Tell me more."

"Not much to tell. He was jockeying a Stratojet at night from London to Kingston, Jamaica. Was carrying over 300 passengers. His last radio communication was 50 miles from Kingston. Said he could see the lights of the city and would touch down in 10 minutes or so. That was the last they heard from him. Right after that the tower lost him on radar, just as if he had blinked out of sight."

"I imagine there was a search," Matt said.

"Search is not the right description," Barrett replied sarcastically. "They scoured that bloody ocean for over a week. They combed ever inch of bottom between Cuba and Jamaica, following his projected flight path. The water in that region is comparatively shallow, and if the plane were down there, they would have surely spotted it from the air. They found nothing. Not even an oil slick."

"You say, *if* he went down. Where else could he go?"

"You may have noticed my sister is very touchy when it comes to talk about UFOs. Supposedly, there was one more radio communication from the Stratojet. A ham operator picked it up from Wheeling, West Virginia, no less. Can you believe that? Some bloody hillbilly sittin' on top of a mountain. And it came five hours later, when the plane's fuel supply should have been long depleted. Sound familiar?"

Matt gave a small shudder at the reminder. He would never forget their harrowing trip through a similar time warp. *If only I could remember what happened in the interim.* "What did the message say?"

"Bright lights approaching all around the aircraft. Don't come after me."

Matt waited for the punch line. There was none.

"That's it!" exclaimed the detective, waving his hands in mock despair.

"Yep, that's it. Strange. It's almost the same words that came from one of the pilots of Flight 19 when he finished his transmission with the same warning, 'Don't come after us.'"

"Was there ever an investigation?"

"Oh sure, but it's like everything else that happens in the Triangle. Oddities abound, but nobody knows what to make of them."

"Did your sister ever remarry?"

"Yeah, to the United States Coast Guard. She dedicated herself to find out what *really* happened to her husband. After receiving her commission, she's requested sea duty down in the islands in one capacity or another ever since. She finally worked her way up to the *Proteus* after many years of commanding smaller cutters. During that time she built her reputation as one of the Guard's finest. She would have never landed the Coast Guard's first atomic-powered vessel otherwise."

"Which brings me to another question, Stu. What the hell happened to the ship's reactor? Some sailor went whizzing by us on the way down here saying there was a leak of some sort." It was just a short while ago that they had gotten underway again, after what had seemed an interminable delay.

Barrett never had a chance to sort out an answer, even if he had one. Suddenly, a nerve-shattering, ear-piercing cacophony of electronic whistles reverberated throughout the ship. To Matt's untrained ears, it was as if a thousand fingernails were being scratched across a mental chalkboard. He was momentarily stunned, and his heart began to pound. "What the hell's that?"

"General Alert," Barrett announced excitedly. "Some bonehead psychiatrist from the Navy Department dreamed it up. He claims it stimulates enzyme emitters in your brain to make you respond faster. C'mon, let's see what's goin' on."

"It could stimulate a heart attack too! Did he ever think about that?" Matt shouted back over the din. He felt as though he was inside a kettledrum as the irritating screeching noise bounced from one steel bulkhead to the next. The sound was certainly stimulating to the nervous system, as witnessed by the added clamor of excited voices and pounding feet all around. Adrenaline surging, the detective followed closely on the Englishman's heels through a maze of passageways and up a series of ladders. *A stranger could easily get lost in this rabbit warren,* Matt thought. Cursing aloud, he tripped over a hatch coaming, skinning his shin in the process. He hurriedly picked himself up and scrambled through a door marked 'Main Deck.'

Stepping outside into the open air was like stepping under an open faucet. Sheets of blinding rain assailed his body, drenching him instantly. Through blurred vision, Matt mechanically continued to follow his companion up more stairs into the ship's superstructure. Before he knew it he found himself standing on the bridge, by now thoroughly soaked. His feet were even sloshing around inside his shoes. He managed to duck inside the pilothouse while Barrett, ignoring the rain, joined his sister and several of the watch officers standing on the port wing.

Matt saw the wind-whipped rain pouring off their ponchos and hoods like miniature waterfalls. He noticed they all had their binoculars trained on something behind the cutter. The detective peered through the rear windshield, but the rain-streaked glass prevented him from seeing any detail. All he could make out was a strange, pulsating glow emanating from the fantail. Curious as to what it was, he resigned himself to getting wet again. *What the hell, I'm already wet!*

As what so often happens in the subtropics, a veritable deluge can miraculously end in seconds. When Matt stepped out onto the bridge-wing, only a light mist was falling. The deck was slippery under his feet as he stepped gingerly toward the small group of officers. Off to the side was a junior officer, shooting video. When Matt saw where the camera was aimed, his heart stopped. Beyond the *Proteus's* radome, trailing some 40 yards behind, was the research vessel, *Explorer*. Its hull and superstructure was aglow with a green incandescent mist. A shimmering whitish-green halo had completely enveloped the ship.

"Bill, get on the horn and find out what's happening over there," Captain Richardson barked out. "Put it on the speakers." In the same breath she ordered the helmsman inside the pilothouse, "All stop!"

Matt learned later that she had transferred a small caretaker crew over to the derelict prior to taking it in tow. He could hear the terrified voice of one of the seamen on the ship coming over the loudspeaker, amidst a background of yelling and screaming. It sounded to Matt as if mass confusion had erupted aboard the towed ship.

"Cap'n. Something strange is happening here. Some of us are starting to … to disappear! I … I can't see Ensign Bernelli anymore, and he was standing right in front of me!"

The captain grabbed the radio mike to the bridge extension. "Get off the ship! You hear me? NOW! Jump overboard and we'll have the inflatable pick you up."

As if by silent command, the XO rushed toward the cutter's stern, snapping orders as he went. Within seconds, the inflatable was in the water and heading toward the *Explorer*. Meanwhile, Matt could discern three frightened sailors jumping over the rail and into the sea, with one following a few seconds later. The decks and hull of the ship were starting to fade in and out, becoming less visible after every pulse. It looked like they got off just in time.

"What the hell's happen' over there?" came a flabbergasted petition from one of the officers. The

Voyage to Oblivion

eerie pulsation was starting to build, casting a pale glow over to where the small group was huddled. By the time the caretaker party was climbing back aboard the *Proteus*, only a hollowed out depression of the *Explorer's* hull in the water remained. Matt couldn't believe what his eyes were telling him. It was as if the research vessel was still taking up space, but had somehow disappeared out of the visible spectrum.

"Where'd the bloody ship go?" cried Barrett.

"It's still there," came a faint utterance from behind them, "only it's not in our space-time continuum anymore."

Everyone whirled around to stare into the wizened face of a Quartermaster 1st Class. He had a sound-powered headset on, and was serving as voice backup in case the ship lost its electric power. Matt recognized him as the sailor with all the hash marks standing on the quarterdeck when he and Barrett first came aboard.

"What do you mean?" Matt asked.

"I was stationed aboard a Light Guided Missile Destroyer years ago. The Navy used the ship to experiment again with electromagnetic force fields. There must be a strong magnetic influence around here somewhere. The same thing that happened to my ship is happening again."

"Then why doesn't it affect us? Shouldn't we be subjected to the same force field as the *Explorer*?" Matt asked as he nodded his head toward the quickly fading ship. The light green mist covering the missing vessel was getting thicker as he spoke. What was so weird was the hollowed out cavity in the water. It was like watching foot tracks in the snow of the Invisible Man.

157

Except in this instance, it was a 2,000-ton floating ship.

"The *Explorer's* been in the area longer than we have," the sailor explained. "Give the Triangle enough time and it will get us too."

Captain Richardson turned around, giving the quartermaster an admonishing look. "Belay that kind of talk, Mr. Palinski. Get back to your duties."

"Yes, ma'm."

Matt saw him slip back into the shadows without so much as batting an eye. *Strange little man*, he thought.

"You'll have to take what Palinski said with a grain of salt," the captain said to Matt, training her binoculars back toward where the *Explorer* once stood. "He's nicknamed 'the survivor' because he's the oldest member of the crew who's served in the Triangle the longest. But he does have a tendency to exaggerate at times."

"Captain, request your presence immediately!" a voice shouted.

The summons had the impact of a gun going off. Without further comment, Captain Richardson spun on her heels and followed the voice back into the pilothouse. Matt followed a few paces behind. As long as he was where the action was, he was going to learn all he could of what was happening around here. It would be something he could tell his grandchildren someday.

"Look at the magnetic compass! And the gyro! They're spinning like tops!" The outcries came from a balding lieutenant, junior grade, who was the officer-of-the-watch. His eyes were as big as saucers, and the rest of the watch-crew stared dumbfounded at the whirling instruments.

From Matt's earlier tour of the bridge, he recognized only a few instruments he could relate to. He had felt like a dinosaur on this modern-day man-of-war, knowing everything he had grown up with had gone out with the typewriter. The *Proteus* employed a plethora of multi-colored consoles, fire-control panels, lighted buttons, and finger-sensitive computer screens that reminded him of the high-tech gadgetry he had seen on the starship *Enterprise*. Color-coded symbols gave easy access to instrumentation dealing with any system aboard, such as engineering, navigation, or ordnance. Every nook and cranny of the pilothouse was filled with readouts, graphs, and oscilloscopes integrated to miles of wiring and computer circuits that were interconnected throughout the ship. Even the overhead was loaded with esoteric telemetry equipment, including panels of various warning lights, signal indicators, and control switches. The only instruments Matt was familiar with were the standard compasses that were now spinning out of control, so he didn't feel completely stupid.

Captain Richardson immediately picked up the telephone that connected her to the chief bosun's mate and his party standing on the fantail. "Chief, cast off our towing line and secure your detail. We're getting underway." Pausing for a brief second while waiting for word the line was free, she then turned toward one of the watchmen. "Ring up full revolutions."

The seaman dutifully complied by moving the hand lever on the ship's control console to FLANK. Within a heartbeat the engines roared into life, spitting out a fresh gush of white water and foam below the transom. Matt could feel the deck come alive again under his feet.

The bewildered helmsman stared at the blank indicators on his steering control console with a perplexed look on his face. Without a compass card to steer by, the man was completely lost. The captain read the helmsman's expression, then gave him an understanding smile. She let her eyes drift toward the darkening sky as if searching for something. The *Proteus* had broken out of the cloud cover and was sailing under a blossoming field of stars. When she seemed satisfied, she turned back toward the helmsman and pointed. "See the pole star coming up over the horizon?"

"Yes, ma'm."

"Steer toward it until I tell you different."

"Aye, Cap'n."

Turning toward the XO, who had just returned to the bridge in a huff telling her Ensign Bernelli was missing, her demeanor exuded the first hint of uneasiness. "I don't think the admiral's going to believe this," she said cryptically. "Take over the Conn, will you Bill?" Her face was especially drawn. Matt sensed she was on a self-imposed guilt trip as she walked back to the radio shack. Who could blame her? Losing a man under such weird circumstances was hard to explain.

Stepping back onto the open bridge, Matt wasn't prepared for the 40-knot wind blowing in his face. It brought stinging salt into his eyes, and he had to turn his head away to avoid further pain. The cutter was plowing through moderate swells in a corkscrewing fashion, throwing up spray as high as the masts. He had forgotten how fast this thing could go. He leaned against the bulwark, waiting for his stomach to adjust.

Peering into the distance, he could barely see the dark form of Puerto Rico as it slowly receded into the background. They were headed away from it, taking a more northerly track. It gave him a sudden sense of abandonment. Getting back home was slipping away faster than the twin shafts were spinning below him, he thought glumly. His eyes involuntarily drifted toward where the *Explorer* should have been ... *had* been. Only a wide swath of phosphorescence trailed behind the *Proteus* to mark the spot.

He was about to turn away, but hesitated. Something had caught his eye just as the last afterglow of daylight was fading over the horizon. *A reflection?* He silently stepped back inside the pilothouse to retrieve the high enhancement glasses. He didn't want to attract undue attention to what probably was only his imagination. But whatever he had seen had piqued his curiosity.

Standing where he had been a moment ago, he cautiously slipped the set over his head and adjusted the focusing knob with trembling fingers. A cold numbness gripped him, changing quickly to incredulity as the scene in front of him zoomed to within arm's reach. He couldn't believe what he was seeing.

The spectral outline of the *Explorer* was hovering just above the waterline, shimmering like a radiant ghost. But it was who was standing on the doomed vessel's bow that made his blood run cold. The glasses were clearly bringing into focus the features of two men gazing back at him from across the widening gulf. Their expressions were deadpan and somber. Matt recognized them as the Mutt & Jeff duo, still in their black outfits and wrap-around shades. The tall one was leaning nonchalantly against a crusty windlass, as though he was resting on the promenade deck of a cruise liner. Was it only a stroke of luck that he caught the last rays of light bouncing off the lens of their glasses? Matt wondered.

He quickly grabbed the arm of one of the bridge watchmen standing a few feet away. He was hoping a more youthful and experienced set of eyes could tell him he wasn't hallucinating.

"Sailor, do me a favor. Take a look behind us and tell me if you see anything." Matt was almost apologetic as he handed his binoculars over to him. He didn't want to sound as though he was losing his mind.

With a conciliatory nod the young seaman deftly slipped them on and began scanning the horizon in a slow, methodical fashion. He was doing a thorough job of it. *Probably ingrained in him from habit*, Matt thought.

The watchman made two 180-degree sweeps before handing the glasses back to the detective. "Nothing out there but empty ocean, sir."

"Huh … okay, thanks. I just thought I saw something." *I should have known.*

Gazing back across the heaving swells one last time, Matt couldn't help but feel a wave of futility wash over him. It was as though he was on a one-way trip, and there was no turning back. He sensed some unusual destiny awaited the *Proteus*. Call it a gut feeling. He

had to call Barb and let her know he wouldn't be home
… for awhile at least. His time had just run out.

The glowing white ribbon trailing behind the cutter
seemed to be the only visible connection he had left with
Barb and the kids. They were back home, in a different
world. A world that for the most part had never heard
of time-space warps, geomagnetic anomalies, and
gravitational aberrations. Stories of unexplained power
failures, glowing mists, and mysterious disappearances
of ships and planes were tales only told by kooks, or
people with overactive imaginations.

Overshadowing them all were the missing victims.
Machines such as aircraft and ships can malfunction
and seemingly vanish from the face of the earth.
Sometimes they're even found. But the common
denominator being no trace of survivors? That was
the real mystery. Matt had read that since recorded
history in this 44,000 square mile area known as the
Bermuda Triangle, disappearances that left no trace of
wreckage or people were out of all proportion to such
recorded losses anywhere else in the world. He only
hoped he would be able to return to that normal world
someday. He couldn't shake the strong premonition of
foreboding gripping his insides like a vise.

The detective tried to shrug it off. Perhaps if he
talked to that sailor the captain had called 'the survivor.'
It was a good chance Matt would find him grabbing a
cup of coffee after his watch. He decided to return
to the mess hall and wait for him there. It would be
interesting to hear how he had managed to survive so
long in a place where others hadn't.

CHAPTER FIFTEEN

Bermuda Triangle -- 20:06 hours

Matt was into his third cup of coffee by the time the man named Palinski came strolling into the mess hall. He was a wiry sort of individual, the kind Matt knew looked like a pushover but was really as tough as nails. Palinski's blackish-gray hair was cut short, almost down to his scalp. *Probably a holdover from boot camp*, Matt decided.

The veteran walked over to a sideboard where a large coffee urn was placed, and helped himself to a steaming cup of coffee. There were also sandwiches and cookies for watch standers coming off duty. Matt waited a few minutes for the man to sit down and take his first sip before walking over and introducing himself.

"Mind if I sit down with you a spell? Name's Benner. Matt Benner." Palinski's firm handshake reinforced Matt's initial size-up of the man.

"No, I don't mind. Help yourself," Palinski replied, indicating the bench seat across the table from him. "I remember you from when you first came aboard. The ex-cop."

"Yep, that's right. I remember you too; the guy with all the hash marks. How many years in service does that make you?" Matt wanted to make the man feel at ease before he started pummeling him with a bunch of questions. He was interested not only in the man's title as the 'survivor,' but also in the man himself.

It seemed Palinski didn't mind talking. Proudly flashing his left sleeve full of gold diagonal stripes, he said, "There's seven of them there, each one counting for a four-year hitch. Not all of them were in the Coast Guard though. I spent about 12 years in the regular Navy. A few enlistment's ago I decided I still wanted sea duty, but closer to home. So I switched branches. Lost a rate in the process but I gained it back within six months."

"Where do you call home?"

"I was born in Jackson, Michigan. But where I call home, I'm talkin' about whatever ship I'm on at the time. I haven't been back to Jackson since I was a kid." He grinned a toothy smile, displaying a particularly white and even set of choppers. *Unusual for a guy who has to be pushing 60*, Matt opined. *Probably dentures*. The fact that Palinski hadn't volunteered his current family status must have meant he was a loner. No sense beating around the bush any longer.

"I'm curious. On the bridge you mentioned something about the Navy experimenting with electromagnetic force fields again. What did you mean by that? Did they try that once before?"

"Yeah, back in '43. Aboard the *Eldridge*, a destroyer escort. It was basically an experiment to induce radar invisibility. Wasn't successful then and it wasn't successful when they tried it 40 years later. I give 'em credit, though. They made my ship invisible longer than they planned. So you can say in that respect the experiment was a success, but the men were a failure. They stayed frozen. Something went wrong, and half my shipmates either vanished or went crazy. I was one of the few lucky ones."

"What do you mean by frozen?"

"Frozen in time. Somehow the force field rearranges the atomic structure in your body. Affects ships too. They end up in limbo somewhere."

"Did any of your shipmates, the ones that disappeared, ever reappear later?"

"Never saw one come back personally. But I heard plenty of rumors. Every once in a while, a man might show up on some ship cruisin' the Triangle. Drives the rest of the crew nuts trying to figure out who he is or where he came from. They usually ship him out faster than it takes to fire a Harpoon missile."

Matt could imagine the confusion running through a man's mind after experiencing such a trip. He could relate to the disorientation, after his own two-hour excursion into a time warp.

He pressed on. "What keeps bringing you back to the Triangle? The captain said you're called 'the survivor' because you've spent the most time out here. Aren't you afraid you're pushing your luck by sticking around?"

Palinski gave the detective a mock look of concern, as though delighting in the fact that he was defying the odds. He then gave an exaggerated shrug. "So they say," he said with a chuckle. He started to get up. "I'm going to grab another cup of coffee. You want another one?"

"Sure, why not? Thanks." Matt figured that once he got tired enough all the caffeine in the world wouldn't keep him from sleeping. He was reaching that threshold fast. He handed his cup to the old salt and watched him as he walked away. Swagger would have been a better description. Palinski had a nimbleness about him only reserved for men who had lived on the sea most of their lives. When he returned, Matt said, "I never caught your first name."

"Stanley. But if you want to call me Ski, go ahead. Everyone else does. Except the captain. She calls every one of the enlisted crew by their last name, with a mister in front of it."

"I was told this was either a hand-picked or volunteer crew. Which category do you fall under?"

Palinski gave Matt a chagrined look. "I guess hand-picked. The captain has a reputation for surrounding herself with personnel who have an open mind. I think she wants to keep me around as a material witness. We go back a long ways."

"That sounds interesting. It sounds like you've served under her before."

"We've shared a few experiences together in the Triangle alright," Palinski said morosely. He started to rub his forehead, as if to stimulate a clearer impression in his mind. Matt got the feeling he was conjuring up a memory that had long been deeply buried. *And for good reason, perhaps.*

"The first time was several years ago," Palinski began, "when we were both serving aboard a Medium class. We were just returning from chasin' down some drug runners that had escaped to Cuba. The ship was somewhere in the Florida Straits when it happened, sometime during the Dog Watch." There followed a drawn out moment of silence as he took a long swallow of coffee. Matt felt like screaming *What happened next?* but bit his tongue. Palinski didn't seem to be in any hurry, dragging out the suspense like a good storyteller.

"It was one of those black nights when you felt like you were sailing in the bottom of an inkwell. There was no moon, no stars, and the temperature was unusually cold for a summer night. All of us had to wear jackets. Captain Richardson, who was a full lieutenant then, was Officer of the Deck. One of the other two watchmen with me actually saw it first."

Matt caught himself holding his breath. "Saw what?"

"An atomic explosion. Oh, it really wasn't one, but that's what it looked like. It started out on the horizon like a large bubble that just kept getting bigger and brighter. It didn't register on radar, but it was definitely solid because it blocked out the darkness beyond and made everything look like the sun was rising."

"Did anybody else see it?"

"Oh yeah. The captain was notified immediately. When he saw it he almost feinted. He thought World War III had started. Lieutenant Richardson had already reversed course and increased revolutions. That's the proper course of action, you know. Turn your ass toward a bomb blast and run like hell. A report was eventually made to the commandant, and it was even noted in the ship's log. That's the last I heard about it."

"Some kind of natural phenomena, you think?"

Palinski looked at the detective askew. "If it was, it didn't make any noise and it didn't create a seiche. It was almost as if it had happened out of synch with our time frame. You know, like we were lookin' at something that happened in the past." The quartermaster wrapped his hands around his cup to savor whatever liquid warmth was left. "It's only a theory of mine, but it kinda confirms what happened a few years later."

"Shoot."

"This time it happened in broad daylight. And not more than 100 feet away from us. I was serving with the captain who was then in command."

"You were on another ship?"

Palinski nodded. "We were on maneuvers near the Windward Passage, if I recall correctly. It looked like an old Fokker warplane from the First World War that came flyin' out of the sun … headin' straight for us with guns a-blazing. There again, we hadn't heard a sound and there was nothing on radar either. Caught us completely by surprise. Before we knew it, the damn thing disappeared straight into the ocean."

"You mean, it crashed?"

"No, I mean the ocean literally opened up and swallowed it without even making a splash."

"That's hard to believe."

"Maybe so, but it's true. When you've sailed or flown over this part of the ocean for any length of time, nothing surprises you anymore. You get to see a lot of strange things that most people only read about in science fiction books."

"Does that include flying saucers?" Matt asked, half-jokingly.

Palinski threw his head back and gave a lusty guffaw. "Mister, I've seen more flying saucers out here than you can shake a stick at. They're so common sightin' them isn't even worth a second look. Some of the ones scanned by sonar have been clocked at speeds of up to 200 knots and tracked to depths of 17,000 feet."

Matt was having a hard time conceptualizing what Palinski was saying. It more or less corroborated the things Captain Richardson and Lieutenant Grissam had reported to him earlier. UFOs were using the waters of the Bermuda Triangle as their own fishing grounds. And they were as prevalent under the water as they were on the surface. The entities piloting them could pluck people at will, while their machines boldly displayed themselves without any fear of retaliation. He suddenly remembered Barrett's strong conviction that UFOs were responsible for the scientists' disappearance. His own convictions were steering in that direction, too. UFOs were probably responsible for the disappearance of countless other people, ships, and planes as well.

Matt held the coffee cup to his lips for an exceptionally long time, his mind locked in concentration, before finally setting the container down. His brain was racing a mile a minute. Even in the U.S. he recalled instances when large UFOs had hovered over major cities for hours on end, and nobody did anything about it. Lame excuses of military flares or helicopters on maneuver seemed to satisfy most of the populace. But not him. If one ever hovered over his house, he would be the first one beating the drum for a full-scale investigation.

At the same time, his training and experience as a private investigator would not let him rest until Tom's ultimate fate was decided. Matt likened the Bermuda Triangle to a gigantic jigsaw puzzle. Each piece represented a small mystery that had to be meticulously taken apart, studied and reassembled before a complete mosaic could be drawn. You had to see the big picture. But pieces of the puzzle were still missing, and that's what bothered him. Under Professor Vail's theory, the entire mystery was wrapped neatly into an event that began 12,000 years ago. The underwater domes could be the missing link, Matt admitted. The detective's search for the truth compelled him to press the old timer for more information. Perhaps he could fill in some of the missing pieces.

"What do you think happened to the scientists, Ski? I'd like to hear your opinion."

"Your guess is as good as mine, Mr. Benner. But I'll tell you somethin'. All the so-called natural phenomena that people fall back on, like storms and pirates and human error, are just copouts." Palinski stopped to take another sip of coffee. He seemed to be getting his second wind. "I'm not sayin' that some of it ain't true. But anybody with half a brain knows you can't hang your hat on that peg forever. They say truth is stranger than fiction. You can believe it out here. A friend of mine told me about the time his ship ran into an enormous fog bank, but a kind of fog he'd never experienced before. He said that once they penetrated it, all their instruments went haywire and didn't return to normal until they left the area. Many of the crew came down with respiratory problems afterward. And then there was another story I heard, where a cutter spotted a large landmass on radar where there shouldn't have been landfall within 50 miles. When they kept advancing toward it, it just kept backing off, maintaining the same distance. They never did catch up with it." The quartermaster paused and gave the detective a hard look. His mouth twisted into a leer. "I got an even better one to tell you if you're interested."

Matt's ears perked up. "I'm listening."

"It happened on our last patrol, not too far from where we are now." Taking another sip of coffee, he continued in a lowered tone of voice, glancing around nervously as if he was afraid to have somebody overhear him. "It was mid-day when we came up to this enormous trench in the water. It must have measured 200 feet wide and half as deep. It was as if somebody had taken a giant bulldozer and cut a swath right in the middle of the ocean. The captain had to stop because she was afraid going over the edge might broach us. We went one way, then the other, trying to go around it, but it must have extended for miles. She even sent the chopper up for a look. After about six hours without finding a way through, we just turned around and went back the way we came. To this day, I still don't know if she ever officially reported it."

"Could it have been caused by some underwater landslide, or maybe a seismic disturbance?"

"Unlikely. The sides were precision cut, and the whole phenomenon lasted the whole time we were there. Who knows how long it had stayed that way before we got there, or after we left? I never heard of an earthquake lastin' that long. Besides, underwater disturbances can't account for the clouds."

"What clouds?"

"You can't tell them apart from the regular nimbo-cumulus that frequent the area. But if a plane flies into one, they never come out. In wartime, they've even been known to descend to the ground and snatch up entire regiments." Glancing at his watch, he gave a twisted grin before stifling a yawn. "I'm pullin' a double watch tomorrow so I'd better hit the sack. It was nice talkin' to you."

He started to get up, then paused. "Oh, by the way, I think you're eligible for this." He reached into his pocket and pulled out a strange-shaped medallion, holding it up in the air for Matt to inspect. It glinted scintillatingly in the overhead lights. It was made of bright silver, and drawn in the figure of an open triangle with the island of Bermuda etched in the center. It was attached to a length of braided black rawhide.

"This one was for Ensign Bernelli. After he saw mine, he asked me to get him one. Tonight was the first chance I had to give it to him before he … had his accident. I guess he won't be needin' it now."

"I can't accept that. It wouldn't be right."

"Why not? It's already paid for. I don't think Ensign Bernelli is in a position to care one way or the other anymore. Besides, mine has brought me luck. They don't call me the survivor for nothin', you know. You might need some luck yourself before this trip is over."

It was an ominous prediction of things to come. But at the time Matt didn't think much of it, sloughing it off as an old sailor's superstition.

The veteran opened Matt's hand and pressed the talisman firmly in his palm. The tiny piece of metal had an odd feel to it. "Luck won't keep the Triangle from trying, though," Palinski said. "Remember what I said topside. If you give it enough time, it will eventually get you too." He stretched to his full height and stuck out his hand. "Have a good trip, Mr. Benner. I'll see you around." He shook Matt's hand and gave the detective an imitation smile before sauntering out the door.

Matt looked down dumbly at the object in his hand, then at the retreating figure. *What an unusual trinket,* he thought. He would never wear it, but he'd keep it handy, if just for nostalgic purposes. It was something he could show his grandkids. He thought back to his earlier assessment. His first impressions were usually on the mark. Palinski *was* a strange little man.

CHAPTER SIXTEEN

Bermuda Triangle -- 02:30 hours

The steady rising and falling of the *Proteus's* prow smashing into six-foot troughs provided a symbiotic accompaniment to Matt's pounding headache. He was lying on top of a bunk bed not much bigger than a surfboard, and just as intractable. He was trying his best to soften the blows by cushioning his head against the pillow and the bulkhead. It was like cushioning his head against a firing 76mm gun mount. In between the reverberating booms and clangs, he could hear Barrett's snoring coming from the bunk below. They had been assigned a stateroom that, if Matt had been claustrophobic, would surely have had him climbing the walls by now.

His forehead felt hot to the touch. The migraine had started about midnight and had been building ever since. His compulsion to cry out warnings of impending danger was insidiously undermining his will to resist. He could feel the pressure behind his sinus cavities slowly seeping into his frontal lobes, as though a giant fist was squeezing his head. After consuming enough aspirins to fill a candy jar, on top of everything else he was starting to feel nauseated. If the seasickness didn't get him, the analgesics would.

He stared absently at the steel casing inches from his nose. Pipes of all colors carrying the ship's vital fluids crisscrossed in their never-ending journeys through miles of conduit. He could hear the water sluicing against the side of the hull, knowing only four-tenths of an inch of titanium alloy separated him from some of the deepest water in the world.

Just before turning in he had decided to visit the bridge again. This sacrosanct space was off limits to everybody except officers and enlisted watch standers. With the exception of the engineering and berthing spaces, he had been given carte blanche permission to roam the ship whenever he wanted, so he was taking full advantage of it. If anything untoward were to happen, the pilothouse was where the brains of the ship gathered, i.e. the captain and XO. Their combined experience made him feel secure, as he knew they were in total command of any situation that might come along. Also, an electronic chart display, which interfaced with the ship's AN/SPS-73 surface search radar, kept him abreast of where the *Proteus* was at all times. It was always good to know where the closest land was.

He had learned they would be passing over a stretch of ocean called the Puerto Rico Trench. Bounded by steep walls and perpendicular cliffs, it was where the continental shelf dropped off to over 5.5 miles deep. Beyond were mountain ridges higher than Mount Everest and valleys deeper than the Grand Canyon.

Particularly in this part of the ocean, he was told, the earth's interior was constantly in motion, creating new rifts and fissures daily.

Matt involuntarily shuddered. It was a sobering feeling to know there was a different world out there in the ocean's bottomless depths, just inches away from his outstretched body.

He repositioned his head again in a feeble attempt to ease the pain. His thoughts kept returning to his conversation with Palinski. It had been an informative session, he admitted, but not very helpful when it came to learning what had happened to Tom. It only proved that it was still a very big ocean out there. Matt could come up with a thousand scenarios as to what tragedy could have befallen his partner, and still not be anywhere near the truth. Then to top it off, later in the evening the metallic voice had come over the PA, asking all civilians to report to the captain's quarters immediately. It had sounded ominous. He remembered the solemn look on Captain Richardson's face as he and the others stood there, expectantly waiting for her to speak. He remembered the impact of her electrifying words on his benumbed brain.

"Gentlemen, we're not going home for another 24 to 48 hours. Since our electronics have been restored, and my radiological officer has assured me the genie has been contained and put back in his bottle, we've been ordered to proceed immediately to our new search grid. We should be there by daylight. The *Rainbow* has been officially declared missing. We have a large tropical depression heading our way, and it's increasing in intensity, so time is of the essence."

Ty Jodouin

"Another hurricane brewing?" asked her brother. "Quite unusual for this time of year, isn't it?"

The captain nodded. "The low pressure system became visible under satellite imagery just 12 hours ago, forming off the Cape Verde Islands with only gale force winds right now but traveling fast in a westerly direction. With the mild winter we've been having, it has a lot of warm water to feed on. It could be a bad one, easily developing into another Category Five. That's the latest report I've gotten."

That means winds over 156 mph, Matt thought.

The captain let her gaze rest slowly on each individual of the group. "So tell me gentlemen, does this change of plans present a hardship to any of you? If so, I can have you taken back to San Juan directly by helo. If not, you're welcome to remain aboard and enjoy the ride. If you wish, you can contact your families via ship-to-shore telephone and inform them of your delay."

Matt looked dumbstruck at the captain, feeling as if he had just been asked to donate a kidney. He knew he could live with just one, but he didn't know if he could survive the operation. His analogy pretty much said it all. It meant subjecting himself to possibly another two days of mental hell.

"I have no family other than you, Sis. I'm not going anywhere," Barrett confided.

Professor Vail cast a doleful look. "My family were my colleagues aboard the *Explorer*, Captain. I will stay also."

"And what about you, Mr. Benner?" asked the captain, turning toward Matt. "What's your decision?"

Matt had done some fast mental arithmetic. Twenty-four to 48 hours from now would put him ashore late Christmas Eve or early Christmas Day. With a little bit of luck with the flight schedules, he could still be home before all the presents were passed out.

"To quote a military cliché, Captain, I'm in for the duration." He spoke with false bravado, hoping he wasn't being too brash. "Does this mean that the Triangle did a vanishing act on the cruise ship too?"

As soon as he said it, Matt mentally kicked himself in the butt with both feet. The loss of the *Explorer* with Ensign Bernelli on board must still have been agonizingly fresh on the captain's mind.

She seemed to ignore Matt's faux pas. "As I explained, Mr. Benner, geomagnetic anomalies are not unheard of in this area. I, for one, was as deeply shocked as everyone else when the *Explorer* disappeared. However, for the moment, a potentially greater one has exceeded its loss. Let's hope and pray that the *Rainbow* did not meet a similar fate."

With that, the meeting had broken up.

Matt swung his legs out of bed and gingerly dropped down onto the cold deck. His feet immediately felt the vibration of powerful nuclear-fueled pistons driving the ship forward. Here below the waterline the sensation was much more perceptible than when standing topside, he noticed. Maybe some fresh air would do him some good. Slipping on some clothes, he quietly sneaked out the door. Red adaptation lights to combat night blindness lighted the passageways. Thankfully, they provided more than enough illumination to walk around without tripping over any more coamings.

After a few practice runs he was able to find his way through the subterranean steel tunnels without too much difficulty. Stepping through a hatchway, he suddenly found himself on the main deck, somewhere on the starboard side, between the mid-ship lifeboat and a Harpoon SSM missile-launcher. The lifeboat, he guessed, was the latest design in survival equipment. It looked more like a giant orange nylon peapod. He let his gaze drift beyond to the signal towers, as they cut a 20-degree arc against a blanket of stars weaving to and fro amidst a smattering of low cumulus. The moon was just hiding behind a surfboard-shaped cloud skimming the horizon. The early morning air felt crisp and clear. He took a couple of deep breaths and found that the enriched oxygen seemed to take the edge off his headache.

When he stepped to the rail, he could feel salt spray from the breaking bow wave dampening his face and arms. The cool mist felt good against his flushed skin. Looking into the distance, his eyesight merged into a vast emptiness. The magnitude of the ocean made everything else seem small and insignificant by comparison. Even the *Proteus*, as fine and magnificent a warship as she was with all her electronic gadgetry and firepower, wouldn't stand a chance against the sea if it ever turned against her, Matt mused. But for the moment the ship didn't seem to mind its shortcomings as it punched effortlessly through the waves. It seemed to enjoy its freedom as it continuously bucked and

tossed in a never-ending ballet. He held on tightly
to the rail for support. The deck was treacherously
slippery. All he needed to do was fall overboard.
Nobody would have been the wiser, and the Triangle
would have mysteriously claimed another victim.

As Matt continued to let his thoughts roam
unhindered, he began to understand why the lure of the
sea captivated some people. As far as he was concerned,
its intoxicating effect kept him from wanting to return
to the confinement of his steel compartment. He let
his gaze slowly gravitate upward toward the emptiness
of space. Strange. The stars, shining like sprinkled
confetti in the velvet blackness, looked lifeless and
remote somehow. They didn't seem to have that
warmth and closeness he was accustomed to seeing in
the desert sky. Even the moon, as it began to peek
out from behind a cloud, seemed nebulous and unreal.
It was as if the entire scene was nothing more than a
surrealistic stage prop.

He tried rationalizing the acute migraines and the
inexplicable fight to keep from losing control of his
mind. He was afraid his will to resist was nearing the
breaking point the deeper the *Proteus* ventured into
the Triangle. He could feel the same warning signals
grating the nerve endings of his brain, as they had before
the video presentation. Perhaps if he could sort out the
litany of flitting shadows playing a game of tag with
his rationale, he could understand what was happening
to him. But for the time being, it seemed hopeless.
It was like watching an old silent movie in which the
characters were out of focus. When he started to realign
the focusing knob, a dark curtain would sweep down,

obliterating the screen completely. It was maddening, and always left him with a deep feeling of dread.

Matt's reverie was broken by a small dark hump, signifying an island, on the horizon. It was only a short step backwards in time to when pirates flying the Jolly Roger made these same coral-encrusted islands their playground, he reflected. He smiled condescendingly to himself after stealing a quick glance at the missile launcher standing invincibly over his left shoulder. The formidable weapon imparted a cogent reminder to him that this was the 21st Century. The *Proteus* was, for its size, the most sophisticated floating arsenal in the world. Yet he felt little comfort from the fact, when comparing it to the waters sluicing under its keel.

Reluctantly, he had come to the realization that whatever mysterious force was operating in the Bermuda Triangle, it was totally evil and far-reaching. Whether it stemmed from ancient earthly cultures or outer space, ordinary defenses had no effect on it. To his bedevilment, as it must have been to others, it emitted a strange siren song that eventually took over the minds of its victims. Distance seemed to have little effect on its power. It had even reached as far as a house in a sprawling suburban development in the Nevada desert he called home.

A boiling rage had seethed inside him when he had heard the sound of his wife's frightened voice over the ship-to shore telephone, just hours earlier. She was beside herself with worry as she told him of their daughter's sudden fixation with the Bermuda Triangle. It had begun the day after he had left. With glazed eyes and cries bordering on paranoia, Stacy kept warning of some awakening force inside the Bermuda Triangle, claiming it would prove deadly to anyone who came near. Barb had described their daughter as schizophrenic, mimicking the zeal of a frenzied evangelist one moment and exhibiting the doldrums of a manic-depressive the next. Stacy also complained of severe headaches. She had been rushed to the hospital and was now home under sedation and careful monitoring.

Matt noted the time of day in which it had all started. He couldn't believe it. Calculating the difference in time zones, Stacy began her neurotic behavior the same time he was going through his own titanic struggle in the wardroom. It seemed uncanny that two people 4,000 miles apart could simultaneously undergo the same neurosis. The doctors at the hospital attributed Stacy's condition to some sort of psychosomatic problem. Something was triggering a violent reaction in her nervous system. *And I bet that 'something' was coming from here*, he said under his breath.

Matt clenched his fists in helpless futility as he tried to erase the image of his daughter lying defenseless at home while he was playing Dick Tracy in the middle of the Atlantic. *I could have taken the captain's offer and been halfway home by now*, he admonished himself. But for some reason, he had to see this through.

Heaving a big sigh, he closed his eyes and let his thoughts travel back to happier times. Christmas was always a special season for the Benner family. Family on both sides came from as far away as Timmins Ontario, Canada and Nokomis, Florida, to celebrate the festive occasion with them. Then there was always the camaraderie he shared with last-minute shoppers such as himself; the bustle of hurrying traffic; the toasting of family and friends around a festive table of food and drink; the delightful look of joy in his children's eyes on Christmas morning. He shook his head, wondering if perhaps he had been too hasty in his decision to stay the course. *Too late now.*

Matt sensed a subtle movement next to him. He opened his eyes, startled to see Professor Vail standing next to him. The Indian scholar was dressed in a black caftan with matching calotte that made him look like an Inca priest. He had a strange, expectant look in his eyes.

"I see you are in deep meditation, my boy. I do not mean to intrude upon your thoughts, but I sense you are troubled. Perhaps I can help. Sometimes if there is someone to talk to, it purges the soul and makes it easier for the mind to heal."

"Oh ... hi, Professor. I was just having second thoughts about my decision to stay aboard. We always celebrate the Christmas holidays pretty big in my family. I'm afraid I'm just getting a little homesick. I'm sure it'll pass. By the way, I'm sorry about the disappearance of your colleagues. It looks like now we both have a cross to bear."

"Thank you, Matt. I feel, however, that my colleagues somehow found what they came to find. I don't place much hope in their return soon. In a way, their contribution to the scientific community was not a complete waste. Future generations will be inspired by their sacrifice to keep the spark of Atlantis alive."

"I never thought when I left home I'd end up believing in the lost continent of Atlantis," Matt averred. "But after watching the tape, your little talk afterward convinced me that a higher intelligence than what is generally believed put those domes down there. Everything I've read in our history books though, says we were still rubbing sticks together 6,000 years ago."

"Yes, very true. Our history books need to be drastically revised. Supposedly, *Homo sapiens* are in the advanced stage of their evolutionary cycle. And yet, we haven't even remotely approached the plateau of knowledge the Atlanteans attained 12,000 years ago. Compared to them, we are still crawling."

"What kind of people were they, Professor? Where did they come from?"

"According to Edgar Cayce, Atlanteans arrived on earth in soul form 10.5 million years ago. However, he also stated that physical life, referring to plants and animals, were already pursuing their evolutionary path on this planet long before the souls' arrival. During a span of 21 years and 650 life readings, Cayce pretty much described Atlantis as the original Garden of Eden. All the pleasures of what Adam and Eve experienced, as stated in the Bible, were theirs for the taking. But some still weren't satisfied. Free from the limitations of a material body, and anxious to experience the physical senses, some souls carelessly projected themselves into other life forms. Over a period of time, souls that projected themselves into animals lost their ability to project themselves out again. For them, the spirit form was irretrievable. As a result, materiality took over. Since souls are androgynous and incorporate both the male and female principles, procreation was not a problem. But once these unholy unions separated the sexes, the offspring were frequently grotesque mixtures of human and animal traits. Cayce called them 'things.' By interrupting the evolutionary cycle of the planet, these new creations were now subject to earthly laws. That was the beginning of a long moral struggle between the Children of the Law of One, and the Sons of Belial. It was the classic battle of good versus evil, carried straight through to the days of Atlantis."

"Who were the good guys?"

"The Sons of Belial were Atlanteans who enslaved the 'things.' Driven by greed and self-aggrandizement, they exploited these pitiful creatures for their own purposes. The Children of the Law of One, on the other hand, were Atlanteans who taught that these 'things' were not objects, but imprisoned souls containing the divine spark of the Creator. There was a constant battle of philosophies between the two groups. But that did not prevent them from using their attained knowledge from the gods to advance their technological achievements to unparalleled heights."

"Which brings us back to the firestones inside those domes?"

The learned sage shook his head deprecatingly. "As I said before, Matt, there is no empirical evidence to support my theory." There was a definite slump to his shoulders as if some secret knowledge he bore carried a heavy burden. "Those domes could very well be nothing more than innocent devices, perhaps astronomical observatories, from some more recent culture—such as the Mayans, for example. They were very adept in astronomy and mathematics, you know."

Matt turned toward the old man, giving him a suspicious look. "You don't really believe that, do you Professor? The argument you propounded that they're Atlantean power sources sounded pretty convincing."

"Yes, that's true. But I only believe what is … "

A deafening silence suddenly engulfed the ship, making the professor cut his words short. The gentle drone of the engines in the background had inculcated their hearing for so long that when the droning stopped, it was akin to donning earplugs. The *Proteus* had unexpectedly cut its speed down to a crawl while muted shouts and commands filtered down from the direction of the bridge. Bells jangled below deck.

Matt leaned over the rail, craning his neck around the gun mount, trying to see what was happening. He spied three uniformed figures standing on the starboard wing, silhouetted against the backdrop of stars. Two of the figures had high-enhancement binoculars and were focusing their attention directly abeam of the ship. He then saw a burly figure join the group. It had to have been the XO, whose arousal out of bed told Matt that this was not a planned exercise. He turned his head, straining his eyes in the direction the binoculars were trained.

At first he didn't see anything out of the ordinary. The moonlit vista of two to three foot waves spread uninterrupted all the way to the horizon in an endless series of peaks and valleys. Whatever was out there had to be just beyond his line of sight. He kept looking. Finally, he spotted something that broke the pattern—

a slight reddish glow in the water that was steadily increasing in size. A moment later, it quickly assumed a luminous halo of incandescent light that reminded him of a flare burning underwater. *This is no flare*, he decided as it kept getting bigger and brighter. It was either gaining in size or approaching at a pretty good clip. The detective had a hunch that a General Alert was imminent. A mysterious unannounced presence barreling toward you represented a potential threat, especially to a commanding officer that had lost her husband under similar circumstances.

Sure enough, seconds later the ingratiating sound of General Alert split the night air, galvanizing everyone to action. Almost immediately, a host of sleepy voices broke out below deck. Shrugging his shoulders in resignation, Matt figured the conversation about Atlantis with the professor would have to wait. With adrenaline pumping through his veins, he and the old man sprinted for the bridge like puppets pulled by an incorrigible puppet-master.

CHAPTER SEVENTEEN

Bermuda Triangle -- 0303 hours

Louise Richardson dreaded this moment. Only once before did she have to be the bearer of bad news, and that was on a different ship, in different circumstances, at a different time. A seaman, coming back from shore leave drunk as a hoot owl, had fallen off the gangplank and cracked his head on the concrete wharf. He was DOA at the hospital from a brain hemorrhage an hour later. She was the XO, and it fell upon her to write a letter of regret to the family, extolling the U.S. Coast Guard's condolences. She didn't like doing it then, and she didn't like doing it now. But this time it was different. She didn't think it was her XO's responsibility to have to do something that, as captain, was her moral obligation to do herself. Knowing Bill Cosgrove, he probably would have objected strenuously anyway. He would most certainly have brought up the fact that Ensign Salvino Bernelli was not officially dead, only missing. And yet, *missing* in military parlance ultimately meant *deceased*, especially under the circumstances Bernelli was last seen. So it was up to her to do the dirty work.

What was even more exasperating, she wouldn't be able to tell the truth.

Captain Richardson readjusted her position on the top covers of the bed. She was sitting up, braced against a couple of pillows with her knees propped. Her hands kept fiddling with the ballpoint pen and the stationery with its decorative Coast Guard logo on top. She hadn't been able to sleep. She had gotten up so many times, she finally decided to get dressed and try to write a letter she knew would be more difficult to write the longer she waited.

She leaned her head back and tried to let her thoughts flow freely. Instead, they kept returning to that eerie greenish mist that had surrounded the *Explorer* before it vanished. She closed her eyes tightly. To have to listen repeatedly in her mind's ear to Seaman Porter's horrific screaming, as he came crashing out of the pilothouse door, still gave her goosebumps. His reaction to seeing someone vanishing before his very eyes was understandable. Mister O'Neill gave an apt description of what had happened next. What torture must have been going through Ensign Bernelli's mind as he saw himself disappearing, limb by limb? It must have been a nightmarish scene.

Her mind skipped backward over the intervening months to a happier time. She visualized the young Ensign standing curtly at attention the first time they met on the day the *Proteus* was commissioned. He was a handsome lad, and quite brilliant, having just graduated cum laude from the Coast Guard's Aviation Training Center in Mobile, Alabama. One of its youngest candidates, she believed. She had also heard he was gifted with a photographic memory. It was on the All Day Dependent's Cruise when Captain Richardson had been introduced to Bernelli's beautiful fiancée, Christina. The captain remembered how proud Bernelli was of her, and his new assignment as co-pilot of the HH-60K Jayhawk. With its new type of long-range fuel cells, lighter frame and advanced design, it was as revolutionary as the *Proteus*. Even more vividly, the captain remembered how young and vulnerable Christina looked. Such a beautiful name, one she would have picked for her own daughter, if she'd had one.

It reminded Louise Richardson of when she was that age, growing up in a man's world. She hadn't gotten over the times when her mother had to scrimp and save to make ends meet after her father disappeared in the Bermuda Triangle. Louise had been too young to remember him much. He was never officially declared dead, so there were no death benefits to make life a little easier for them until much later. Unconsciously, Louise had developed a toughness that masked the deep hurt she felt when her mother unexpectedly died in a traffic accident. The burden of raising her eight-year-old brother, Stewart, suddenly fell on her shoulders. Now, years later, after achieving a position of status, the hurt still lingered. It all came flooding back as she pondered what she would say to Christina.

It became even more painful when she thought of her poor husband, Ian. Losing him under similar circumstances as her father was almost more than she could bear. She gazed across the room at where Ian's picture stood on the cabinet. Although she couldn't

Ty Jodouin

see it in the darkness, she had memorized every nuance
of his captivating eyes and sweet lips. She had been so
much in love with him then. As with every young couple
in love, they had exciting plans for the future. That
had all crashed in less than a year, when he vanished
into oblivion. It irked her to think that the official
register listed her father's and Ian's disappearances as
occurring under natural, but yet unidentifiable causes.
What an oxymoron. And now, Ensign Bernelli would
have the same stigma of respectability. That was what
the U.S. Coast Guard Department would want you to
believe, anyway. But Captain Richardson knew better.
So did thousands of other people, who had witnessed
for themselves the strange phenomena that plague the
Bermuda Triangle.

Prior to the mid-20th Century, disappearances in
this ignominious region of the world had been mostly
reserved to small boats and aircraft. Every once in
awhile a larger prize disappeared under mysterious
circumstances, such as the U.S.S. *Cyclops,* a Navy
collier with 309 people on board, or the H.M.S.
Atalanta, an English training ship with 290 hapless
souls.

But only when Flight 19, followed closely by a series
of civilian passenger planes, including her husband's,
vanished without a trace, did the rest of the world wake
up and take notice. And yet, as frustratingly simple
as it would be to systematically explore the region
for answers under the aegis of scientists of different
disciplines, the resolve was sadly lacking. The people
who could do something about it did nothing except
shrug their shoulders in futility and shake their heads.

Without government backing, they were helpless to tackle such a complex undertaking. The military had other axes to grind.

Louise Richardson was not in that camp. She had promised herself 30 years ago she would not rest until her fathers and Ian's loss was avenged. Now she could add Ensign Salvino Bernelli to the list. But she needed something concrete she could hold onto, proof that something unworldly was happening out here; what scientists called empirical evidence. Since the chances of capturing an alien or recovering a crashed UFO were remote, to say the least, she decided on the next best thing. That's when she started taking videos of every anomaly she encountered in the Bermuda Triangle.

She had quite a library of documentation already, she realized. The scientists' record of their dive among the domes and the recent video of the *Explorer's* disappearance was more ammunition. After this trip, she figured she would be ready to present her case. Palinski, as well as several others of the crew, had served with her since the first day she began her quest. Their eyewitness accounts would prove invaluable in corroborating her testimony in front of a Military Board of Inquiry. Moreover, she had made many friends over the years, some in influential places in the Navy Department. *After all this work ... all this time ... they'll have to listen to me*, she pleaded silently to herself.

However, a more pressing demand occupied her mind for the moment. The *Rainbow* was still listed as overdue. And the most recent weather report didn't sound encouraging. They wouldn't have much time to search. *Whoever was flying the UFOs must be licking their chops at that smorgasbord of humanity*, she thought wryly. Notwithstanding Professor Vail's theory, nobody could deny that extraterrestrials were responsible for many of the disappearances. She was convinced that's who had taken her father and Ian away, among others. But for what purpose? That was the question. She was even more convinced that the missing people were still alive out there somewhere, but unable to return to this world or dimension again.

The commanding officer of the *Proteus* paused in her reflections when the room suddenly became deathly still. With the ship's heartbeat stilled, her first thought was that they had to off-line the reactor again. Deciding to wait for confirmation, the silence was suddenly interrupted by the intercom buzzing loudly next to her ear. She answered immediately, her finger already poised on the switch.

"Yes?"

"Cap'n, sorry to bother you. There's an unidentified underwater light bearing 90 degrees off our starboard beam. Range, 9,800 yards. Sonar is tracking it. Seems to be heading toward us."

Louise Richardson immediately recognized the voice as her XO's. There was a trace of urgency in it. "Be right there, Bill," she said. "Sound General Alert."

CHAPTER EIGHTEEN

Bermuda Triangle -- 0346 hours

From his higher vantage point, Matt was able to see that the strange light was definitely underwater, and drawing nearer to the *Proteus* with every heartbeat. There was some sort of nebulous middle to it that gave it dimensional form; at first he thought it might have been a moving gas cloud. Sharply defined spokes of light radiated outward from its center like searchlight beams, each one approximately the length of a football field, spinning slowly counter-clockwise. He estimated the beams to be 15 to 20 feet wide and symmetrically spread apart the same distance, illuminating the black sea for half a mile in all directions. It reminded him of a gigantic pinwheel. At the same time, streaks of flashing red, green, and yellow brilliance was spewing from around its periphery like a Roman candle.

"What is it?" an officer asked.

"I know what it isn't," exclaimed another. "It's nothing from this world."

As the glowing object kept narrowing the gap between them, its radiating beams virtually lit the ocean depths as if it were daylight below. Soon the mysterious object's reflection was close enough to bathe the ship in an ethereal ghostly light, casting weird shadows on the bridge. Matt could plainly see the looks of amazement mirrored on the faces around him. They were all forced to shade their eyes as the luminous hub began giving off spectacular bursts, like a dying star reaching the status of a supernova.

"The bloody thing's ready to explode," exclaimed Barrett as he came up and stood next to Matt. In the artificial light, his flaming red beard and mustache reminded Matt of their encounter with St. Elmo's fire in the Cessna not so long ago. By now, he could roughly gauge the object as having a 50-foot or better diameter.

"Look! Some of the beams are starting to bend," someone shouted.

Sure enough, as Matt studied the scene with a pair of high-enhancement binoculars he had confiscated, he saw for himself what was happening. Some of the beams were curving inward, not unlike a giant version of a Catherine wheel rocket he had seen at fireworks displays. Meanwhile, the center of the lightwheel was continuing to approach the *Proteus* with pinpoint accuracy. Already, the tips of its elongated spokes were starting to pass under the ship's hull like reaching skeletal fingers.

As far as Captain Richardson was concerned, that was close enough. "Left full rudder, all ahead flank!" she barked vehemently to a lean, blond-haired youth stationed at the helm. Almost immediately, the *Proteus* lunged as if a tiger had just been freed out of its cage. A powerful roar erupted from the stern. The vessel's twin screws bit deeply into the water as its atomic reactor powered up the 32,000 horsepower turbines to their maximum revolutions. Everyone on the bridge had to grab for a handhold as the hard turn and unleashed power drove the starboard side of the ship 50 degrees closer to the waterline.

"You have any idea what it is?" the captain asked Professor Vail. She had to raise her voice above the increased drumming noise beneath their feet. "Could it be a marine organism of some kind?" It seemed to Matt she wasn't ruling out any possibilities.

"I don't know, Captain," the professor replied. "But if I remember correctly, in the *Explorer's* log there was mention of their spotting a genus called the Noctiluca."

"Well?" Captain Richardson snapped back somewhat exasperatingly. "Is that what it is?"

"No, I don't believe so. Noctiluca will not pattern themselves in such numbers. I believe what we are witnessing is something totally unknown to science. If it is organic, it boggles the imagination to think such a monstrous creature inhabits our ocean."

"Whatever it is, there's more of 'em," announced a dour-faced officer hunched over a SURTASS LFA sonar unit, a towed Array Sensor System that provided both active and passive detection. "Thirty points off the port bow. Range, 1,000 yards. Speed, 30 knots. Depth, 45 feet. I'm reading another one keeping station behind us. Same depth. Range, 1,200 yards."

Everyone turned to the new coordinates. There was no mistaking the configuration of another giant lightwheel on a collision course with them, with another one following close astern. To Matt it almost seemed as if they were purposely trying to maneuver the ship into a box. Next to him was the ubiquitous officer with his camcorder, recording the action. The detective figured he must have standing orders to start shooting every time they ran into something not written in the ship's plan of the day. *It's a wonder he hadn't run out of tape yet.*

"Come to bearing zero-two-zero!" the captain yelled to the helmsman through the open door of the pilothouse. Matt could read the puzzlement on her face. She had probably reached the same conclusion; they were being shepherded into a trap like a hunted animal.

As the cutter swung to the new course, more sonar sightings were being reported coming from all points of the compass. To Matt, the perplexed officer sounded as if he was reading off a list of attacking undersea kamikazes.

"Hard right rudder. Steer course one-four-five degrees." This time there was growing concern in Captain Richardson's voice. She hurriedly flipped the intercom switch to the reactor room. "Emergency speed, Harry! Give me all you've got!"

Matt could hear more bells jangling in the background. He didn't think it possible, but the artificial breeze blowing in his face freshened just a bit more as the *Proteus* found new life. The reverberation of the thrashing screws radiating through the deck left a tingling sensation in his legs.

After several more wild maneuverings by the *Proteus*, Matt realized that the captain was fighting a losing battle. The converging lightwheels were closing in on them from all sides. He could hear the hard-pressed sonar officer calling off coordinates as he desperately tried to keep up with all the white pips materializing like live maggots on his screen.

"Bearing zero, zero, zero. Head on, skipper. Range, 2,000 yards, depth, 25 feet. Closing fast. Wait a minute. There's ... there's another one behind it. Range 2,200 yards. There's several on the port quarter. I make out three ... no, four more. Damn! Two are coming up on the starboard side. Range ... 1,900 yards. Speed, 40 knots. Jesus ... they're all around us!"

Matt quickly came to the realization that the *Proteus* was surrounded. They couldn't outrun the lightwheels, and they couldn't outmaneuver them. The cutter was caught inside a giant closing net. There was no escape. He could see the reluctance to admit defeat etched on the captain's face.

She finally gave in. "All stop! Belay any more readings. Reel in the Array." The decisiveness of her words sliced through the enclosed space like a surgeon's scalpel. Almost immediately the *Proteus* fell away sharply, while bells deep within her bowels echoed their acknowledgment. A deathly stillness settled over the ship. The backwash of waves slapping against the hull was the only sound Matt could identify. Everyone seemed to be holding their breath to see what would happen next.

It didn't take long before the first of the luminous spokes began passing under their keel. The lightwheels came in groups, sometimes three and four of them at a time, crossing over and under each other like maddened hornets. With amazing alacrity, none of the hubs ever came close to hitting one another, Matt observed. With all their cavorting, one had to assume they were under some kind of intelligent control. Every time a spoke flashed by, Matt and the rest would have to shield their eyes from the blinding glare. The entire ship basked in their eerie glow.

"Looks like a fireworks spectacular on the Fourth of July," commented one of the officers. Matt had to agree. The exhibition was a mesmerizing display of pyrotechnics that would have evoked ooohh's and aaahh's at any Fourth of July celebration.

For approximately the next hour the *Proteus* played host to whomever, or whatever, was behind the strange force operating the lightwheels. At about five-second intervals, the luminosity from one of the spokes would sweep up one side of the ship and down the other. Each time it occurred, Matt could feel the electricity in the air. It was like being subjected to a high-energy field; the hairs on his body stood on end, just as he had experienced in the Cessna. But this time, there was something different. He began to experience a warm, relaxing sensation slowly seeping into his body. He wondered if anyone else was experiencing it. He started to ask, but thought better of it. Everyone was too absorbed in the undersea light show to pay him any mind, he decided.

Occasionally, one of the lightwheels would reverse course and retrace its path under the ship, while others would simply reverse their rotation and fly off in a different direction. It almost seemed like a game to them, as if the strange objects were challenging the captain to chase them. But the *Proteus's* leader wasn't biting.

At one point, everyone on the bridge had a chance to examine one of the hubs up close when it suddenly dimmed and hesitated ever so briefly under the ship's hull. If there were any skeptics in the crowd who doubted UFOs were real, what they saw would have made them instant converts, Matt opined. The core appeared to be solid and elliptically shaped, about 50 feet in diameter, and circumvented by apertures emitting an intense kaleidoscope of colors. By spinning on its axis at a tremendous rate, the colors solidified, producing the mysterious beams of dazzling light that were making the ocean around the lightwheels look like an underwater sunburst. When the hub suddenly accelerated, it was as if a thousand light bulbs had exploded in their faces.

"Well, I'll be ... " gasped a gawking officer standing next to Matt. "I would have never believed it in a million years."

"Look! The magnetic compass and gyro are going nuts again!" someone cried from the pilothouse. Matt stepped back inside and overheard someone else exclaiming that the microwave linkup with a Celestial Tracking and Relay Satellite, one of the ship's electronic eyes, was also showing anomalous readings.

"That's impossible," muttered Lieutenant Grissam savagely. "That satellite is in a geosynchronous orbit 600 miles up. There's no way any interference from earth could affect it."

Ty Jodouin

"Our GPS screen is blank. No signal coming in," came another announcement. These all sounded to Matt like a rehash of the mysterious glitches Barrett and he had experienced aboard the Cessna.

Captain Richardson turned toward a balding baby-faced officer standing within earshot. "That's your department, Merv. Check it out."

"Aye, aye Cap'n."

A long moment later, a puzzled look was on the captain's face as she returned from the radio shack. Picking up the radiotelephone mike, she turned a knob that would let her tune in directly to the carrier. You could always hear lively chatter between conversing ships on the different frequencies while in the military bandwidth. This time, only ominous crackling static could be heard from the overhead speakers. The airwaves had inexplicably gone silent. While reflected shadows danced across the room, the captain's face took on the haunted look of someone whose perception of reality had just been deeply shaken.

"It seems we can't reach the admiral or anyone else for the time being," she said detachedly as if voicing her thoughts aloud. "Which means we're completely incommunicado with the outside world." For the first time, Matt saw that the captain looked ill at ease. It made him feel jittery. When the XO stepped over and said something to her in hushed tones, it must have been something she concurred with, for she nodded as if complying.

Then somebody outside cried out, "Look, they're leaving!"

Sure enough, by the time Matt and the rest in the pilothouse rushed back to the bridge wing, the last of the lightwheels were fading from sight. But unlike their arrival, their departure seemed to be governed by a single mind. Simulating a squadron of batfish, they all sought the shelter of the depths at once. Within seconds the last of their blazing centers were extinguished by the all-consuming blackness below. The stars and moon and the surrounding vastness again reasserted themselves, as if nothing had happened.

When the captain spoke again her voice carried her old self-assurance, which Matt found extremely comforting.

"I expect to get our communications back soon, gentlemen." She deliberately paused for effect as she studied each individual officer around her. She got what she expected; their faces in total concordance with her assessment. "In the meantime, I'm sending the chopper as a courier to the admiral. It will leave at daybreak, which ... " she glanced with a practiced eye at the first vestiges of pink spreading over the horizon, " ... will be very shortly. Our mission has not changed. We must have an update on that low-pressure system off the Cape Verde Islands. It will determine how long we can stay out here." She turned to her brother. "Stewart, I want you to accompany Lieutenant Washington as backup pilot. He will inform the admiral of our situation and get the latest dope as to what's happening with the *Rainbow*. Get your coordinates from Lieutenant Grissam."

Matt could see Barrett's face light up like a kid's in a candy store. It was his chance to get back into his own element again. Having Barrett ride shotgun in the place of the missing Bernelli was probably the captain's best bet, the detective surmised. Normally civilians weren't allowed to fly military aircraft, but Matt got the feeling Captain Richardson was playing her best hand, relying on her brother's flying experience to even the odds.

Once General Alert was cancelled and only the watch-standers were left on the bridge, Matt decided to hang around awhile. A resurgence of fleeting memories was somehow trying to resurface from somewhere deep in his consciousness. He needed desperately to sort things and start putting together more pieces of that puzzle. But first, he had to stop and reevaluate his own situation. Amazingly, something fortuitous had happened to him. The stimulation of the crisp morning air was bringing in a flood of new energies. The dull ache in his head and the somewhat lesser scourge in his stomach— things he had learned to live with for so long that he had begun to think were normal— were completely gone. Vanished, wiped out, just like that. He felt rejuvenated. Maybe it would be short-lived, but he didn't think so. He had heard stories of the recuperative effects UFOs had on people. Some terminal diseases were even cured by their intercession.

In his pocket, he fingered the talisman Palinski had given him. It had a cold, slippery feel. Apart from the magical power it promised, it was hard to believe it could protect him from the forces behind the demonstration he had just witnessed. There was little doubt left in his mind that the Bermuda Triangle and

UFOs were inexorably linked. One more piece of the puzzle had just fallen into place.

In the background, Matt could hear the thump-thump-thump of powerful rotors chopping up the cool pre-dawn chill. Hints of a new day's sun peeking over the earth's curvature were harshly reflected by a splash of brilliant magenta lighting up the morning sky. A red blinking strobe light on the Jayhawk's rotor tail lifted into the air as the 22,000-pound machine rapidly gained altitude. Once it was silhouetted against the waxing sunrise, the sleek bird reminded Matt of an eagle leaving its nest for a day's hunt.

As the last of the chopper's thundering engines faded in the distance, Matt suddenly began to feel very tired. He had to hold on to the bulwark for support. His energy level was slipping fast. It was as if he had just swallowed a bottle of sleeping pills. His legs were rubbery, his arms disjointed. *Maybe a delayed reaction to getting soaked last night. No, that's stupid thinking*, he told himself. *It certainly wouldn't make me feel like I haven't slept in a week.* He shook his head, trying to clear the cobwebs. But it did no good. He was sliding down a deep, long, dark tunnel … fast. It didn't make sense.

Wait a minute! Through the debilitating fog muddling his brain was something else that didn't make sense. The direction the *Proteus* was travelling. If they had maintained their northerly course, as the captain had ordered, why was the rising sun facing him on the port side of the ship? He was on the port side of the ship, wasn't he? He glanced toward the bow and saw that he was. His befuddled thoughts could only come up with one answer. They were going back the way they came ... back to the domes.

That was unacceptable. He had to make the captain aware of what was happening. He was certain that blundering back to the vicinity of the domes would be catastrophic. Carol and the kids were depending on his return by Christmas. *He* was depending on it.

That was the only reality he had left to hang on to in this crazy, topsy-turvy world. Slowly, painstakingly, he groped his way back to the pilothouse.

Matt was tripping over his own feet by the time he reached the door. As he stumbled back into the room, he was in for the shock of his life. Everywhere he looked, the watch-standers were staggering around like a bunch of zombies. Some were lounging against whatever kept them propped up, while others had simply slumped to the deck and were apparently fast asleep. The helmsman had already collapsed at his post. Matt took a quick glance at the control panel and saw that the man must have thankfully put the ship on autopilot before passing out.

Matt grabbed the officer nearest him by the arm and spun the man around to face him. The poor guy's eyes were glazed and distant, with the disheveled look of someone in a state of shock. Matt recognized him as the man with the video camera.

"What's happenin' to us?" the detective demanded.

"I ... I don' know ... somethin' strange."

"Have you notified the cap'n?" Matt slurred. His tongue was starting to feel too big for his mouth.

"Yes ... I tried reachin' her ... over the squaaawk box."

"Whereee is she?"

"In ... her quartersss." That was the last of the man's speech as he gently slumped to the deck, pitifully sliding his hand down the detective's pant leg until stilled by unconsciousness. He laid there softly on the deck with his eyes closed and a composed look on his face. Matt saw he wasn't dead, only sleeping. *Thank God.*

Matt managed to stagger back out to the bridge wing. The fresh breeze blowing in his face didn't seem to help. Everywhere he looked on the deck below he saw men stretched out at their post, either asleep or in the last stages of consciousness. He himself was fast approaching the somnambulistic state of a sleepwalker. His eyelids felt like lead shields. He knew he was not long for this world. He only hoped he wasn't taking that assumption literally. Perhaps none of them would ever wake up again.

Blundering down a short companionway, he succeeded in reaching the passageway leading to the captain's stateroom. But that's as far as he got. His legs finally gave out. He could feel the strength draining from his body as he slumped to the deck. He found the hard surface of the cold steel not as uncomfortable as he had first imagined. Curling up in a fetal position, his brain clouded over and a deep dark tunnel awaited him. His last remaining thoughts were of Barb and the kids, having Christmas dinner without him.

CHAPTER NINETEEN

Bermuda Triangle -- 09:17 hours

The beating of the giant rotor above Stu Barrett's head was like music to his ears. Half a lifetime ago he had been in a different kind of chopper and in a different part of the world, but still, it was all the same— the exhilaration of a full-thrust dawn takeoff, the boundary layer of air pushing the nose at over 200 mph, the sea and sky melding together in a cornucopia of morning colors. But there were differences.

For one thing, the modified HH-60K Jayhawk, with its light alloy fuselage, powerful turbojet engines, flight control computers, and high-tech avionics, was like a Rolls-Royce compared to the lumbering Apaches with their archaic hardware of the Gulf War. What hadn't appeared in the press reports or on CNN was what still kept him awake at nights— the deadly white contrails of ground-to-air missiles, the rattle of ground fire, and the shouts of wounded comrades.

Although the Jayhawk's fuselage was insulated with soundproof baffles, Barrett could still feel the scream of the air intakes sucking up voluminous amounts of air through the thin titanium shell. This upgraded version, with its larger fuel cells, could stay in the air longer than anything he had flown before. His and the pilot's white helmets, with *USCGC PROTEUS* stenciled across the front, were also engineering marvels. Built-in digitized sensors enabled them to have normal two-way conversations without throat mikes, while high-enhancement night-vision visors allowed long-range visibility in the darkest of nights. Barrett almost felt omnipotent.

He gave a measured glance at the young black pilot seated next to him. Although his boyish features belied the fact, Lieutenant Fletcher Washington was hardly a rookie. He had flown over 150 combat missions with UN peacekeeping forces as well as Afghanistan and Iraq before 'volunteering' to join the *Proteus*. Barrett had learned that the veteran pilot had served with his sister when she was captain of a 270-foot Medium Endurance Cutter, the *Bucyrus*. He also found out Lt. Washington didn't care much for female commanding officers, although he took exception with Captain Richardson. He once referred to her as having 'balls.' Washington was cool, calm, and collected, the epitome of military bearing and self-assurance ... and self-centeredness, Barrett was forced to include in his analysis. Washington's taste in women was not lacking, however. Stuck in the overhead panel was the photograph of a young bathing beauty in a scanty bikini, striking a most voluptuous pose. Her mahogany skin suggested she was a native Carib, or perhaps even Cuban.

On the side of Washington's helmet was painted, in flamboyant script lettering, *Black Angel*. It was also the chopper's official call sign, with a picture of a black angel painted alongside the tail assembly. If that wasn't enough hubris, they both wore highly reflective orange nomex flight suits that made Barrett feel like a lit-up neon sign. That was the whole idea, according to a leading psychiatrist lauding the psychological impact it would have on a survivor in the water. A bit overdone perhaps, but effective, Barrett conceded. Probably the same bloke that thought up the General Alert ear-buster. The only people missing were the mechanic and rescue swimmer who normally sat in the empty seats behind him. You don't need extra baggage on a courier mission, his sister had explained. Still, he missed the companionship. Washington wasn't much of a conversationalist.

Looking out through the Lexan canopy, Barrett saw that the complexion of the ocean had changed little since the days he flew rescue missions over the Persian Gulf. Nothing broke the pattern of cerulean except the random patches of phosphorescent water streaming like endless white ribbons in the distance. Some called the glowing streaks 'white water,' and they were the last light on earth astronauts could see on their way into space.

The Englishman studied the airspace surrounding their tiny world. There wasn't a cloud in the sky, and the limitless sea showed no breaks except the parade of small whitecaps that stretched all the way to the horizon. He was surprised the place wasn't teeming with ships and planes looking for the lost cruise liner.

213

Time seemed to be standing still. From the amount of hours they'd been in the air, they should have been well over the Bermuda Islands by now.

Nonchalantly he shifted his gaze to the white vastness below, then frowned. "What do you make of the color of the water down there?" he asked. For some reason it had a different look.

The pilot shrugged as if flicking off a fly. "Can't figure. Been around since Columbus's day as far as I know. Maybe even longer."

"Strange. The whiteness is much more radiant than I've seen it before. And I've been flying this ocean for a long time," Barrett reminded him.

"Some attribute it to banks of small luminescent fish, marl stirred up by fish, or radioactivity in the water," Washington expounded. "Take your pick."

Barrett sensed none of those explanations was what caused him to have doubts about the glowing waters. But in five minutes the phenomenon had passed out of sight, and out of mind. *We should be coming up on the carrier soon*, he thought. He was growing restless. He was a pilot and was born to fly. He didn't like the inactivity of simply being a passenger, having too much time to think about events in his life that he would just soon forget. By habit, as he did when he needed a diversion, he let his mind rove. He never tired of summoning from his subconscious the relaxing calm of a tranquil sea, or envisage a painter's palette of exploding colors blazoning a breaking dawn. It awakened his artistic senses every time.

Except for today. Something about the blood-red sunrise had bothered him. There wasn't the splash of soft reds, oranges, and golden yellows he was accustomed to seeing; instead, it was as if a gaping wound had opened up in the eastern sky. Barrett figured unusual atmospheric effects were the cause.

He fidgeted in his seat as he recalled something even more unnerving. By the time he and Washington had reached the helipad on board ship, they were almost asleep on their feet. Both had the strongest desire to just lay down under the shelter of the helicopter and take a nap. Thankfully, the feeling dissipated quickly once the pilot got the Jayhawk into the air and away from the general area where the lightwheels, i.e. UFO's, had been last seen. Perhaps the unworldly objects had something to do with it, the Englishman opined.

The ionization from the UFO's could also explain why some of the helicopter's electronics were fried. It was similar to what he had experienced in the Cessna. The nose-mounted AN/APN-217 Doppler Search and Weather radar unit with its infrared thermal imager, integrated to operate inside its own nonconductive pod, was the only thing on line besides the gyro and magnetic compass. Their most reliable navigational instrument, the GPS, which was tied in to four NAVSTAR satellites orbiting above them, was showing a complete vanishing act. So was the VOR, which should have been receiving telltale navigational signals from several base stations around the globe to help them pinpoint their exact location.

Barrett casually glanced at the quivering needle of the magnetic compass. It was behaving erratically, but was showing a northerly course, as was the directional gyro. He let his gaze roam to the small green fluorescent oscilloscope squeezed in between electronic moving map displays that had gone ominously blank. For the last several minutes he had been watching for signs of the carrier, but all that was showing on the edge of the radar screen was an oval shaped blip, signifying a mid-size island. *Could be part of the Bahama chain,* he opined.

With the helicopter travelling at an airspeed of a little over 180 mph, it wasn't long before he saw a swelling blotch of green and brown racing up to meet them from 800 feet below. *Wait a minute!* Barrett sat up straight. A flyer's sixth sense had just been activated inside his brain. Something didn't add up. Glancing at the instrument panel with unbelieving eyes, he finally fixed his gaze on the island once again. It didn't take long before his suspicion was confirmed. They were flying south instead of north.

"Fletch, I hate to tell you this, old man, but we're going the wrong way."

"Huh." In Washington's vernacular, that was equivalent to an expletive. The pilot reached over and tapped the compass glasses. "Of course we're going the right way, man. The mag and gyro say so. Besides, look at the sun." The officer nodded toward the glowing orange medallion rising over his right shoulder. "It's coming out of the east, just like it's supposed to."

"I don't think so," Barrett retorted. "See the island coming up? That's Caldera Island. Just north of Cap Haitien. Its geological features are unmistakable. An almost complete ring of coral surrounds the bay. Used to be a volcano before it blew its top. I've flown over it a thousand times."

Washington studied the doughnut-shaped spit of land through his visor. The configuration of volcanic rock almost jumped into his lap. "Yes, I recognize it. But if that's true, why is the sun rising from the west instead of the east? It doesn't make sense."

Barrett tried to read his companion's thoughts. The pilot's eyes were hidden behind the shaded lens, but the Englishman would have bet they were harboring the same sense of bewilderment. Washington was right—it didn't make sense.

It became even more bewildering when the pilot checked the radio. After several failed attempts to contact the carrier through the normal UHF military channels, he tried calling the *Proteus*. The mother ship was showing the same disregard for their presence.

"For Crissake man," Washington said, "I can't get anything. It's as if all the radio bands have gone dead."

Barrett's gut instinctively cringed. This whole scenario was starting to give him a sinking feeling in the pit of his stomach. "I think it's time we abort our mission, mate. I don't like the bloody looks of this." His voice had the steadfast tone of a flight instructor ready to take over control if his student didn't comply to his instructions immediately. Something was crying out in his brain to turn back before their window of opportunity escaped them completely. He couldn't shake the memory of a similar feeling in the Cessna.

"You got that right, man," Washington rejoined. His body had snapped to full alert. It was obvious a red flag was waving frantically inside his head as well. He whipped the cyclic in a vicious left turn, while simultaneously increasing the throttle and collective pitch of the blades. The combination of moves sent the machine in a steep bank, like a panicked condor. An uncomfortable feeling of foreboding passed between them. It portended an ominous beginning to their trip. Barrett couldn't help but wonder if his realizing their mistake hadn't come too late.

CHAPTER TWENTY

Bermuda Triangle -- 11:05 hours

They started out as five shining specks in the sky. Their contrails showed that they were in echelon formation, approaching rapidly from the northeast. On their present course and speed, Barrett estimated they would cross over the helicopter by 500 feet at a distance of 1,000 feet within the next minute and a half. The Jayhawk's radar was capable of painting a target as far away as 300 miles, but surprisingly these blips didn't appear on the screen until they were barely within visual range. To be this far south they must be returning home, the Englishman decided. He also thought them to be military. No civilian pilots in their right minds would fly in such a tight formation. It was also odd that they hadn't been able to communicate with them. Washington had activated the radio scanner and had caught an exchange of voices at one of the lower VLF frequencies. They could hear them chattering like a bunch of magpies, although the reception was extremely weak. When Washington tried to break in on the standard military frequency of 243 megahertz, he got no response. He then turned to several VHF civilian bands but, as was the case earlier in trying to reach the carrier and the *Proteus*, the radio seemed to be transmitting into an empty void.

"Keep trying, old man. Maybe we can find out where the bloody hell we are," pleaded Barrett. He tuned in his headset so he could pick up what the pilots were saying.

At first their conversation was unintelligible, but as the distance narrowed between aircraft Barrett began making out definite words. The voices sounded frightened, disoriented. He caught his breath as he suddenly realized the impact of what he was hearing. *These guys were lost!*

"Calling tower. This is an emergency. We seem to be off course. We cannot see land ... repeat ... we cannot see land." There was a slight pause, as though whoever was speaking had been listening to another voice before replying. "We are not sure of our position. We cannot be sure just where we are ... we seem to be lost." Another pause. "We don't know which way is west. Everything is wrong ... strange ... we can't be sure of any direction ... even the ocean doesn't look as it should."

Barrett and Washington exchanged stupefied looks. What the hell was going on?

It was when the mysterious aircraft came to within a mile of the chopper that Barrett almost swallowed his tongue. He had flipped down his visor, bringing into focus what he thought was going to be a gaggle of warbirds, probably F-16s, returning to base. At first, he couldn't believe his eyes. He waited while the scene in front of him enlarged to giant-sized posters before the last shred of doubt was erased from his mind.

The words tumbled out of his mouth. "They're Navy Grumman TBM Avenger Torpedo Bombers. World War II era." He recognized their markings with the star emblem and large white numerals emblazoned on their solid dark blue fuselages. The sun was gleaming off their canopies like flaming metal. "Now where the bloody hell did they come from?"

His first thought was that they were from the Confederate Air Force, a group of veteran pilots who flew vintage aircraft for movie productions and at air shows. But as he continued to stare at the flying anachronisms, Barrett suddenly realized he was witnessing the real thing. It could explain why their radio transmissions to the carrier were not being received. Unbelievably as it sounded, he and Washington had been transported back in time, back to the day of December 5th, 1945. They were watching Flight 19, the most celebrated of all the Bermuda Triangle mysteries, reenacting its fateful journey.

It was the continued conversation among the aviators in the doomed planes that convinced him. It appeared that Lieutenant Taylor was the lead pilot. He wanted them all to stay together so when they ditched, their chances of being found would be greater. It was a well-known fact that a TBM's reputation for staying afloat was no better than that of a chunk of granite. Thirty to forty-five seconds was all they had to free their life rafts from a rear storage compartment. To hear their desperate appeals for help, knowing their fate was already sealed by history, gave Barrett a helpless feeling. He knew the script by heart. The flight controller at the Fort Lauderdale tower would try his best to bring them home. His repeated instructions had been simple enough to be understood by the most disoriented flyer. "Assume bearing due west."

Due west ... that was the key!

"I say, old chap," said the Englishman almost flippantly. "Since we know the sun isn't where it's supposed to be, let's try to make it right for those chaps. If you can get through, tell them to assume a bearing *due east* instead." *But will it create a paradox?* he wondered. If Flight 19 was found because of their interference with the natural chain of events, like a domino effect, might the whole world turn out different?

Washington gave his companion a sidelong look before switching his gaze back to the Avengers. He had to crane his neck and squint, as their shadowy outlines were now back-lit against the sun, placing them about 45 degrees above the level of their own flight path. Their combined flyby of over 300-mph would rocket them out of sight within seconds. He quickly pressed the radio mike button on his control stick.

"United States Coast Guard helo, calling Avengers. We are directly below you off your starboard wing. Identify yourself, please. Repeat. This is the United States Coast Guard. Identify yourselves."

After several attempts had failed to establish any response, both pilots realized it was pointless to continue. Flight 19 was quickly slipping out of radio range. Already the strength of their signal was extremely weak, as though coming from a long distance. It was obvious they hadn't heard Washington's hailing calls, or spotted the big orange and white helicopter speeding past them.

This was the first chance Barrett had to see an Avenger up close, other than in a museum. He was surprised at how graceful they looked in flight. It was like watching a life-sized replica of his favorite boyhood model airplane come to life. Naturally, it was induced by the fact that his father had been lost looking for the same type aircraft that comprised Flight 19.

"We're losing them," Barrett announced flatly as he craned his neck to see past the tail rotor. He could faintly overhear snatches of the doomed pilot's strained conversation coming through his earphones. "We are not sure where we are ... we are completely lost ... " And then, toward the end ... "entering white water."

The Englishman felt a deep sadness. Both pilots had just borne witness to a tragic piece of history that, unfortunately, was a common theme in the Bermuda Triangle. A vision of the Avengers crash-landing in the water flashed in his mind. The thought suddenly struck him that he and Washington might end up doing the same thing. Jayhawks were not able to perform water landings. That was a standard edict in the Flight Manual. Somehow, they had to get back to the *Proteus*.

"Let me have a try at reaching Mother, will you mate?" Barrett keyed the radio mike and repeated the familiar cry for assistance. It was met with the same disturbing silence as before. It was like trying to establish contact with the moon.

"If we don't get back soon, we're going to end up in the water like those poor bastards," Washington stated in a flat monotone. Barrett picked up a disquieting edge to the pilot's tone that compared with his own set of jittery nerves. The pilot nodded toward the fuel gauge.

Barrett found it buried amongst a darkened array of electronic digital displays and graphic visuals, the likes of which were barely comprehensible to him. Lit up and working they would have presented an even bigger challenge, he thought. As much as he hated to admit it, technology had soared past him since the days he flew Apaches.

Since the normally lighted digital gauge wasn't working, it seemed the engineers, in their eternal wisdom, had placed a color-coded scale alongside in case of emergency. It was as if they had earmarked the most important instrument to have its own fail-safe system ... just in case. *Must have had the Bermuda Triangle in mind,* he thought. Barrett saw that the brighter the scale, the closer they were to fuel depletion. It was at the pink stage right now. He hadn't a clue as to how much longer that meant they had, and he didn't care to ask. "What do you think is going on?" he asked, trying to find assurance that everything was not as bad as it seemed. "If I didn't know any better, I'd say we slipped into some kind of time warp, mate."

"What do you mean?"

"It's as though we're reliving the past somehow. Seeing Flight 19 proved it by me."

The pilot looked at Barrett as if he was seeing him for the first time. "You mean those aircraft we saw was actually Flight 19? I thought they were a Confederate search team that got lost."

Barrett responded with an impatient grunt. "Figure it out for yourself, old man. The bloody sun is in the wrong direction. That's why Flight 19 was never found. They turned the wrong way. They must have gone down somewhere in the middle of the Atlantic when their fuel ran out. Nobody would have thought of looking for them out there."

"Then what are they doing here ... with us?"

Barrett looked at his companion as if he were suffering from brain lock. "Don't you get it? Our navigational equipment is acting as if instrument flying hasn't even been invented yet. Our radio is completely useless. What we were listening to was some residual radio waves floating around in the atmosphere in a wavelength only used by the military in the 1940s. I'm afraid it's us who have joined Flight 19's airspace."

"If what you say is true ... if we're in a different dimension, then Mother will be too, right?" The imperturbability of the man who called himself the Black Angel was starting to show stress cracks, Barrett thought. Still, who could blame him? Even he was starting to feel a cold trickle of apprehension running down his backside.

"I would think that's a fair assumption. We might be able to make radio contact when we get closer to her. Keep trying."

Washington nodded, at the same time pressing the transmit button. "This is Black Angel calling Mother. Come in please ... " And so it went for several minutes, until a faint beeping on the display panel interrupted the pilot's appeals. Barrett realized it was the thermal imager picking up something. A small white blip had simultaneously appeared on the top edge of the radarscope.

"Looks like we got something dead ahead," he said. "Whatever it is, is generating heat. Could be the *Proteus*."

"Too big to be the *Proteus*," the pilot shot back. "More like an island with volcanic activity."

"There's no such islands this way," replied Barrett.

"Hate to disagree with you man, but this is the signature of a land mass … and a damn big one at that."

Barrett studied the slowly mushrooming blob taking shape. He had to agree. It indicated a heat source significant enough to register on their radar. Yet, the only land with volcanoes that had been in this part of the ocean had sunk 12,000 years ago. He wished the blob to go away by shutting his eyes and praying it was only a false echo. But when he reopened them the blob was still there, and getting bigger. That meant they had either discovered an uncharted island, or a new one had just thrust itself out of the deep.

He closed his eyes again and settled back in his seat. That he was trapped inside another time anomaly was something his mind was finding hard to accept. What was even more unacceptable was what was churning inside his imagination— that he and Washington had somehow entered a rip in time, a different dimension that was slipping them further back in earth history the longer they stayed in the air. *Impossible!* Yet the thought would not go away. If that were the case, his suspicions would be confirmed shortly. He only hoped his sister was seeing the same thing. Otherwise, he was afraid it was going to be a long flight home.

CHAPTER TWENTY-ONE

Bermuda Triangle -- 12:42 hours

Matt woke up with a start. A strange whooshing sound had suddenly pierced the fog clouding his mind like a thick blanket. A split-second later another sound, that of a loud splash, followed by what sounded like the hull being pounded by a sledgehammer. What the hell was going on? He lay there for a moment, trying to clear the cobwebs in his brain as another whooshing sound split the air, followed by another splash. Thankfully, this time the water hammer striking the hull sounded muffled, as if there was more distance between them.

His vision suddenly tilted as the deck slanted beneath him. He found himself in an empty passageway, bracing his feet against the bulkhead until the deck leveled out again. Then came the ingratiating sound of a General Alert bleating in his ears. That, above everything else, cleared his mind, giving him new energy. He then heard distant yelling in the background as the whooshing sounds continued, but seemingly distancing themselves after every splash. He automatically ducked as a group of sailors came storming toward him, leaping over his prone body as though he were a hurdle on a racetrack. They quickly disappeared around a corner and were gone.

He glanced down at his watch in the artificial light, blinking in amazement. He had been unconscious for almost seven hours. He faintly remembered the struggle of willpower that had brought him this far. In fact, he recalled the whole crew had been behaving as if they were acting out a Stephen King novel. He rolled to his feet and stumbled up the nearest companionway. The raucous-like screeching bombarding his senses made him move as fast as he could to get topside, if only to escape the pricking needles stabbing his eardrums. *This is getting monotonous*, he thought. What could be so blasted important that they couldn't just announce whatever they had to say slowly and calmly over the PA, like civilized people? Weren't a vanishing ship, a disappearing sailor, and an underwater fireworks display enough for one trip?

When Matt finally made his way to the bridge, he found a replay of a Greek tragedy that he had witnessed earlier. He recognized the same cast of players milling about, but somewhat in a more ordered state of confusion this time. At first he didn't see anything out of the ordinary that would have everybody getting so excited. Then he heard another whooshing sound splitting the air over his head like a howitzer shell, followed almost instantaneously by another splash. This time it was much louder and more deadly sounding, coming from about 50 yards off the ship's port quarter. He could hear Captain Richardson inside the pilothouse calling orders to the helmsman.

"Hard right rudder. Steer course 0100 degrees." Her tone of voice was decisive and commanding—a good sign that she had all her faculties, *and confidence* back, Matt thought.

"Why don't we just harpoon the son-of-a-bitch?" someone said. "One missile is all it would take."

Matt still didn't understand what was going on. He had already figured by the splashes hitting the water that they were being fired upon by some big guns. But who?

It was when the *Proteus* turned to face her adversary that Matt's chin dropped to his knees. At first he thought he had walked in on a movie set. He was gazing at a ship about a mile off their starboard bow that looked like it had just sailed out of the pages of *Treasure Island*. It seemed to bear the description of a three-masted wooden schooner under full sail. The square-rigged main and foresails were billowed and stretched as if a strong following wind were propelling it. Yet there was no wind that Matt could determine.

When he slipped on a pair of high-enhancement binoculars, the detective was in for even a bigger surprise. Flying high on the mainmast was a large black flag, stiffened out in the breeze like a giant flashcard. It was what was painted on it that made Matt do a double take—a white skull and crossbones. Pirates! "You gotta be kidding!" he gasped. His mind grappled with the notion of seeing Blackbeard the Pirate strolling out on deck, gripping a pistol with one hand and waving a sword with the other. What he did see through the magnified lens made it seem even more unreal. Mixed with the swirling smoke of the cannons were several swarthy looking men running around, naked to the waist. Some wore pantaloons, while others were garbed in flashy blouses or pullovers with bandannas draped around their heads. Red flashes ignited like fireworks around them, with black puffs of cordite streaming from the guns like an elaborate movie production. Matt held on tightly as the *Proteus* made another sharp turn. An eerie sound of rushing air could be heard, followed immediately by a splash as a huge fountain of white water rose high in the air where the cutter had just been. *Those are real shells*, he kept telling himself, still not fully believing what was happening. He could make out a double row of at least 20 cannon sticking out of the vessel's side before the ship began a sharp tacking maneuver toward them. Guessing the same number on the opposite side, he concluded the pirate ship would have been a formidable opponent in its time.

Wait a minute! *In its time!* He had to remind himself this was the 21st Century. Yet as he watched the strange scene being played out before him, he was forced to admit that the *Proteus* might have already left the 21st Century behind. In some inexplicable manner, while everyone was asleep, the ship had somehow crossed over into that etheric world Professor Vail had talked about.

Meanwhile, the pirate ship was not going away. It kept cutting across the cutter's bow in a vain attempt to train its full complement of guns on them. But Captain Richardson was not falling into the trap. She seemed to combine concern over her crew's safety with coolness and daring. Matt found it fascinating to watch her shrewdly finesse the ship back and forth like a duck in a shooting gallery. He wondered what the pirate captain must have thought of a ship with no sails and the speed to outmaneuver him like a mouse outrunning a cat. Although the cannon shot sounded menacing as the pirates continued their deadly target practice, Matt knew the chances of one hitting the *Proteus* was virtually nil. The cutter was too fast and too maneuverable to be hit by such archaic artillery. Yet there was always the lucky hit, he conceded.

The reason for hanging around instead of just outdistancing the marauder was made clear when Matt saw an officer standing in the corner of the bridge taking video footage. It was the same officer that had taken footage of the lightwheels and the *Explorer* when it disappeared. It seemed strange to keep such a meticulous record of what was happening out here, and Matt suspected the captain was acting under some kind of hidden agenda. In any case, the video would make for some interesting conversation back home. That is, if they ever made it home.

Matt overheard that same fear being addressed by Professor Vail to one of the officers.

"As I explained in the wardroom, young man, it's all based on Einstein's 'unified field' theory. The principal comes from the three universal forces: electromagnetic, gravitational, and nuclear. His theory was based on the first two. Time distortion can result."

"What are you saying, Professor? That we're in a different dimension?"

"Yes, I believe so. One of the observable properties of Einstein's theory would be coexistence in another space-time continuum. The extreme tiredness we all experienced was probably a byproduct of the powerful electromagnetic field produced by those underwater objects we saw. There is no way to determine its long-term effects."

"Does that mean we're stuck here … forever?" The officer, whom Matt remembered as the snickering skeptic in the wardroom, was now on the verge of hysteria.

Captain Richardson stepped over and placed a hand gently on his shoulder. "That's enough questions for now, Phil. We'll get through this okay. Stand easy." Her calming words and relaxed composure seemed to break the tension that had been quickly mounting among the bridge crew. The unspoken consensus was that if the captain wasn't worried about it, why should they be? Some even broke out in hopeful smiles, glancing at each other confidently. *John Paul Jones had spoken,* Matt thought.

After ordering another course change to the helmsman, she hollered through the pilothouse open door to the officer with the camcorder. "Gary, you have enough to convince them yet?" Matt later learned the captain was referring to the Military Board of Inquiry, whom he gathered was the reason she seemed to be paying so much attention keeping an accurate diary of the trip.

"Cap'n, I have enough recorded tape to show a full-length feature of Terry & the Pirates if necessary." Just then another whooshing sound screamed over their heads, followed by another geyser of water and a bone-jarring thump hitting the hull. That was the closest one yet.

"Good. Let's get out of here before our friend gets lucky." She gave a quick glance to check the pirate ship's location. It was just starting another run toward the *Proteus* in a desperate effort to cross their bow. "You have to give credit to his persistence, anyway. Left full rudder, all ahead flank. Let's get back on course 0100 degrees."

A cryptic voice suddenly came from the direction of an officer hunched over a DSP radar unit. "Bearing 0010 degrees, Cap'n. Dead ahead. One hundred-forty miles out. A landmass of some magnitude. Looks to be a large island."

Murmurs of disbelief circulated all around him. "There's no island out here," someone declared.

Captain Richardson reacted to this startling revelation without batting an eye. Matt was beginning to understand why the crew trusted her so explicitly. Her experience at handling fluid situations was obviously a morale booster to them. It certainly made his heart feel good.

"Steer to new course 0010 degrees. We'll stay at full revolutions." She then walked over and peeked over the radar officer's shoulder. Matt had the feeling she had trouble convincing herself that the unit was giving an accurate reading. She turned to her navigation officer. "Bob, check the plot again. Find out if we missed something." Matt had been told the ship had the latest up-to-date telemetry encoders. If there were anything happening different on the ocean's surface, satellite imagery would have relayed it to their onboard computers within nanoseconds.

"I've been checking it ... can't seem to get a reading. I'll keep trying." His bespectacled features had the harried look of a lost traveler who had just discovered he'd made a wrong turn 50 miles back. In what seemed an afterthought he added, "If the professor is right, Cap'n, our eye-in-the-sky hasn't been invented yet."

"Could be another Surtsey," someone piped up. Matt saw it came from an older officer with flowing sandy hair and bushy eyebrows that made him look regal. The man went on to explain. "It was an island that formed off the coast of Iceland in 1963."

"Quite true," Professor Vail continued. "This part of the ocean, near the Mid-Atlantic Ridge, is laced with underwater volcanic activity. Volcanism is earth's bedrock. Similar islands have also risen near the Azores and South America. Even the Hawaiian chain is being extended every day with a new island called Loihi."

The professor paused for a moment as if flipping through a mental data bank. "Seismic activity also plays a significant part. Violent upheavals in the earth's history are not uncommon. It has always been suspected that fluctuations in the earth's magnetic field have been the cause."

"Now we're back to magnetism again," Lieutenant Grissam complained. "It seems when everything else fails, scientists find magnetism to blame for earth's anomalies."

"And for good reason, my dear man," Professor Vail soothed. "It is because core samples taken in the earth's mantle have shown that the magnetic polarity of the earth has changed over 300 times in the past 200 million years. The sun has reversed directions many times."

"What causes this to happen, Professor? Aren't they just natural occurrences?" asked the captain. Her attitude toward the scientist assumed an indulgence that Matt sensed was more of a concern to keep everything in perspective. She understood the need for caution, knowing full well that everyone was under a great deal of strain.

"Nobody knows for sure, Captain. We all know the history of meteors striking the earth, or of planetoids veering into our path. It could even be a grand alignment of the planets pulling the earth out of balance, or perhaps a slippage of the polar ice cap caused by an overheating sun." Professor Vail gave a meaningful pause. "On the other hand, it could be something not indigenous to our solar system ... maybe something intelligently controlled."

The professor's subtle reference to unworldly activity affecting earth history made everyone's head turn.

"You mean those lighted objects we saw?" Grissom shot back. "You really think a colony of little green men are driving around underwater shooting off magnetic beams, Professor?" It was obvious that the navigation officer was not a big fan of the extraterrestrial theory.

"Who says they have to be little green men?" Professor Vail countered. "After all, haven't we already witnessed the results of ancient man's ingenuity on this voyage? The domes on the bottom of the sea floor were certainly beyond our imagination. Perhaps the land mass we are approaching will contain more proof of our ancestor's accomplishments than some of us are willing to acknowledge."

With that thought-provoking note, the exchange of words ended. Matt drifted back onto the bridge wing, trying to collect his thoughts. The professor's latest hypothesis had hinted of a world none of them could ever imagine. It evoked imagery of H. G. Wells' novel, *The Time Machine*. Now he must try to deal with it. The entire crew had to deal with it.

The overhead sun seemed to beat hot daggers into his brain, making it difficult to concentrate. He sighted the pirate ship's masts slowly dissolving over the horizon, the sounds of cannon-shot already taking a back seat in his mind. In its stead new sounds emerged. Thankfully they were sounds his overtaxed brain could attune to—the steady swish of the bow wave, the deep thrumming of the turbines, and the monotone announcements of the radar officer reading off the coordinates of a mysterious blob growing steadily larger on the monitor in front of him.

CHAPTER TWENTY-TWO

Bermuda Triangle -- 15:50 hours

The thin wisp of vapor at the edge of the horizon materialized quickly into a full-fledged plume of smoke as the *USCGC Proteus* edged its way closer. With the high enhancement binoculars bringing everything to within arm's reach, Matt saw it to be a massive volcano spewing hot gasses into a self-forming cloud suspended over its summit. Still, with several miles to go, Captain Richardson reduced the cutter's speed to a crawl. It probably was a wise precaution. They were in uncharted waters. It would be disastrous to be waylaid by some hidden underwater obstacle at this stage of the game.

So far, so good. Side-scan sonar and a sub-bottom profiler to sweep the ocean floor projected a clear path ahead. A slow approach also enabled the crew to get better acclimated to what could only be described as an unprecedented landfall. Many of them had lined the rails, some with their cameras and camcorders, drinking in the harsh beauty of a newborn island. That was the original consensus, but some of the old hands knew better. It took virtually thousands of years for a chunk of lava to cool and solidify into a tropical paradise like this one appeared to be.

In fact, the mass of jungle stretching for miles from one side of the compass to the other made one doubt its legitimacy as an island at all. Matt was starting to believe it wasn't an island, but a continent. It was enormous, going on for miles, and its lush vegetation indicated it had been here for some time. A thin white strand of sand beach lined its circumference like a bleached necklace. Everyone was asking himself the same questions—what island was it and was it inhabited?

The giveaway came when the ship got closer and Matt discerned an artificial wall through the dense foliage. It stood about 30 feet high and half as wide. Watchtowers were placed at strategic locations along its length. It reminded him of the Great Wall of China, except instead of brick and masonry construction, it had a bronze cast to it. That was the general consensus, anyway. It gleamed in the late afternoon like a gilded snake as it wound its way through a series of rolling hills and valleys for miles in either direction. The vegetation within its borders seemed to be extremely wild and impenetrable. The scene exuded a peculiar aura that made one think of a landscape indigenous to an alien planet. Strange looking plants with colossal leaves and trees with giant roots were nothing Matt had ever seen before. There didn't seem to be any sign of life.

That all changed when the *Proteus* circumnavigated a rocky headland and found itself in the middle of a wide

estuary. Anchored in the sheltered waters were dozens
of various merchant craft of all shapes and sizes. Some
were entering and exiting a wide channel cut deep
into the interior. Smooth stone blocks, indicating the
passageway was manmade butted its sides. To Matt,
none of the ships looked to be of familiar design. One
or two approximated an ancient caique or tireme he'd
once seen as mockups in a museum.

There were people aboard. Up close through the
high enhancement binoculars, they looked like they
just stepped out of a history book. *Why am I not
surprised?* Matt thought. If he had to guess, he would
have described the people on some of the vessels as
Egyptian, from the time of the pharaohs. They were
short, black-haired, olive-skinned, and dressed in
traditional knee-length togas and sandals. On other
ships the crews were either Caucasian or black, some
even with a bluish caste, with blond hair and blue eyes.
Their dress was more conventional, with trousers,
sleeveless shirts and feet wrapped in leather thongs.
Both sexes were mixed together. There didn't seem
to be any distinction between male and female. Some
had long hair tied in cords behind their heads; others
wore the type of headgear typically worn by Egyptian
slaves. *Maybe that's what they are.* It seemed all of
earth's indigenous races were represented.

But one race stood out above the others. They were
travelling aboard a vessel larger than the rest, and of
much different design and make. It came charging out
of the channel with streamlined prows both fore and
aft, cutting a huge bow wave like a maddened beast. It
was made of metal or some other such element, looking

more like a submarine with its top half sheared off; a veritable ocean greyhound crewed by a race of red-skinned giants. Matt didn't have to be told they were Atlantean. The detective estimated the males to be at least seven-and-a-half to eight feet tall, the women somewhat shorter. Both sexes had flat faces with high cheekbones, lower jaws squared, with noses somewhat narrowed and eyes spaced far apart. Except for their size, their facial features very much fitted the mold of the American Indian. Their hair was several shades brighter than their skin, which most wore skewered into large buns or knots atop their heads. It reminded him of pictures he'd seen in *National Geographic* once of the giant statues found at Easter Island. They had red topknots atop their heads. That race had mysteriously disappeared. *Was there a connection?*

The Atlanteans' dress was also very different from the rest of the ship's crews. They wore a loose fitting silvery material that gave off a shiny luster, looking more like an astronaut's jumpsuit than anything else. The way the detective distinguished between the sexes was the jewelry worn by the females. They were the only ones that sported rings and bracelets, and their ears were wrapped in gold.

Without ceremony, Professor Vail began reciting a parable from the Book of Genesis: "The Sons of God seeing the Daughters of Man, that they were fair, took themselves wives of all which they chose. Now giants were upon the earth in those days. For after the Sons of God went in to the Daughters of Man, and they brought forth children, these are the mighty men of old, men of renown."

Voyage to Oblivion

The old man then made a grand gesture with his arms, reminding Matt of a circus ringmaster introducing the next act. "Welcome to Atlantis, gentlemen," he said with a gleeful smile.

Everyone looked at him with frozen stares, as if in shock. Even Matt had to let the words' impact run their course while a cold shiver ran through his body. He noticed that no one attempted to challenge the professor's statement.

As the *Proteus* slowly moved past the flotilla, Captain Richardson ordered the 76mm and .50 caliber machine guns manned, just in case. It soon became apparent, however, that the seamen aboard the ancient craft were oblivious to their presence. Matt thought everybody seemed to be operating in a vacuum. He couldn't hear any sound coming from the shouting workers as the *Proteus* came within earshot.

"Why can't they see us?" someone queried. "And why can't we hear them?" Everyone automatically turned toward the professor, waiting for an answer. It seemed he had unwittingly become the official spokesman for the scientific community.

He countered by giving a helpless shrug. "You must realize gentlemen, that this is more in the field of quantum physics. However, I have formulated a theory you may want to consider," the sage said unassumingly. *He isn't fooling anybody*, Matt thought. *He's bursting with answers.*

"Go ahead, Professor," pressed the captain.

"Einstein was right. A conversion of energy can take place. We are living examples. Our vibratory rate and that of the ship have been altered to correspond

243

to another time, another world, coexistent with ours—a parallel universe, if you will. It was in this same area of the ocean where the continent of Atlantis once flourished. We are gazing upon some of the merchant ships that traded with them as well as one of their own craft. Atlantis was reputed to have been the mightiest sea empire in the world. I believe we're at the outer approach to their main canal, which was used as a means of entry into their inner zones."

"But why can't they see us?" someone repeated.

"Our vibratory rate has not yet had time to adjust to the Atlanteans' space-time continuum. However, the longer we stay, interspaces between the cell nucleus and the electrons of our bodies will continue to increase in density. When the transformation is complete, our subatomic particles will be equal. Then they will be able to see us and we will be able to hear them."

Listening to the professor's explanation, Matt felt as though he had just been given the last rites.

"What about the pirate ship?" a plaintive voice inquired. "We were plenty visible enough for them to take pot shots at us."

"Yes, very true. But they were pirates from a more recent period in our dimensional travel. Since then, it seems we have slipped further back in time. It's a fair assumption to say that the lingering effects of the force field are still altering our bodies' molecules. Right now, we are somehow maintaining equilibrium outside the Atlanteans' visual spectrum. For how long is uncertain—several minutes to perhaps several hours. Our two presences are like the sound and video of a movie film that are being played out of sync.

Eventually though, I would imagine we will be able to see and hear each other—and most important, to communicate."

"The whole thing's impossible!" somebody blurted.

"Impossible or not, you're here, aren't you?" came a cynical retort.

"I wonder what their reaction will be when they do realize we're here?" someone else asked.

"It will be a wonderful experience to exchange ideas and learn about our past," Professor Vail replied in glowing terms. "Just think of what they could teach us."

Captain Richardson came up and stood next to Matt. She had her brow furrowed and her mouth set. "What's wrong with that picture?" she asked. She nodded toward the Atlantean ship that had just exited the canal and was passing them off their starboard beam at a good clip. The question was directed to no one in particular, but everyone knew that was her way of making a point.

She answered her own question. "It has no visible means of propulsion—no sails, no oars, nothing extraordinary except that silver colored sheathing plate covering its bow. And only the Atlantean ship has it."

"The Atlanteans were known for their engineering skills, captain," Professor Vail said. "One of the means they used to power their conveyances was electricity. That's probably a conductor of some sort. Their power centers, which we have already learned to appreciate, could energize their vehicles very much the same way we recharge our batteries."

By now the *Proteus* had slipped past the anchored fleet and was entering the canal. Captain Richarson had decided, with Professor Vail's urging, to follow one of the entering vessels in, although she was staying behind at a discreet distance. Matt calculated the width of the canal at not much larger than the length of a football field, which didn't allow much maneuvering room for passing ships.

As they looked ahead they saw that the waterway seemed to stretch through the countryside forever. The scenery had changed to that of a collage of fields, forests, and lakes taken right out of *Field & Stream*. The detective saw that most of the crew still lining the rails didn't seem to be overly concerned by the captain's decision to explore. They were drinking in the strangeness of this exotic land as if mesmerized by its beauty. It did seem to have an alluring quality about it. *What's to fear?* Except for the bridge personnel who had overheard the professor's remarks, Matt guessed most everyone else thought the captain was just taking a short sightseeing tour before returning to homeport. Everything was under control.

He shook his head in wonderment. It wasn't hard to understand why they placed such faith in her. He was starting to get a strong feeling of dependence on her too. No matter how skilled and resourceful she was, though, he knew Captain Richardson had her limitations. It didn't surprise him to learn that she was keeping a tight lid on their true status. The lightwheels had knocked out half their electrical systems, and most of the navigational equipment was down. Without computer backup, they were virtually deaf and dumb.

Radio communication was nonexistent. She had been trying for hours to contact both the carrier and helo without success.

Matt was sure everyone would learn soon enough just how serious their situation really was. Once it sunk in that they might never see their families again, it would understandably present a problem. Not carrying trained psychologists on ships operating in the Bermuda Triangle was definitely a military oversight. Even he was starting to feel overwhelmed by it all. It was as if part of his brain was trying to convince him that traveling in the fourth dimension was a normal manifestation; all part of the tourist package graciously supplied by the Bermuda Triangle Chamber of Commerce. The other part was telling him he was playing a fool's game. He would never see home again. He didn't like the feeling, and he quickly tried to dispel it from his mind.

He could feel a slight rumbling deep in his gut. He couldn't believe he was actually hungry. For the first time since the voyage started, his stomach felt normal again. Perhaps if he got something to eat, it would perk up his spirits. All he could see for the moment was jungle on either side of them. Sightseeing could wait.

He had already reached one of the hatchways leading to below decks when, within his peripheral vision, he spotted movement on shore. A tall grassy plain was just starting to come into focus on the starboard side. He stepped closer to the rail to investigate. His heart caught in his throat. In a small clearing he saw an elephant as big as a house. It had exceptionally large curling tusks that brought back memories of pictures he had seen of prehistoric mammoths. He thought it was only a single animal at first, until it moved away and he saw there was a whole herd lumbering through the underbrush. There was no sound of bleating or trampling feet as the surrounding trees eventually swallowed up the large pachyderms. *Like watching a silent Tarzan movie*, Matt thought. All that remained to complete the picture was for a loin-clothed figure to come swinging out on a vine beating his chest.

Hurriedly, Matt resumed his trip to the mess hall. If the ship did get stuck here permanently, he was going to make damn sure he ate his share of the food before it gave out. He wondered if he would ever develop a fondness for elephant steaks.

CHAPTER TWENTY-THREE

Atlantis -- 17:33 hours

They were approximately five miles inland when Matt saw his first ziggurat. It instantly brought to mind what he, Barb, and the kids had once seen at the Mayan ruins in Chiche'n Itza, the temple of Kukulcan. This stone pyramid was even more impressive as it stood in the middle of a large open clearing. It was taller than a 40-story building, and its diameter, he gauged, measured 500 feet or better at the base. Steep steps and narrow bands that tapered symmetrically all the way to the top encompassed its sides. At the very summit stood a small, flat-roofed structure surmounted by a ball-shaped object the size of a Volkswagen. It had an incongruous appearance. The way the sunlight reflected off its rounded surface gave Matt the impression its purpose was as some sort of marker or beacon.

"Look in the sky!" someone cried. "Nine o'clock!"

All eyes swiveled left. Matt had to shade his eyes against the fierce luminosity of the sun as it hung low on the horizon. He managed to spot a black speck emerging from out of the brightness. When it began its descent, coming closer to the ground and out of the sun's direct glare, its features became unmistakably clear. It was an aerial machine of sorts, with a fuselage about 15 feet long mounting a pair of swept-back wings that reminded him of a delta-wing jet fighter aircraft. The nose was also curved back and appeared to have the same shiny metal covering that had been attached to the Atlantean ship. A long flame was shooting out the back. It had an open cockpit. Sitting inside was a giant of a man, holding between his knees a vertical rod that looked similar to the control stick of a modern helicopter. His red hair was tied back in a knot, and his dress was similar to that same silvery garb Matt had seen on the other Atlanteans.

An identical scene he had seen on Mayan friezes instantly jogged the detective's recall. Their architecture abounded with pictures of aerial flight, which most archeologists mistook for religious rituals. He marveled at how smooth the Atlantean glided the vehicle into what apparently was his destination atop the pyramid. There was no hesitation on his part as the airship silently hovered in the air for just a brief second before gently settling down next to the ball. After he climbed out of the craft, the stranger proceeded to walk only a few steps before disappearing inside the structure.

Almost everyone, including Matt, was holding their breath, waiting for the Atlantean to reappear. He never did. When the pyramid finally faded from sight around a bend Professor Vail said almost reverently, "We may have to change our preconceived ideas of what those temples atop the ziggurats were used for. It may be they're a means of housing a secret tunnel that allows access into some inner chamber."

The comment was left unchallenged as more pyramids began to appear on both sides of the canal. Some of the others looked like the more common ones one might expect to see in Egypt and elsewhere, Matt thought, matching and some even exceeding in beauty the Giza complex, as well as the great pyramid of Cholula in central Mexico. *The approximate same size as in the video.* They were all covered with polished facing stones that blazed in the sunlight like giant flaming torches.

Scattered among them were the mysterious domes the professor suspected were used as energy sources. Some of the roofs were partially rolled back, revealing in the shadowy interior of the closest one a tapered crystalline object seared with light. A firestone! Even from a safe distance Matt could feel the electrically charged atmosphere reaching out and tickling his skin. As far as he was concerned, the firestone confirmed the professor's claim that the Atlanteans had learned to harness the earth's nuclear furnace for their own energy needs. His body involuntarily shuddered at what it might do to exposed flesh and bone. He was thankful the *Proteus* wasn't passing any closer.

As the ship continued further inland, more airships were spotted. But they were of a different kind than the delta wing everyone had gawked at earlier. These new aeriforms reminded Matt of an International Balloon Fiesta of hot-air balloons shaped like animal characters. They invoked the same surrealistic touch as being in Disneyland.

"Looks like an aerial circus up there," someone commented. Matt concurred. Many of the airships were patterned after bulls, horses, elephants, and camels, plus a variety of birds and snakes. Other balloon designs didn't make any sense to him at all. Some balloons were as big as dirigibles with enclosed, bus-sized, torpedo-shaped capsules attached underneath. Most all had viewing ports on the side, some stacked four and five rows high, presumably serving as observation windows. As if tied to invisible strings, they all seemed to be travelling under power, although none of them showed any visible means of propulsion except the ubiquitous energy sheath attached to their surfaces. The professor appeared to be right on that score too, Matt thought. The conductors were obviously acting as the vehicle's power source.

As the amount of traffic increased, Matt figured they must be approaching a major population center. The sky was starting to get congested.

Large fertile fields began dominating the landscape, crisscrossed by long, narrow irrigation channels. There were figures tilling the land, looking like neither human nor beast. Everyone's mouths fell agape as the cutter passed by several of these creatures. They were of much smaller stature than the normal person. Some had on only the barest of essentials for privacy. They trod behind machines evidently made for earthmoving, as the fields were being neatly furrowed by dozens of these devices. Many of the creature's pitiful bodies were covered with incrustations resembling fish scales.

Others had bird plumage sticking out of their buttocks. The most gruesome sight was the third type of mutant. It was mostly beast, with the body of a goat and the head and appendages of a human.

"What the hell are those things?" inquired one flabbergasted officer next to Matt. "They look like they belong in a freak show."

Professor Vail's voice held a trace of bitterness as he spat vociferously, "That's what they were called—*things*. Atlanteans used those poor devils for slaves. They tilled their soil and dug their mines such as your country did to their slaves two centuries ago." In a more conciliatory tone he added, "Their appearance does provide a key though, to what many have believed to be only folklore and legend. Since Athens was a major Atlantean colony, these unfortunates could have been the Pans, centaurs, and satyrs of Greek mythology."

Everybody was caught unprepared as the canal suddenly emptied into a large circular basin that extended about two miles across. A wall, which looked identical to the one they'd seen earlier, circumvented a steep hill beyond. Below lay a vast assembly of docked ships, swarming with workers. Gazing through the high enhancement binoculars, Matt saw that they were loading and unloading large crates and bundles from the ships with the help of those strange-looking creatures they'd seen in the fields.

He could pick out the Atlanteans easily. Because of their size, they stood out like Sequoias in a stunted forest. Some of them were using hand-held levitating devices that shot beams of light, lifting the merchandise in and out of the cargo holds as if they were made of feathers. The cargo was then placed inside large boxcar containers suspended by hovering airships, before silently taking off to unknown destinations further inland. Other airships, looking more like floating platforms, were shuttling their goods like a fleet of automatons to what appeared to be an odd assortment of buildings and towers perched on raised terraces overlooking the harbor. Matt guessed them to be storehouses of some kind. On both sides of them, spanning the harbor as far as the eye could see, were metal-covered bridges that looked like brass worms. They were spaced not more than two to three miles apart, looking more like an engineer's nightmare than anything else. They showed no girders or crossbeams signaling any means of visible support. Their polished exteriors reflected the late afternoon sun like large freestanding tubes of opalescent glass.

"This could be the outskirts to their capitol city, Semira," the professor said excitedly to the captain. "We must find the continuation of the main canal that will bring us deeper into the citadel. There we will find the greatest building ever built on earth, the Temple of Poseidon." His face beamed with anticipation.

"All right, Professor," Captain Richardson said. "But at the first sign of trouble, we're turning around and heading back."

Matt knew she was caught up in the moment like everyone else. More so was the professor, as he kept fidgeting with his hands like a schoolboy getting ready to open presents on Christmas morning.

The captain then gave orders to the helmsman to steer a course around the harbor, staying well clear of the litany of ships plying back and forth like a regatta on parade.

The *Proteus* passed many more docked ships lining the inner wall before it came to the next canal. This waterway also measured the same as the first, as if someone had dissected the island in two with a giant bulldozer. Professor Vail went on to mention that there would be three adjacent islands altogether, each one separated by a concentric ring of water smaller than the one before.

The cutter no sooner entered the second canal before the first glimmerings of a bustling metropolis began to materialize. It was as if suddenly awakening and finding oneself in the Emerald City of OZ. Nobody had expected to see architectural grandeur on such a massive scale. Matt and his shipmates stood speechless, beholding wonders never before seen by modern man. Buildings of majestic proportions, composed of thick, white coralline walls, fronted by intricate archways and polished stone terraces glided by on either side of them. Some were resplendent with marbled columns holding up massive vaulted roofs of silver and gold. The city seemed to be arranged in wide circular boulevards, with magnificent complexes and broad paved courts adding to the impression of magnitude. What he was observing swept away any preconception of concrete and glass Matt may have expected to find in a high-tech society. Buildings of such intricately cut stone blocks were put together with such amazing craftsmanship that they dominated the landscape by their exquisite grace and beauty alone. Many of the structures were constructed of white, red and black granite; some intermingled for the sake of ornament, while others portrayed a grid-like pattern suggestive of a giant checkerboard.

Some architecture was indescribably futuristic, overwhelming the senses by their powerful symmetric designs. Pyramids that could have dwarfed any of the formations in Egypt, China, or South America were dotted across the landscape like silvered mountains. A commensurate sized pool of water was displayed in front of each one, apparently being used as reflecting mirrors, but for what purpose no one could imagine. The luminosity of the facing stones of the monuments themselves was bright enough to be seen for miles around. At the end of each pool were tall onyx obelisks that punctured the sky like black needles, as if giant seamstresses had placed them there. Mammoth circular buildings, ringed like the planet Saturn, with airy stoops and rounded openings, reminded Matt of tremendous squatting beehives.

Large portions of the panorama were interspersed with expansive gardens flowing with exotic flowers and shrubbery. Their verdant foliage extended to a wide assortment of luxurious palms and other tropical trees not found in modern arboretums. Among what looked like large public baths, both open and roofed-over, were indications of a sophisticated aqueduct and plumbing system. Where buildings looked as if they were made of steel and concrete, it soon became evident that their principal construction material was finely-hewed stone, but used in ways that were architecturally impossible to duplicate even in the 21st Century. Megalithic blocks weighing thousands of tons apiece comprised the foundations of many of the buildings, with ornate facades of gold, silver, and bronze giving them a rich, stately appearance. The strange black and red stonework called orichalcum, which Matt recalled seeing in the video, was also a dominant feature. Next to gold, it was the Atlanteans' most treasured metal. One of its major uses was for bases supporting multi-storied platforms. These seemed to be strategically located near major groupings of buildings, somehow giving him the impression they were used as helipads.

A moment later, as if on cue, an Atlantean landed on top of one with a jetpack strapped to his back. It was like watching a Buck Rogers movie. Slipping the unit off in a shrug, the airman then disappeared into what appeared to be an attached elevator on the side of the platform. Within seconds the aeronaut descended to ground level and instantly merged with the multitude of pedestrians making their way along the wide boulevards.

People of all races were represented, each in their own distinctive wardrobe and makeup. But it was the Atlanteans who seemed to shine above all the rest when it came to dress. The silver jumpsuits Matt had seen worn by the pilot and ship's crewmen were exchanged for colorful flowing robes and elaborate headdresses. The colors were more vivid, more vibrant than anything he had ever seen in movies or photographs. The costumes had a light translucent texture that seemed to soothe and caress their bodies as they walked. The Atlanteans looked noble and aristocratic. The women in particular, Matt observed, wore fancy footwear, flounced skirts, and lavish jewelry as if they were in a fashion parade. Some had their hair held up in poufs or covered in tiaras of precious stones.

"The Atlanteans had a caste society," Professor Vail explained. "Ninety percent of the population lived in the rural areas. Only the sons and daughters of the gods lived inside the cities."

It seemed to Matt, however, that travelling by air in some form or another was the main mode of transportation. The sky was inundated with multi-tiered lanes of traffic that would have rivaled a modern superhighway. At the lower levels were the jetpacks, which buzzed around like flies. On the ground he spied egg-shaped vehicles riding on invisible curtains of air, powered by those same enigmatic conductors. Also prevalent were people racing around on scooter-like devices that looked like floating skateboards.

Exactly two hours had elapsed since the *Proteus* first entered the outer zone. After an almost continuous string of ooohhs and aaahhs from a crew still bug-eyed with amazement, the cutter finally reached what Professor Vail declared to be the innermost sanctuary of Atlantis. The ring of water that surrounded this last island bastion was somewhat narrower than the rest, although the fathometer had registered a constant 100 foot depth the entire distance. A wall also surrounded it, this time made up of rich orichalcum. The harbor was conspicuously absent of the international montage of cargo ships that had been scurrying about the outer harbor. It seemed only Atlantean vessels, with their distinctive metal hulls and energy conductors were allowed to ply the hallowed inland waterway. The aerial parade had also taken a detour. It was as if anything above the innermost island was restricted air space.

The *Proteus* was approaching the island cautiously, bringing slowly into focus a towering mountain pasted against an azure sky, its summit shrouded in a curtain of mist. It actually was an active volcano that was still percolating, Matt surmised. More cheers and applause erupted from an already overdosed crew as the gulf between it and the cutter steadily narrowed. Gasping in delight, Professor Vail related it to be the fabled Mount Atlas, the largest of a series of lofty peaks that descended to the other side of the island all the way to the sea.

But as grandiose as the mountain might have been to the professor, Matt thought it paled in comparison to the edifice squatting beneath its shadow. The detective found himself catching his breath. He didn't have to be told he was gazing upon the famed Temple of Poseidon, named after the founder of Atlantis. The citadel's size overpowered the senses; its dimensions could easily incorporate several city blocks. The entire exterior was coated in silver, and the pinnacled towers, covered in gold, soared into the heavens like New York skyscrapers. Even from a distance the sweeping magnificence of the legendary temple looked as if it belonged in a fairy tale.

"The temple was built in honor of the god Poseidon and his wife Cleito," Professor Vail said. "Its original dimensions were a stadium in length and half a stadium in width, with each successive generation of kings adding to the palace's size and beauty." Remembering a stadium to be a little over 600-feet, Matt knew without having to be told that the temple, in its earlier development, hadn't been much bigger than the Parthenon in Athens. It was obvious that the elegance of the final version overshadowed anything the modern world had to offer, rivaling and even exceeding the luxuriance of the Taj Mahal.

With the aid of the high-enhancement binoculars, Matt was able to see with lucid clarity the fabled inner sanctum of Atlantis itself. Although the island was comparatively small, it soon became apparent how much emphasis the Atlanteans put on sporting events. Their huge arenas encompassed mammoth structures; one they were passing, the granddaddy of them all, he guessed, could have housed the New Orleans Superdome. What looked like an open-roofed amphitheater, on the same lines as the Roman Coliseum, glided by like a modern-day acropolis. A large racetrack for horse racing unveiled itself as encircling the greater part of the island while a spacious garden covered the remainder. From the plush variety of its flowers and plants, Matt suspected even Van Gogh would have had trouble duplicating on canvas its luxurient beauty. It almost seemed as if he could smell its succulent fragrance as the cutter drew nearer.

Inside the garden, purple-robed figures walked about on smooth stone pathways. Their heads were covered with hoods so he couldn't see their faces. But their presence immediately sent a shock wave through his subconscious. Memories came flooding back, memories that had once been blocked, suddenly released. In his mind's eye he saw himself laying on a laboratory table.

Standing around the table are alien creatures resembling insects. They stare at him with black, limpid eyes. A robed giant is bending over him, thankfully more humanlike, but still unrecognizable. A cowling hides his face. The figure leans closer over him. Thought processes begin pummeling his brain. *We are the Caretakers. Heed our warning. Humankind is not ready for the power of the crystals. All will suffer who come near. Stay away.*

CHAPTER TWENTY-FOUR

Atlantis -- 2000 hours

"Caretakers, you say? And why would they warn us to stay away? They do not even know we're here." That was the immediate reaction from Professor Vail after Matt had finally voiced out loud what had been bottled away in his mind the entire trip. The memories were back—the mind's camera unreeling in fast-forward the sequence of events that led to his obsession with imminent disaster. He confided to the professor about the robed figure in the cave, and the device implanted in him and his daughter.

"The Caretakers do know we're here, Professor. They knew we were coming. That's why my daughter was programmed, to warn me of the danger. It was why I was programmed—to warn people to stay away."

"Nonsense, my boy. The robed figures you see are the high priests. Every ancient culture had them. Their job was to educate people in the ways of moral and religious philosophy, not implant strange devices in their heads."

The professor sounded a little exasperated at him, Matt thought. It was obvious to him from the start that Professor Vail would not hear his story. Or perhaps, could not. The learned scientist was enamored with the discovery of Atlantis so strongly that his mind refused to listen. Matt could see the gleam of expectancy in the professor's eyes. His whole body quivered with excitement. His life-long dream of witnessing the creations of his past life, as described by Edgar Cayce, was about to come true.

"We must take sufficient time to explore the temple, Captain," the professor said. "It is an opportunity of a lifetime that we may never have again." Matt could overhear his pleas to Captain Richardson, beseeching her to send out an inspection team. Reluctant at first, the captain finally agreed. The inflatable was ordered over the side.

"I see no harm in sending a landing party, Professor," she said. "I'm sure you can appreciate the significance of our discovery better than the rest of us. But you must realize we cannot stay long. Our presence here could cause irreversible changes that could impact future generations." The captain then glanced at the sun still clinging to the edge of the horizon. She wore a puzzled expression. Its magenta color mixed with gold bathed the gardens and surrounding landscape in a brilliant tapestry. Over the treetops the temple's spires beckoned to them like Cinderella's castle.

"I want to be in the open sea before nightfall," she continued. "Daylight's holding out longer than I expected, so I can give you two hours to be back aboard. To accompany you I'm sending Lieutenant-

Commander Cosgrove, who will carry a walkie-talkie and stay in touch with me at all times. Also, my photographer, Lieutenant Chaney, who will be doing the video, and my public affairs assistant, Ensign Berkholder, who will be recording everything on a transcriber. An armed guard will escort you."

"I'd like to go too, Captain," Matt pleaded. He must have sounded like a little kid who was afraid to be left behind on a family picnic. He didn't mean to sound so anxious, but he was having a hard time masking a strong case of nerves. He had an uncanny feeling of foreboding. A momentous event was about to happen, and it was important he be there when it did.

Captain Richardson turned to look at him, fixing a studious gaze on him like an inquisitive mother hen. A tight frown creased her forehead. "If you wish, Mr. Benner. But I seem to detect a trace of apprehension in your voice. Will you feel comfortable going along?"

The captain's astuteness made Matt blink in surprise. He didn't think his fear was showing through. He gave a sidelong look at Professor Vail, who was standing off to the side. The scholar's focus of attention was thankfully directed toward the activity on deck. The detective knew that if he came on too strong about his premonition, the captain might have second thoughts about letting him go. Worst still, she might even cancel the mission. *The professor would really be pissed at me then*, he thought. *I have to tread carefully.*

"I have no problem with that, Captain. It's just that I can't seem to shake this strange feeling I've got."

"What kind of feeling?"

"Well, ever since I left home I've had this feeling of guilt in the back of my mind. I think I would best serve my purpose for being here by going ashore. Something is telling me I would be of more use there. Perhaps it's just my imagination getting the best of me. You know ... losing my partner and everything ... " It was a lame excuse, but it was the best he could come up with at the spur of the moment.

Captain Richardson laid a comforting hand on Matt's shoulder. "This little diversion has been unexpected for all of us," she confided softly. "And losing loved ones on top of it all is never easy to accept. Perhaps getting your feet on dry land for a couple of hours will do you some good." She gave his shoulder a slight squeeze before turning away. Matt appreciated her concern. *If only she knew the real reason.* He tried shaking it off as he made his way down to the main deck. The inflatable was already in the water waiting for him as he clambered aboard. The professor looked impatient. Matt couldn't blame him. This moment was what the scholar had lived for his whole career.

It took only a few minutes for the small party to traverse the narrow gap that separated them from the island. A rich verdure of green sorghum the thickness of deep pile reached all the way to the water's edge where they stepped ashore. Meanwhile, Captain Richardson had the cutter turned around for a fast exit.

As Matt stepped out of the boat, he happened to look up at the temple towering over them, 40 stories tall. The ornate walls exuded a feeling of elegance and invincibility. It was a breathtaking sight. Now he knew how Jack felt when he climbed off the beanstalk and saw the giant's castle for the first time.

The group saw that a narrow footpath led directly across the garden to the temple. Matt noticed other footpaths branching off to the sides. Each one overflowed with different kinds of beautiful flowers and shrubs he would have a hard time describing to anyone. Trees with pinkish leaves and tall fronds stood plentiful like blossoming corn stalks. The garden also contained cisterns of both hot and cold water supplied from underground springs, as well as a variety of graceful fountains. A common feature was statues of bearded Atlanteans, some astride horses and brandishing swords as if they were ready to do battle. Others were standing stoically, with expressionless faces of marble and stone.

The Atlanteans seemed to revere bulls, Matt discovered. There were several statues of them, large creatures with sharp horns and blazing eyes that made him feel as if they could come alive at any moment.

Hustling along to keep within the time constraint, it wasn't long before the landing party found themselves standing at the garden's edge. Facing them was a broad paved court, about a city block in diameter, which wrapped itself around the temple like a concrete apron. Except it wasn't concrete. Matt knelt on one knee to feel the surface. It was made up of superbly cut ashlar blocks so smoothly butted together that it looked like a terrazzo floor.

"It's amazing what they could do with stone," Professor Vail remarked. "They molded and shaped it like we do plastic."

Everything they had witnessed so far was nothing compared to what was barring their path ahead. Fronting the temple were two 50-foot tall Sphinxes that measured the length of football fields. Their close proximity to one another gave Matt and the others the impression of confronting a pair of enormous bookends. One had the head of a man and the body of a lion. *Just like the Sphinx in Egypt*, Matt thought. The one opposite had the head of a lion and the body of a man. Both were constructed of stone that had the sheen of white agate. It immediately brought forth an exclamation from Professor Vail. Matt could tell he was beside himself with excitement.

"I believe we have found the key to the Riddle of the Sphinx," the professor said. "It confirms one of the theories bandied about for years, of the Dendera Zodiac, which deals solely with cataclysms. According to the Zodiac, major earth changes occur when the vernal equinox is in the constellations of Leo and Aquarius. See … " he said pointing toward one Sphinx, then the other. "That's what we have represented here. Records have shown that just in the past 12,000 years, the sun has twice risen where it now sets. I must tell you that the date of the cataclysm that sank Atlantis was in the sign of Leo. By taking a ruler and looking straight across the Zodiac, we see Aquarius, the sign of man. If the last cycle of earth changes began in Leo, astrologers say the next movement of the heavenly bodies will be in Aquarius. For those of you who believe in astrology, our 21st Century is currently in that house of stars."

The professor's little dissertation left a queasy feeling in the pit of Matt's stomach. *The pieces of the puzzle are all nicely fitting together.*

Matt and his companions started across the open span until they came to the sweeping entrance of the temple itself. A row of 39 dressed columns supported an arched entryway reaching 10 stories in height. The giant pillars sat atop an immense flight of steps, giving the temple the visage of enormous breadth and scope. Climbing them prompted a footnote from Professor Vail that it reminded him of the Temple of Artemis at Ephesus, only 10 times bigger in scale. Matt had to use his own imagination to visualize what the professor was referring to. *He never heard of the Temple of Artemis.*

When the gathering reached the top of the landing, the colonnade towered over them like a row of missile silos. Upon closer inspection they discovered the pillars were individual blocks of highly polished white marble, carved with figures, some in high relief that resembled three-dimensional artwork. Furbished on top were elaborate motifs and petroglyphs that possibly had meaning to no one but the professor, Matt guessed.

"I never saw such architectural grace and beauty in all my life," exclaimed Professor Vail in an awed voice. "These sculptured columns are unequaled in the world. Why, these stones must weigh several hundred tons apiece."

In between each one were 20-foot tall bronze statues of Atlantean kings and their wives, guarding the palace like brooding sentinels. From the portico the group entered a long, wide corridor lined with 10 taller statues, this time fashioned in orichalcum. There were five on either side. All were garbed in luxuriant ceremonial dress, with glassy eyes staring vacuously into space.

"The 10 antediluvian kings," Professor Vail announced. "The god, Poseidon, begat five pairs of twin male children by a mortal woman. It was he who divided the continent of Atlantis into 10 portions, and his eldest son, Atlas, he made king and named ruler over the rest."

It was when the corridor emptied into a large rotunda that the honor and importance the Atlanteans placed in their originator was realized. The group all stood in awe at the breathtaking 50-foot statue hovering over them. It was made of solid gold. It was the first patriarch, Poseidon, standing in a chariot drawn by six winged horses surrounded by sea nymphs riding on dolphins. His gold-crowned head almost touched the domed ceiling, which was made of crushed lapis lazuli. The ceiling itself was star-studded with jewels that glittered like cut glass. In one hand the great being held the reins of his steeds, while in the other a giant trident held sway over them. A strange light was playing over the entire scene, although Matt couldn't tell where it was coming from. He could hear the photographer's camcorder whirring in the background while Ensign Berkholder, speaking into the recorder, was trying to do justice to his duties as official chronicler. It was a thankless job, Matt decided. There was no way in the world one could describe with words the opulence they were witnessing.

Circumventing the dome's alabaster-covered walls, richly decorated with gold leaf and exquisite enamel tiles, were a number of smaller statues and frieze paintings that Professor Vail recognized as depicting Greek gods. He listed several by name, which made Matt think the kings of Atlantis and their descendents had metamorphosed themselves into gods of other cultures as well. A large bas-relief adorned one wall that showed several ferocious-looking bulls milling about inside a ringed enclosure. An Atlantean was holding a long rod, and by his stance he looked as if he was ready to do battle with the large creatures. Matt could see spectators sitting in tiers looking down on the spectacle. *A bullfight?* He didn't have time to mull over the scene, as the XO kept everybody moving. The man kept checking his watch, making sure he had enough time left to get them back within the allotted deadline. At 10-minute intervals he would check in with the captain, assuring her that everything was okay.

Branching off the rotunda was a grand staircase made of pure ivory. It was the principal entrance leading deeper into the temple, Matt concluded. Its pearly steps ended under a corbel-vaulted ceiling with lavishly decorated beams and painted frescos that called attention to pictures he had seen of St Peter's Basilica.

As much as Professor Vail pleaded for them to explore the upper sanctuary, where possibly the grand altar stood, Commander Cosgrove desisted. Instead, the XO shepherded his entourage toward an arched portal that led to an open courtyard guarded on either

271

side by life-sized sculptured winged bulls. Matt thought the decision seemed to be the safer alternative. Off in other directions were dark passageways that begged caution to anyone venturing deeper into the citadel without fear of getting lost.

The courtyard measured no more than the size of a skating rink. It was empty except for what was standing in the middle, and which immediately captured everybody's attention—a 15-foot tall stele made of pure diorite. Diorite was one of the hardest stones on earth, far harder even than iron. It bore strange inscriptions that looked like gibberish to Matt. But to Professor Vail, it was like finding the Rosetta Stone. The man went absolutely ecstatic when he started interpreting the weird symbols inscribed on it. It was a form of Sumerian cuneiform, he elucidated to the curious crowd around him, and in the same breath reported how exceedingly old it was. Sumerian was unrelated to any known language on earth. It was left by the *Nefilim*, the first celestial travelers who visited Atlantis.

Matt could see the professor's hands virtually tremble as they brushed over the raised lettering. "The Ancient Land," he read aloud, "when men came down from the stars; the Middle Land, when men reached the stars; the New Land, when men embraced the stars." The three Lands, Professor Vail surmised, had to have been when Atlantis broke into three separate islands at various stages throughout its history. Each succeeding culture that arose delved further to understanding the universal laws that controlled the universe. They had the help of the *Nefilim* that visited the earth long before, when there were only crude life forms occupying the land. Mixed with animals and plants, the life forms had no purpose until new DNA was introduced, which proliferated into what eventually became homo-sapiens. But it took many millennia to perfect, the inscriptions said. As the professor read, it made Matt feel privileged to know that his species wasn't just a mistake that had accidentally congealed itself together after crawling out of the ocean.

Professor Vail's voice continued to crack with excitement. "The inscriptions are followed by none other than the Ten Primary Laws laid down by the *Nefilim*." *Strange that it was the same number of commandments received by Moses from God,* Matt thought. As the professor extrapolated their meaning, Ensign Berkholder, apparently afraid he might miss every nuance, almost stuck the microphone up the sage's nose. Several of the group broke out in smiles, but the professor was oblivious to the intrusion and kept reading. Matt found the information fascinating. The words struck a chord he had learned in bible school when he was a kid.

"Unto your opponent do no evil; your evildoer recompense with good; unto your enemy, let justice be done." The professor paused as if trying to sort out in his mind what he was interpreting next. "It talks about intelligence evolving on 12 original planets. Earth was one of those planets. It says, 'The individuality of the soul was the *Nefilim's* greatest gift to humankind, thus insuring his place in the universe.'"

"All very interesting Professor, but we must move along," Commander Cosgrove cut in, glancing at his watch. "Time is running short, and there's a lot more to cover."

Matt felt sorry for the gifted scientist, who obviously would have been content to camp at the foot of the stele overnight. But the XO was right. Time was of the essence. Already long shadows were beginning to feel their way across the compound. But a bizarre thing was happening. The stele was acting as a shadow marker. As the sun's rays reflected off the monolith, an oblong shadow emerged, pointing a dark finger to one of the doorways lining the enclosure. *Almost as if a higher force is pointing the way for us,* Matt thought.

They entered. Acclimatized to the brightness outside, everyone had to adjust to the subdued light as the passageway inside the doorway gently sloped downward, leading them deeper into the citadel. To Matt, it felt as if they were walking into a burial chamber. They passed a maze of small windowless rooms connected by light wells cut into the ceiling that allowed the only light to enter. The rooms had no clear purpose other than for meditation, the professor suggested. The fact that they were bare of any furniture or decorations added to the mystery. "What did these people do, sit on the floor?" one of the guards asked. One curious feature they came across, however, was a pedestal formed of shining glass standing in the middle of one of the rooms. Atop its surface was attached a black cube shaped device with a transparent mirror attached. Everyone was of the opinion it was either a computer monitor or a television receiver. No one could have known that a secret passage connected the room to a massive golden altar where sacrificial rites were performed.

The passageway ended at a large cylindrical room that measured seven stories high and was cut into solid rock. By this time they were well below ground level. There was no doubt in anyone's mind that it was an underground vault of some sort. A strange dim light emanating from tiny apertures in the ceiling gave the chamber a soft, warm glow. It reminded Matt of a giant time capsule. In honeycombed walls that seemingly stretched into infinity were hoards of artifacts stashed in their own individual alcoves. The objects ranged anywhere from gold chariots decorated with embossed designs of jeweled sequins to shields and priestly vestments inlaid with precious gems.

The further in they went, the more arcane the objects became. Sinister-looking translucent cylinders and tube-like laser guns with electrically coiled barrels suggested awesome firepower. Some included machines that none of them could even remotely identify. It was also their first sight of iron-made products. A facsimile of the one-man delta-wing airplane and the wheel-less vehicles they'd seen floating off the ground were equally represented.

But as the group ventured deeper into the chamber, they found something even more remarkable. Layered in rows, covering both sides of the walls, were poster-sized ledgers stored in niches, which reached all the way to the ceiling. They weren't just ordinary ledgers, but pliable tomes bound inside gold-leafed fasteners with luminescent monogrammed symbols on the cover. They were as light as a feather, Matt discovered as he lifted one out. The pages were brittle, as if made of a thin metal, and were written with the same hieroglyphics as on the stele.

Professor Vail's eyes lit up with passion as he delicately began turning the pages. He paused and pointed with a shaking finger to a spot on one of the pages. "In this particular passage it tells of a war between the *Devastas* and the *Daityas*. The *Daityas* were Atlanteans who fought against the gods ... who must have been the *Devastas*. They were the 'others' who came from another galaxy. Terrible destruction reigned in annihilating the earth of all living things." He looked up with tears in his eyes. "My God, the ancient texts don't go far enough to explain what really happened." He suddenly lapsed into silence as he delved deeper into the book, all the while shaking his head.

Matt pulled out another volume and flipped it open. The first thing he saw was a diagram of an elliptically shaped machine that looked very familiar. It had features similar to the one he'd seen the night before, with portholes along the side and a round cupola on top. Underneath the diagram was the same unintelligible writing, presumably describing its features.

"Look, Professor. What do you make of this?"

Professor Vail seemed unmindful of the interruption. Matt had to repeat himself to get the scientist to break his concentration. Once the sage finally stopped to examine the diagram Matt was holding up, his interest suddenly piqued. He assiduously inspected the ancient symbols. "The Atlanteans called this a *Shem*, my boy, an aerial car that could reach the outer planets. It was a gift from the *Nefilim*. It even describes how the vehicle was powered. Absolutely amazing!"

He turned to the rest of the group gathered around him. "Look at this, gentlemen." He beckoned toward another volume he had opened. "This is a book on human diseases and ailments. It gives a breakdown of what herbs and plants to take to eradicate ulcers ... how to cure specific types of cancer ... what foods to prepare to prevent the common cold." His body shook with emotion as he gazed wonderingly at the voluminous collection of books looking down at them. "I would imagine this whole library contains information our doctors and scientists would dearly love to examine. It probably shows how to build machines of technological superiority we have not yet even imagined."

He paused for a moment to catch his breath. Matt could see the professor was having a hard time containing his emotions. "I do believe we have stumbled upon the Hall of Records. Here resides the wealth of accumulated knowledge possessed by the Atlanteans, handed down to them by the gods. There are secrets buried here that unlock the mysteries of the universe. If only we had more time ... "

"I'm sorry Professor, but we don't," said Commander Cosgrove. "We only have a few minutes left before we start back."

Reluctantly Professor Vail conceded, tailing behind the group as they followed the commander through another passageway that led out of the chamber. It branched off the main corridor and seemed to lead to a higher elevation of the temple.

Before they knew it, they were inside a huge cave-like room. The roof soared over their heads like an aerodrome made for the space shuttle. Matt decided it had been made for something of that order. It had side-rails and crossbeam construction that indicated it was built to open and close automatically. A dozen or so airships were sitting on elevated platforms, looking like a collection of floats getting prepped for the next air-balloon rally.

But the object parked at the far end of the gallery was what attracted everybody's attention. It was a large metallic ellipsoid, which had striking similarities to the diagram they had just been marveling at in the ledger. It was about 50 feet in diameter, and around its periphery blazed a series of colored lights, spinning in alternating patterns around a central axis. A faint humming noise could be heard emanating from its interior.

"Am I seeing what I think I'm seeing?" exclaimed Commander Cosgrove. It was a sentiment that hardly needed elaboration.

"Anybody who had any doubts as to how far Atlantean technology advanced before now have just been enlightened," proclaimed Professor Vail solemnly.

Suddenly, a beeping sound began emanating from the XO's walkie-talkie. It was a pre-programmed signal, telling them it was time to return to the *Proteus*.

"Let's get back to the ship, people," Cosgrove announced. "Our stay in Disneyland has just expired."

CHAPTER TWENTY-FIVE

Atlantis -- 21:02 hours

Without warning, a booming voice filled the air. "JALMIN!"

The name echoed across the stone chamber like a ricocheting bullet.

"JALMIN VAILSHOCKI!"

Again, a human reverberation of sound shattered the sepulchral quiet. The small cadre of men had already started retracing their footsteps when they all stopped and looked at each other in astonishment. It was as if the voice of God was calling to one of His chosen. It was the first sound they had heard, other than their own voices, since they had entered the temple.

Professor Vail responded in an obedient croak, "Who's that?"

Matt turned around just in time to see a fairly tall, balding man with a spade beard and thick horn-rimmed glasses come striding down a ramp that had magically appeared out of the spacecraft. There were five other men just making an appearance at the entranceway.

When Professor Vail saw him, he started running toward him, letting out a shriek. "SERGEY!"

There was a flurry of handshakes and bear hugs as the rest of the missing scientists congregated at the bottom of the ramp. Matt could see tears of joy streaming down many of their cheeks, as he and the rest of the landing party stood discreetly off to the side.

"Tell me ... what happened to all of you?" Professor Vail implored.

"We are guests of the *Asuras*, Jalmin ... extraterrestrials who have come from other worlds, other space-time continuums. They came back here to wait for you."

"Who ... who are you talking about?"

Professor Valekovsky didn't have to explain any further. Standing atop the ramp looking down at them was a tall figure with blazing eyes. He was dressed in a purplish robe and had on a strange headdress that covered his ears. His face was gaunt and lean, with long flowing hair the color of amber. Except for the burning intensity in his eyes, Matt thought he very much looked human. The detective sensed he was the same kind of entity who had stood over him in the cave. It was one of the *Caretakers*. Psychic impressions flashed inside his mind—of lying on a cold slab, of having an implant shoved up his nose, of being programmed to warn others to stay away. A cold chill ran down his spine. Now it was too late.

"We must leave this place, Jalmin," the Russian scientist implored. "You must come with us."

"Why ... what is going to happen? I have many friends aboard ship. I cannot leave them."

"I am sorry about your friends. But you mustn't concern yourself with people you cannot help. You ... all of us ... have still much work to do. It has been the responsibility of the *Asuras* to act as Caretakers— to help preserve the technology that was begun here in Atlantis. We have been chosen to assist them. Sometime in the future, when the human race is ready, the seeds of enlightenment will again resurface in the consciousness of man."

"How can that be?"

"What you see here is only the beginning of their vast achievements, Jalmin. In previous earth changes, the Atlanteans were warned in time and many of them escaped, taking their knowledge with them to start new colonies ... new civilizations. Their descendents now live under the earth's oceans in harmony with the *Asuras*, who originally came from a star system many light years away. They have been at war for centuries with a hostile race of beings that want to take over earth's resources. They are creating a hybrid race to accomplish that goal ... to act as their workers."

To Matt, it sounded like a comic science fiction plot. Except nobody was laughing.

"We must leave," the Russian scientist pleaded again. "While there is still time."

Why? What's the rush? Matt's sense of self-preservation began to stir tiny neurons in his brain, and every one of them was waving a red flag. "Professor Valekovsky," he said, "what is it you're not telling us?"

The Russian gave Matt a discerning look before replying. Through his thick lenses, his eyes were as big as saucers. "A large asteroid the size of our planet has broken away from Jupiter. In our time frame we called that asteroid Venus. It will eventually settle into its own orbit, but not before it passes within 10,000 kilometers of the earth. Its effect will be catastrophic. Massive seaquakes will cause huge tidal waves, devastating the planet."

"When?"

Professor Valekovsky wore a pained expression. "It has already begun … in the eastern Atlantic area. The repercussions from it are inescapable." He turned back to his colleague. "That is why we must leave now, my friend."

It was obvious the old man was torn between his peers and his loyalty to Captain Richardson. Commander Cosgrove placed a hand on the sage's shoulder. "Leave with them, Professor," he said. "It was our job to deliver you to them. We have accomplished our mission. Now it's time for us to part ways." He then began talking into the walkie-talkie, explaining to his superior in clipped tones what had just transpired.

It turned out to be a painful exchange of farewells. Everyone on board the *Proteus* had grown to like the Indian scientist, with his quick smile and gentle demeanor. When it came to Matt's turn to say goodbye, he had to swallow several times. The detective had come to consider the scientist a friend during these trying hours, and he knew he would never see him again. The last glimpse he would ever remember of Professor Vail was the look of incredulity on the old man's face as he stepped aboard the spacecraft.

Commander Cosgrove led the group back the way they had come. It was a somber procession as they raced through the empty chambers and winding corridors. The words of Professor Valekovsky kept ringing in Matt's ears like a death knell. It answered why the earth's magnetic pull switched poles when they did, and why the sun had a tendency to reverse directions every few thousand years.

When they reached the Hall of Records, the XO ordered everybody to carry back as many books with them as possible back to the ship. Ones in particular that he grabbed were the books Matt and Professor Vail had singled out. Cosgrove saw no reason why mankind couldn't benefit from the invaluable wealth of information these two volumes alone could provide. Matt had to agree. Knowing how to cure cancer or build a vehicle to the stars was priceless.

But they no sooner stepped outside the temple, than the sacred manuscripts virtually disintegrated in their hands. All that was left was a pile of ashes lying at their feet.

CHAPTER TWENTY-SIX

Atlantis -- 20:30 hours

To Barrett, every hour that had passed since he and Washington first spotted the strange blip on the radar screen had seemed like a lifetime in a microcosm. It felt like they had been going in circles. Although the aircraft's compass was pointing due south, he was silently praying it wasn't their true direction. If he had misjudged in his analysis, their chances of getting back to the *Proteus* were fading fast. Eventually they would be forced to land on an uncharted island in the middle of nowhere. That is, if they didn't run out of fuel beforehand and be forced to land in the ocean. Sink in the ocean might have been a better description. According to his cohort, they were still good for another two hours in the air. *Thank God for small favors.*

Ahead lay a tiny smudge of smoke on the horizon that tantalizingly reminded Barrett of civilization. But he knew that what he was looking at was not a campfire or smoke from a chimney. That would be asking too much. He would have bet a shilling or two their original assessment was correct. The smoke was volcanic in origin. *The whole bloody ocean is made up of islands sprouting from under the sea*, he mused.

Then something else gave him an uneasy feeling. A strange white line had suddenly materialized at the edge of the oscilloscope. It was slowly but inexorably advancing toward them from the east, at approximately 220-mph. *Nothing in nature can go that fast*, his mind kept repeating. Which meant it was something unnatural. It extended unbroken all the way across the north-south axis of the compass. Too far away to get an exact signature, but whatever it was, it was colossal. What gave him a sinking feeling in the pit of his stomach was the fact that it kept increasing in breadth and scope with every passing second.

"Can you make out what it is, Fletch?" he asked. "It's either a glitch in the unit, or something mighty big is coming out of the ocean to greet us. I'm putting my money on the second one."

"Whatever it is, it's not going away." The pilot's voice sounded hoarse and tired. *Too many hours on the radio*, Barrett thought. Too many hours of fruitless searching the airwaves trying to get a response, any kind of response that would tell them they were back in their own time … in their own sane, rational world again.

Washington leaned forward to peer under the lip of the Lexan. "Look at the sky ahead of it, man. It looks like a bucket of shit just spilled over the horizon."

Barrett couldn't have used a better choice of words. The sky was roiling with gigantic splotches of black and yellow cumulonimbus clouds. Not at all indicative of the tropical depressions he was used to flying through. This was something different. He could see strings of bluish-white heat lightning flash like varicose veins across their path. Even from a distance, he could feel his skin beginning to tingle. The storm had to have been manufacturing enough power to light up the entire island of Puerto Rico. It was the kind of phenomenon he and Benner had experienced in the Cessna—atmospheric aberrations that left a hellish path of burned-out circuitry and anything else that relied on electrical energy for power. The Jayhawk stood little chance against it. And radar was showing something piling behind it that could conceivably even be worse.

While the Englishman was mentally reducing their chances of survival from slim to none, Washington had turned his attention to the fuel gauge. It had turned a brighter crimson since the last time he looked. He eyed the distance remaining to what he suspected was an island that fortuitously was offering them a chance to escape crashing into the sea.

"We better hurry up and land this baby soon," he said, "or we'll be making a meal for some fish down there." For some inexplicable reason, he'd always had an unnatural fear of sharks. Ever since he'd seen the movie *Jaws*, every body of water he flew over reminded him of his phobia. He had the chopper at full throttle. Because of its top-heaviness, both men knew an ordinary HH-65 Jayhawk was not made to land on water. In any kind of rough sea, it would turn turtle in a matter of seconds. *With this new bird, however, we might stand a better chance,* the pilot countered. The redesigned undercarriage, with its lowered center of gravity, was stable enough to nullify the most moderate seas.

The machine continuously sent subliminal vibrations through their bones as the super-charged turbines churned the dead air. Straight ahead, the landmass was starting to show recognizable features along its coastline. Barrett saw that a large canal had been cut into the interior. It was too smooth and straight to be anything but manmade, he judged. But he spied something else. Further inland. A reflection of silvered light, as if someone was signaling them with a mirror. It seemed to be pointing the way for them. *Just like the portal in the sky*.

"Head for that light, Fletch. Something's over there," Barrett said, pointing.

The pilot wasted no time in swinging the nose of the chopper toward the intermittent flashes. As soon as the helicopter came into direct line with the mysterious phenomenon, the flashing stopped. It could have been the refracted light playing tricks on them, but to Barrett, it was a sure sign something extraordinary was waiting for them. As they advanced closer, his hunch proved correct. It was a beacon of some sort. A man-made beacon.

A familiar beeping sound suddenly interrupted their concentration. It was coming from the RDF. Washington had left the scanner operating in the VLF bandwidth, hoping somebody ... anybody ... would have a channel open he could lock onto.

The pilot immediately banked the Jayhawk and dropped to a different altitude so their flight path would coordinate with the new frequency heading. The beeping suddenly settled into a steady hum. Barrett knew it had to be originating from the *Proteus*. His sister must have left the radio transmit button open, using it as a homing device, so if the chopper got within range, they would pick up the signal. *Smart gal*, he chuckled silently to himself.

He saw that the new heading was leading them directly toward the canal. He gave a sidelong glance at the radarscope. The unwavering white line was slightly behind the aircraft now, but still driving relentlessly toward them like a fast moving freight train. The misshapen clouds had swollen even larger, pushing a wide swath of tortured air directly into their path. It was going to be a tossup as to which one got to them first.

All of a sudden the humming stopped and a crackling voice broke through their helmets. It was like tidings from heaven. *"Black Angel ... this is the Proteus*. We have you on radar. Am approaching you from the northwest through the main channel. Your flight path is in convergence with ours. Maintain your present course. By the way, where have you guys been? Over."

Barrett jumped in first without preamble. This was no time for military protocol. "Hi, Sis. It's good to hear from you again. Listen. Don't stop for us. I repeat, DO NOT STOP. There's a bloody storm front coming in fast that's lookin' pretty nasty. And there's an anomaly on our radarscope trailing right behind it. We haven't figured out yet what it is. Are you registering it on your scope? Over."

There was a slight pause. Barrett figured she was checking with her radar officer. She was back on the air within 10 clicks. "We don't have it. Too much ground clutter. What kind of anomaly? Over."

"Hard to figure. Could be a tsunami. But if it is, it's one for the books. You'd better get into open water fast. And here's one to hang your hat on. Have you checked your navigational instruments lately? Ours have completely gone bonkers. It's a crazy world out there. We think the sun has reversed itself. Oh, and guess what else. Fletch and I saw Flight 19. They flew right by us like a squadron of ghosts. Over."

"Professor Vail thinks those underwater objects that passed under us this morning are responsible," Captain Richardson responded. "They threw up a tremendous electromagnetic field, affecting the molecular structure of everything it touched. Somehow, it opened up a dimensional doorway. It seems we must have passed through it. Over."

Both pilots mirrored each other's dumbfounded looks. It took several minutes to digest what their leader just said. *Why are we surprised*? thought Barrett.

Washington took over. "Hello Mother, this is *Black Angel*. Have you determined your position yet? My heat sensors are having a hard time picking you up. My GPS is down. So is my VOR. Keep your radio channel open. It's the only thing I got left to find you. Suggest you send up flares to give us a visual. Over."

Leave it to the military mind to keep the conversation focused, Barrett thought.

"Good idea, Fletch, but it won't be necessary," replied Captain Richardson. "There's only one way in and out of this place. Am following the canal. Tracking you 30 miles out. Bear one … zero … zero until you reach the outer estuary. We will rendezvous with you there. Over."

"Roger that. But you'd better hurry. We're under two hours from ditching." He paused and leaned forward over the control panel. A long, golden thread was just starting to emerge wraithlike through the jungle growth. "By the way, Mother. What island are we talking about? It's not marked on any of my charts. Over."

Both pilots could have sworn they heard a faint exhalation of breath filtering through the airwaves. "I thought you would have guessed it by now, fellas. Haven't you ever heard of Atlantis? You're looking at it. Over and out."

Again, both pilots had to stop and adjust their minds to what was turning out to be a waking nightmare. The world had been turned upside-down, and waiting for them on the other side was a land only found in fairy tales. Irresistibly, their gaze gravitated toward a magical green carpet spreading out like a welcome mat before them. The last rays of a dying sun were bouncing off a great barrier wall, transforming the golden metal into a glittering necklace. Off in the distance, the pinnacle of silver that had originally drew their attention kept signaling to them like a beckoning finger.

CHAPTER TWENTY-SEVEN

Atlantis -- 21:33 hours

Matt walked into the pilothouse just as Captain Richardson was hanging up the radio mike. Word had circulated quickly throughout the ship that the captain had reestablished contact with *Black Angel*. This was the first time he had occasion to hear of the fearless rescuer and his unique call sign. He was intrigued with the name and the fact that, being awarded a ton of citations for his bravery under fire, the pilot had attained somewhat of a celebrity status. The detective wondered how much of an impression that would make on his English buddy. He had gauged Barrett to be not much of an idolizer.

Believe it or not, Matt missed the bond of intimacy he and Barrett shared. They had become members of an elite club. They had gone through a time warp in the Bermuda Triangle together and lived to tell about it, presumably suffering no ill effects. Now, along with the *Proteus* and her crew, they were experiencing another one, this time, unfortunately, lasting a great deal longer. Hopefully, their chances of getting through this one would be just as good. But after having heard the Russian professor's warning, it seemed their trip to Atlantis was nearing a climatic ending…fast.

He could tell the crew suspected the captain had received bad news. Something unexpected was about to happen. It was no surprise. This was not the world they were accustomed to. Now that the excitement had worn off, they were ready to be back in the open sea and heading for home. Matt figured Captain Richardson had the same thoughts. No sooner had the shore party arrived back aboard than she had ordered the *Proteus* at full revolutions. The speedy vessel was soon racing up the canal like an express train. The deck vibrated beneath his feet like a tuning fork. The metropolis of Atlantis whizzed by, its causeways and plazas strangely deserted, the sky overhead devoid of traffic. It seemed even the Atlanteans were getting ready for what was ordained to happen, Matt thought.

Suddenly a loud cry erupted from the radar officer. "Holy Toledo! Look at this, Cap'n. This must be what your brother was talking about."

He hurriedly stepped aside as the captain bent over the scope, trying to judge for herself what the strange blips on the cathode-ray tube implied. The unit was operating at its maximum setting. She recognized the familiar storm cloud pattern, but by the look of puzzlement on her face Matt drew the conclusion she was not sure what to make of the wavering line behind it.

Then her uncertainty changed quickly into comprehension. The detective recognized the subtle stiffening of her shoulders, the defiant look in her eyes. The ex-cop knew it was in response to an alarm bell ringing in her subconscious. It had happened to him more than once in his career. To anyone else it would appear that there was no interruption in her cool, methodical approach to the crisis. In people like her, he knew that once the danger was identified, and the decision to act was made, experience and training would automatically take over.

She flipped the intercom switch. "Commander Cosgrove, report to the Conn." Within 30 seconds the executive officer was standing at her side. "Take a look at this, Bill. If my guess is correct this confirms my brother's assessment. It's a tsunami, and a mighty big one at that."

The burly officer studied the radar screen closely before answering. He adjusted a few knobs before bringing it back to where the return echo was strongest. "Impossible, Captain. It's registering over 2,000 feet high. The highest ever recorded was 500 feet. It must be a glitch in the unit. I'll get Henderson to take a look at it."

Matt had the sinking feeling that the reading was correct, and he suspected the captain knew it too. It explained the worldwide traditions of floods inundating whole continents. He remembered reading where entire islands in Northern Siberia were made up of prehistoric animal bones that had been washed up and cemented together with hoarfrost. It seemed reasonable to assume that in the last axial shift, the earth had suffered a catastrophic flood. Its advancing wave descended like a raging monster, sweeping the land clean, leaving only remnants of its inhabitants behind in a mass grave of petrified fossils. Although Atlantis hastened its own destruction by pillaging the earth, even super civilizations were not immune to wholesale obliteration from the skies, Matt realized. *Look what happened to the dinosaurs.*

"First things first, Bill," the captain said. "If that's what it is, make sure everybody has their survival suits on and are ready to deploy the life-pods as soon as the order is given. Get guys up from below decks. We may not have much time if we can't ride this thing out … but we're damn sure going to try."

"Aye, aye Cap'n." His craggy face imparted a look of approval. Matt could tell they also shared a bond between them. Neither one of them would admit defeat until every option was spent.

Captain Richardson then turned toward Matt, who was trying his best to remain innocuous. "You've heard we have a large tidal wave bearing down on us."

"Yes, ma'am."

"Well then, I don't have to tell you the seriousness of the situation. And I'm not going to insult your intelligence by telling you this is something we deal with every day. But the fact remains, as a civilian, your survival has priority over the rest of the crew." It seemed to be a long-standing tradition on board U.S. naval vessels that civilians were not allowed the privilege of the same death as their military comrades. Matt should have felt relieved. Instead, he felt only a sense of detachment from the drama being played out before him. It was what a condemned man in the electric chair must have felt waiting for his executioner to pull the switch, he mused.

Captain Richardson stared at him with those piercing green eyes, almost as if trying to decipher his thoughts. "That means that if I give you the order to abandon ship, I expect you to follow my instructions explicitly. Do I make myself clear?"

Matt wasn't sure exactly what she meant by abandoning ship, but he nodded his head mechanically anyway. Somehow, the act of clinging desperately to a ladder from his fingernails by a swaying chopper briefly formed an image in his mind. But it was only a passing illusion, because he had a sinking feeling the chopper wouldn't make it back in time anyway. Each one of the captain's words sounded to him like a nail in his soon to be watery coffin.

He managed to smile weakly and mumbled something about following her orders to the letter. He could tolerate people pointing guns and knives at him, but drowning was not part of his job description. He would gladly leave the ship if he had to.

A cry of alarm suddenly cut through the tension filled pilothouse.

"Cap'n! It's picked up speed! I now estimate the wave travelling at better than 230 knots. It's going to reach us in about seven minutes."

"I've checked the radar unit for range and velocity resolution, Cap'n," another officer cut in with a hackneyed expression on his face. "Everything checks out."

An additional voice sliced into the fray, this time from the navigation officer. He was standing next to the plotting table with a pair of calipers in his hand. His words hung in the air like the sword of Damocles.

"We're not going to reach open water in time, Cap'n. We still have 6 miles to go before we reach the outer harbor."

Captain Richardson looked back at him, but said nothing, her face deadpan. The rest of the bridge personnel fidgeted where they stood. They were already travelling at flank speed. They couldn't go any faster unless the ship sprouted wings.

"Are you sure?" she said finally.

"Yes, ma'am."

Captain Richardson then calmly flipped the switch activating the PA system. A small feedback echoed eerily throughout the ship. "Attention crew ... this is the captain."

Matt noticed her composure, that of someone completely devoid of fear or trepidation. He had to applaud her courage. The crew continued to have absolute trust in her abilities to pull them through whatever happened. She was counting on that mindset to maintain discipline. But Matt had to wonder if, this time, their fate was in somebody else's hands.

She continued the announcement. "Radar shows a large tsunami approaching us from the east. We have less than seven minutes to prepare. Right now we're in too shallow a water. It's unlikely we'll reach deep water in time, so I don't know what's going to develop. However, this is a military ship and everyone on board volunteered to accept whatever risks came along. We will proceed according to whatever dictates the best course of action. My intentions are to face the bow in the tsunami's direction and throw out the anchor and use it as drag. When the wave starts lifting us we'll use all the power the *Proteus* has to get us over the top. Do what you've been trained to do, and with a little bit of luck and God's guidance, we'll get through this in one piece. Make sure you have your survival suits on, and life jackets properly secured. Be prepared to brace yourself when the time comes. Now, let's get to it. Set the Anchoring Detail. All personnel below decks, lay to topside on the double. Deck crew, break out the pods."

Someone shoved a survival suit in Matt's direction and helped him put it on. It felt like he was wearing body armor, although the material was light and flexible and held together around his wrists and ankles by Velcro and zippers. *At least I won't freeze to death.* Then came a lifejacket, the straps of which he surprisingly managed to secure satisfactorily by himself.

The sound of running feet filled the silence immediately following the announcement, as sailors and officers alike rushed to their stations. To the detective's relief, there was no shriek of a General Alert to accompany their frenzy. It was a calm, orderly exercise. He could still read the expectation of hope in their faces as they scurried past. No matter. It didn't take a rocket scientist to figure out what their chances were, including his. Facing a tsunami almost half a mile high, in any depth of water, was like a minnow being swallowed by a whale. He was going to go down with the ship the same as everyone else … and, sickening as it sounded, he was going to drown the same as everyone else.

A strange calmness slowly worked its way through his body. He was surprised at his approach to certain death. The thought of drowning certainly didn't sound very appealing. The muscles in his body would twitch and jerk involuntarily until the last remaining pockets of consciousness were sifted out of his brain. He would hopelessly gasp for air until the last bits of oxygen were expunged from his lungs. Yet somehow, in the back of his mind, he knew that this moment had to come. The whole trip had served some Machiavellian purpose, in which he had played an important but inconsequential part.

Orders were being barked in the pilothouse behind him as Matt stood off to the side on the bridge wing, waiting patiently. An eerie, expectant silence had fallen over the ship. He instinctively braced himself as the *Proteus* suddenly slowed before turning to face the onrush of black, angry clouds that were just starting to make their appearance over the eastern horizon. Their presence blotted out the last dab of daylight remaining, turning the sky to the color of molasses. With the tsunami being pushed from behind by a 230-knot tidal force, Matt realized it would be upon them before they knew it. It was almost a certainty that he and the crew of the *Proteus* would not survive, their numbers becoming fresh statistics among the thousands of souls already claimed by the Bermuda Triangle.

An offshore breeze, mixed with the smells of lush vegetation, made it even more poignant as the first wafers of the whirlwind to come reached his nostrils. In his mind's ear he thought he could hear the pounding of the surf on a Catalina beach where he and Barb had spent their honeymoon many years ago. It's funny how things like that stuck inside your consciousness just before the final moments.

Like tuning up an amplifier inside his head, the pounding surf swiftly magnified to a loud rumble, then to a discordant howl as it suddenly burst all around him. The wind sounded like the roar of a thousand jet engines in flight. A black pall had settled over the *Proteus*. Jagged sheets of lightning stretched across skies turned ugly with rage, while claps of thunder whipped the air like the beat of kettledrums. Through it all, the rattle of the anchor chain slipping through the hawsepipe sounded like the ship's death knell.

Matt suddenly felt an odd presence. It was when he happened to glance toward the bow of the ship that he saw them again—the same peculiar characters that had been on his tail since he left home. They were each sitting on a bollard, seemingly unconcerned with the calamity about to befall them.

He looked around, and finally realized he was the only one who could see them. And now he knew the reason why. They were part-and-parcel of the Bermuda Triangle enigma. They represented the personification of all the human tragedy that had taken place in the area. Whenever one saw them, it meant the warning signs had been ignored. He felt guilty he hadn't done more to make Captain Richardson and Professor Vail aware of what was happening, knowing deep down it would only have fallen on deaf ears. Now the Devil was here, to collect his due.

A far-off murmur, similar to the sound of rustling tree leaves, infiltrated his ears. The murmur became a flutter, then a steady hiss, like sand washing on a beach.

The detective's eyes were irresistibly drawn beyond the pair to a scythe-like watery beast cutting a deadly swath across the landscape. Partially obscured by darkness, an incensed mountain of water was reaching out a hammer-like fist toward the *Proteus*. On either side there was a long line of breaking waves that stretched as far as the eye could see. Matt realized the tsunami was approaching with the force of a Category Five hurricane. He managed to catch a last glimpse of a pyramid on the mainland pointing a defiant finger skyward moments before being swept away.

It was like snuffing out a candle. Matt's slowly diminishing world was quickly reduced to a microcosm. The roar was beginning to drown out all other semblance of sound, reaching cacophonous proportions. Rain began falling, pelting his body in horizontal sheets as he stood resolutely still, the salt stinging his eyes and mixing with tears of regret that had surprisingly formed on his cheeks. Strangely, he felt no fear, only a deep sorrow that he would never see his family again.

Suddenly, a tremendous force rent the air. It was like waiting for a monstrous living thing to show itself. Matt became transfixed as the storm clouds broke clear to reveal a cataract of indescribable fury. He watched in fascination as the liquid behemoth continued its upward climb, like a waterfall in reverse, exposing the full extent of its deadly power. Simultaneously, the rampaging wind was doing all it could to devour *Proteus's* tiny patch of ocean, choking Matt assiduously, stifling the very air he breathed. The creature had metabolized into a cacophony of hissing snakes, while millions of tons of seething, demonic water loomed over him. It was a creature Matt thought only existed in nightmares. His heart began pounding in painful throbs. He pleaded with God to strike him down with a coronary and mercifully end his misery now.

The deck beneath his feet began to vibrate uncontrollably, the likes of which he hadn't experienced since he came aboard. Out of the corner of his eye, he could see Captain Richardson yelling into the intercom to the reactor room below for more power. He couldn't hear her voice but he watched her mouthing the words. Then they locked eyes for a brief moment. She was pointing to something in the sky.

Matt looked up, but saw nothing except a watery hell poised to strike. Movement around him stopped, as if in suspended animation. The noise was becoming indescribable. He forced his numbed brain to concentrate. His feeling of hopelessness grew with every pounding heartbeat. The wave bearing down on them looked insurmountable. He could barely see the top, curling inward and breaking sharply, like a coiling snake ready to strike. At its very lip, white spume cascaded like an avalanche of snow thundering down a mountain slope. If they couldn't scale the top of that crest, Matt conceded, they would be smashed like pulpwood. Ten thousand years from now, perhaps another team of scientists would find their pulverized bones crushed together into a new chain of frozen tundra.

As the *Proteus* began to valiantly, ponderously claw its way upward, Matt held on for dear life as the deck sharply pitched backward. He knew the captain was desperately trying to keep the bow head-on into the curving sheet of water. It seemed like a losing battle. The tsunami's bulk had risen almost perpendicular to the ship, as if a cliff of solid rock stood in its path. A wall of white-green ocean streaked with uprooted trees and boulders reached around them like a set of pincers. There was no escape. If one of those boulders hit them, it would be all over before the liquid hammer even reached them. *Maybe that would be best,* Matt thought. *Send us to the bottom quickly.*

The blinding spray stung the detective's skin like hot pokers. A great sucking noise reached his ears as billions of gallons of water was lifted into the air, collapsing upon itself in one thunderous roar. Matt had a death grip on the railing, shutting his eyes and delighting in the storm's unfamiliar siren call. The wall of death hung there for one heart-stopping moment, like a guillotine ready to drop. He instinctively held his breath and waited.

It wasn't long in coming. The weight of the monster was all-consuming, all-encompassing, infiltrating his entire being. Suddenly the railing he was clutching was ripped out of his hands. A powerful force picked him up and flung him into the air as if he were a piece of flotsam. He almost reveled in the sensation of falling as he somersaulted end over end into a wet, bottomless void.

CHAPTER TWENTY-EIGHT

Bermuda Triangle -- 21:49 hours

The fall seemed to take forever. When Matt pierced the icy water, it was as if a thousand fingers were instantly clawing at him, pulling him down. His body felt as though it were cloaked in cement. Torrents of water gushed up his nose and into his mouth, choking him, gagging him. The water had even seeped under his clamped eyelids, the salt unmercifully stinging his eyes. His lungs burned as if they were on fire. All the air had been knocked out of him upon hitting the water. Thankfully, his life vest kept him from sinking to the bottom. The layer of floatation wrapped around his chest was counteracting the pressure, inexorably lifting him upward. But it would do him no good if he couldn't get life giving air into his lungs, and fast, he thought desperately.

He opened his eyes to a blurry, topsy-turvy world of strange images, darkness all around. Reflexively he grappled and clawed in whatever direction his arms would take him. He thought he saw an indistinct cone of light floating elusively just out of reach on the surface. He reached for it in a hopeless attempt to break free from the iron fist that was squeezing his body like a vise. He began to gag and swallow water. He realized his futile efforts were sapping whatever strength he had left. He was starting to feel his limbs grow numb with fatigue. They were getting extremely heavy. The torture in his lungs had now descended to the fiery pit of hell itself. Darkness was encroaching on his sensibilities; his ability to even try to save himself.

A long moment turned into a century. Time had stopped for Matt Benner. When time resumed its painful progression, the furor in his brain had miraculously stopped. A warm, pleasant feeling spread through his body. The relentless pressure crushing him from all sides had subsided. In its stead came an overwhelming desire to sleep. He finally quit struggling and relinquished his last lucid thoughts to that of Barb and the kids.

Suddenly and without ceremony a pair of powerful hands had him under the armpits, and were jerking him upward. A rush of warm, moist air splashed on his face. His lungs immediately began sucking in huge gulps of air. He gasped and choked as his body responded instinctively.

Matt looked up into the red-faced countenance of Stu Barrett. The big man was clinging to him from inside a rescue basket in what seemed a precarious position. The scene was being played out inside the beam of a powerful searchlight. A long, black line stretched up behind the co-pilot to the waiting Jayhawk above. The drumbeat of its powerful turbines and the thumping downdraft of its blades sounded like a musical chorus from heaven.

"By Jove, look what I just caught!" exclaimed a tugging Barrett as he made a signaling motion to somebody on top to start reeling them in. Matt was so weak from exhaustion that he had no energy to respond. He just gave the Englishman a thankful look and let him manhandle his body into the chopper.

Another pair of hands grabbed at him as soon as they reach the open hatch. It was Palinski, the old timer, the one the captain called 'the survivor.'

"Are there any others?" Matt choked. He needn't have asked, for he saw no sign of the ship in the maelstrom below. But it did his soul good to mouth the words.

"No others, mate," replied Barrett. "We were bloody lucky to clear the wave ourselves. It was just by sheer chance that eagle-eyed Palinski here spotted you when he did. It doesn't look like you could have held your breath much longer." Matt discerned a tight smile play on his friend's face. In spite of the circumstances, he found it hard to imagine the Englishman could still retain his sense of humor.

Once aboard, Matt gazed dumbfounded as bolts of lightning danced a patchwork of weird designs inside the darkened aircraft. Glowing banks of digitized lights and computer screens were reflecting off the sweating features of a black officer sitting in the pilot's seat. The man seemed to have his hands full bucking a wildly gyrating control stick. Surprisingly, the pilot was managing to keep the aircraft straight and level, although at times the machine would buck viciously, trying to succumb to the strong wind shears pummeling it.

Matt found a seat across from Palinski, who gave him a curt nod. Peering through the side window, he shuddered in contemplation. The man just liberated from a drowning death saw how dark and empty the world had become. The intermittent green and crimson flashes had created a ghostly waterscape. The reflected light had turned the heaving swells into a sullen leaden gray, with phosphorescent whitecaps limning the tips. He blinked several times to clear the cobwebs still fogging his brain. He thought he spotted a ball of white light hovering near the surface of the water. He had trouble keeping the object in focus. It stayed motionless for only a brief second before shooting straight up and disappearing into the clouds.

Matt looked at his companions to get confirmation of what he had just seen—or thought he had just seen. Barrett was busy securing the cargo hatch, while Palinski was seemingly absorbed in his own thoughts. *Must have been a trick of light.*

Looking over the pilot's shoulder at the turmoil raging outside brought to Matt's mind a similar scene not that long ago. He didn't feel any more relieved now than he did then. Massive formations of black swirling clouds were racing menacingly to block them off, their turbid insides lit by a continuous barrage of electrical energy. Matt could smell that familiar stench of burned ozone in the air. Lieutenant Washington, the *Black Angel*, seemed to be holding his own under the circumstances. Occasionally the detective would hear him curse under his breath, as a particularly bad wind gust would catch him unawares. Matt had no perception of how high they were, or where they were going. All he knew for certain was that he was extremely thankful to be alive. He shivered under the warmth of the blanket Barrett had wrapped over his shoulders.

As the minutes dragged, Matt could sense a feeling of dejection among his fellow passengers. The storm was not letting up. In fact, it seemed to be getting worse. He had to put on his seatbelt, otherwise his head would have been bouncing off the top of the fuselage every time the chopper made an unexpected dip. Other than the muffled screaming of the air intakes, Matt could hear no other sounds penetrating the cocoon-like interior. The strained conversation between the pilots was barely audible as they tried to sort out their predicament. What he did overhear didn't sound encouraging.

"I never saw anything like this in my life, man," Washington was saying to Barrett as another stroke of lightning sizzled past them. "Those mothers are getting awfully close to baking our asses. Maybe you'd better get the life raft out of the back compartment and have it ready. It doesn't look like we're going to be able to stay in the air much longer."

Matt guessed the man wasn't referring to his lack of flying skill. There was a bright red gauge on the control panel that seemed to be crying out for his attention. He didn't hear Barrett's reply, but the Englishman must have concurred with what the pilot had suggested. He unhesitatingly unhooked his shoulder harness and was in the process of climbing out of his seat when he spotted something in the water below. His eyes widened in surprise. Pointing, he said to the pilot, "Look down there, mate."

Everybody took the cue, leaning forward in their seats to follow Barrett's unsteady finger. The lightwheels were back! They appeared to be the same glowing manifestation—doing their same crazy pirouetting and playing tag with one another as the night before. Their illumination blazed with the same intensity. Strangely enough, the ocean seemed to have returned to some semblance of normalcy. Wave heights didn't look as forbidding as they had when Matt had first looked. He remembered what Professor Vail had said about the lightwheels' influence on the molecular structure of man and his machines.

Apparently, Barrett was prepared to unwittingly accept the professor's hypothesis at face value. "Head for the deck, Fletch. Those bloody things could be our only ticket out of here."

That was all the pilot had to hear. With a twist of his wrist and a steady pull of his arm on the collective, he caused the giant helicopter to slue sideways, as if it was sliding down a slippery ski slope. The craft dropped like a falling brick. Matt could feel the centrifugal force pressing his body against the safety strap. The vibration in his feet ran all the way up his backside as the chopper shook under the strain of powerful crosscurrents rushing up to meet them. The sound of the turbines took on a different pitch as the rotor bit deeply into the highly charged air. As far as Matt was concerned, the aircraft had become an extension of the pilot's hands and feet as he skillfully maneuvered the machine toward the turgid water below. There was no unnecessary pitching or yawing as the big Jayhawk plummeted at better than 50 feet per second.

The lighted ocean came up fast—too fast, in Matt's judgment. He was afraid the pilot wasn't going to pull up in time. Matt's stomach leaped to his throat.

At the last possible second the chopper shuddered to a stop like a shaking dog, the landing gear just skimming the tops of six to seven foot swells.

"We can float in relatively minor chop but we'll be taking our chances with these babies," Washington declared. He hovered the helicopter inches above the highest crest, waiting for a well-placed moment to land. The fuel gauge on the control panel was bright red. They had only seconds left before the fuel cells were completely depleted.

"Might as well set her down while you still got power, old chap," Barrett said, almost resignedly. "I'll get the raft ready."

As the co-pilot slid in between the two passengers, Matt felt a light squeeze on his shoulder. The detective gazed up appreciatively, detecting a sense of reassurance from the Englishman. He said nothing, but Matt could discern a look of determination in the man's eyes. *Must run in the family.* It gave him a comforting feeling to know he wasn't in this thing alone.

As the pilot lowered the Jayhawk inside two vertical troughs that completely blocked out their view, he gave one final surge of power to the turbines before the machine settled gently into the water. It was a nice piece of timing, Matt thought. He knew he wasn't in the air anymore when his stomach started rolling in

Ty Jodouin

unison to the wave action. He felt as if he was suddenly riding in a roller coaster.

The whining sound of the turbines retreated into the night like the gasp of a dying pterodactyl, the 54-foot rotor blade drooping like a giant ice-laden tree branch. A strange leaden silence instantly fell over them. The lightning continued to flash in silent volleys, as if maddened gods were throwing fiery bolts at one another. Matt jumped as the loud hiss of carbon dioxide cartridges blowing up the six-man life raft infiltrated the tiny space.

It took less than a minute for the raft to be fully inflated and secured next to the chopper's cargo hatch. "All the comforts of home, mates," Barrett said as he plopped back into his seat.

"I don't know how long we'll be able to stay afloat," Washington announced for the benefit of Matt and Palinski as he finished flipping off the switches on the control panel. "This machine was installed with extra flotation chambers just for such emergencies. But I don't think the manufacturers had this in mind." He nodded toward the high-breaking waves marching in serried ranks beneath them.

After one particular precipitous climb followed by a stomach-wrenching drop, Matt's face contorted in agony. Palinski must have noticed Matt's discomfort because the detective suddenly found several individually wrapped saltine crackers pressed into his lap. "Take these. I never leave home without them," the quartermaster said, his mouth twisted in a sardonic grin.

Matt wondered how the veteran could have possibly carried the wafers without crushing them, but he had learned a long time ago not to look a gift horse in the mouth. He gulped them down gratefully, nodding his thanks. After a few minutes, his churning stomach returned to a steady pattern of indiscriminate rumbles.

Now that the helicopter was in the water, the lightwheels seemed to sense their presence. Their frolicking took on an even more frenzied pace. Their radiance was no less irritating, Matt discovered, as he still had to shield his eyes from their fierce glare every time one of them made a close pass.

"Why don't we try and get some rest before morning?" Washington tiredly announced. Matt noticed how withdrawn and haggard the pilot's face suddenly had become. "At dawn we can assess where we are. We should have enough provisions in our survival kits to last us for several days. Hopefully, we can make landfall by then."

Palinski broke out of his shell in a burst of pent-up frustration. "What makes you think there's land out there, Lieutenant? Even if there is, how we goin' to get back to our own time?" His panicky voice carried resonantly through the enclosed cabin. He was asking questions none of them yet had time to contemplate. After shock, denial, and anger, comes acceptance. Matt assumed the little man was still stuck in the anger phase.

Lieutenant Washington gave his subordinate a castigating look that would have melted ice. "We'll work that out when the time comes, sailor. In the meantime, chill out." He then turned to his other passengers in a more conciliatory tone of voice less hardened by military protocol. "I suggest we each take two hour watches until daybreak. If this mother starts sinking, we have to be ready to bail out fast. One of us needs to stay awake so he can warn the others."

"I'll go first, Lieutenant," Matt volunteered. "The way my stomach is acting up, I couldn't sleep anyway. Oh, by the way, the name's Matt Benner. I don't think we were properly introduced." Matt stuck out his hand.

The pilot managed a tired grin as he returned the gesture. "Just call me Fletch," he answered amiably.

Matt could tell the man was almost out on his feet. The stress of keeping them in the air as long as he had must have tapped his reserves to the limit.

Meanwhile, the luminosity of the lightwheels had irradiated their surroundings to that of broad daylight. Their dizzying antics had reached that of a shark feeding frenzy. Their gymnastics were even more pronounced since the chopper sat so close to the water. Matt couldn't help but start to feel overwhelmed by it all. The security of a state-of-the-art warship like the *USCGC Proteus* beneath his feet had been reassuring. So had the intimacy of such experienced officers as Captain Richardson and Lieutenant Commander Cosgrove to lend support. Matt gave an involuntary shudder. Now they were gone … all gone. Inescapably, the fate of everyone on board had been sealed the moment the ship had sailed into the Bermuda Triangle.

Not to be denied was Professor Vail, who had lent credibility to this upside-down, chaotic world. Matt wondered where the scientist's celestial journey would take him—that is, if he and his fellow colleagues had escaped at all. From the guarded conversation between the pilots, the tsunami had virtually wiped out everything in its path. Even if the *Proteus* had managed to reach deeper water, Matt entertained little doubt the ship still would have foundered. Nothing could have survived such a deluge. *Except perhaps the Atlantean spaceship. The white light he had seen ...*

Just as mind-boggling was the fact that, in a blink of cosmic time, Matt and his shipmates had borne witness to an epic in human history—the destruction of Atlantis. The mightiest civilization of the primeval world had been vanquished by the very powers the Atlanteans had not yet learned to suppress. Outer space was limitless, and so were the forces that controlled it.

Matt shook his head. He must have dozed off for a few seconds in his ruminating. He was having a hard time keeping his eyes open. His eyelids felt like lead weights. He dazedly looked up. Slowly registering in his brain was the fact that he was enveloped in darkness. The lightwheels had mysteriously disappeared, and the only light entering the cabin was coming from the fusillade of stars breaking through the clouds. The only sounds he heard was the deep breathing coming from the curled-up forms around him, and the gentle lapping of waves against the fuselage. He struggled to get up, but he didn't seem to have the energy. His entire body was infused with a strange complacency. His mind refused to collect the random thoughts floating lazily inside his head and place them in rational order. He shrugged his shoulders half-heartedly after giving one last satisfactory look around. *Everything seems okay,* he told himself. Before his head touched the floor, the detective had once more slipped into a dreamless state of bliss.

CHAPTER TWENTY-NINE

Twenty-seven years later: San Juan, Puerto Rico, St. Joseph Cemetery — 10:45 a.m.

The day was cold, blustery, unusual for this time of year, he had been told. It was three days before Christmas. Maybe the early wintry blast from the Canadian regions had something to do with it. The whole upper half of the U.S. was in a deep freeze. Matt Benner stood off to the side with his wife, Barbara, listening half-heartedly to the eulogy being spoken by a priest over his departed friend, Stu Barrett. It had been an emotional funeral service, sprinkled with sobs and an unabashed bout of crying from Stu's many friends. The guy had made many through the years, Matt noted. The entire morning he had been rubbing shoulders with islanders from all over the Caribbean. But the detective also knew the Englishman would have preferred less fuss over his death. After all, he had once told his close friend, he lived a full life and had no regrets save for the loss of his sister. He had never married, and did only what he loved to do best—fly.

Ty Jodouin

But losing his only sibling was a tragedy Stu had never fully recovered from, Matt suspected. Every Christmas Stu would throw a wreath somewhere over the middle of the Bermuda Triangle to commemorate her death. His old friend was probably with her now, Matt figured, recounting one of the off-color witticisms that he loved to torment her with.

All of a sudden he realized he was standing next to the casket alone. The priest had finished eulogizing, and the honor guard from the local VFW Post had retrieved the American and British flags that had been draped over the coffin, and silently withdrawn. Everyone else, it seemed, including Barbara, had drifted away or were grouped together in quiet conversations. Others were piling into cars to take them back to where they still had lives to finish. He wondered how long he had been standing there alone. It really didn't matter. Stu's funeral was the last of the 'Fateful Four,' as they called themselves, that he would have to attend.

He reflected on the past several years. Lieutenant Washington, the *Black Angel*, was gone, killed in another United Nations-sanctioned police action, this time in the jungles of Africa. Guerrillas had used a SAM missile to bring him down when the valiant pilot was trying to rescue a downed flyer off the coast of Mozambique. Palinski was a career man and had stayed in the Coast Guard, reaching Chief Quartermaster status before retiring. Ironically, he mysteriously disappeared shortly after that. The last anyone saw of him, he was heading out in his boat to Moselle Reef in the Bahamas on a deep-sea fishing expedition. He always said that if you stayed in the Bermuda Triangle long enough, it would eventually get you. *He was right,* Matt mused.

His reminiscing of the old-timer jogged his memory of something else, something he had been carrying around for a long time. He pulled the shiny talisman out of his pocket and gazed at its worn surface. He had continuously polished it over the years, never wearing it, but keeping it ready ... just in case. Oddly enough, the good-luck charm had brought him a measure of protection over the years. *I'm still alive and kicking.* Now it was time for him to return it to its rightful owner. It had been a long time coming. Matt's notoriety as being the lone survivor of the *Proteus* had been short-lived since Stu's death. It was over the moment he had picked up the morning newspaper at the airport. Now, he and Barb had another stop to make on the way home.

Matt glanced up at the heavy overcast. It threatened rain, but if looks alone were the only criteria, he probably would be wrong again. It was the same kind of curious-looking sky that had greeted him and his companions when they woke up in the chopper 27 years ago. The sky today looked as bleak and depressing as it had then. None of them had had any idea where they were or even what dimension they were in until they saw the *U.S.S. Powell* come steaming over the horizon.

Matt remembered his shock when they had been informed that the *Proteus* had been listed missing for the past five months. *Five months!* The ship, along with its officers and crew, had been relegated to the category of 'unexplained disappearances.' It was just by chance that the carrier was in the area at the time. One of its search planes had spotted the chopper as they were conducting what had become commonplace in the Bermuda Triangle—a search and rescue mission. A Lear jet filled with businessmen had mysteriously vanished between Puerto Rico and Miami, as well as a yacht full of party revelers celebrating San Juan Bautista Day.

Nobody would believe their story about Atlantis and the 2,000-foot tsunami. It was more convenient to the Naval Board of Inquiry to chalk up the entire episode to mass hallucinations. After all, spending five months in the open sea could do strange things to a man's mind. Oddly, no mention was made of the fact that none of them had grown facial hair over the supposed five month period, that it was inconceivable that the chopper could remain afloat for that long, or that their survival packs had remained untouched.

When he had arrived home, Matt was also not surprised to discover that his daughter Stacy's mysterious "mental illness" had disappeared, signaled by a brief nosebleed, exactly five months before he had been rescued. *But that was neither here nor there*, he thought, heaving a long sigh. It had all happened a long time ago.

It was getting late, and he and Barb had a plane to catch. Whispering a final goodbye to his friend, he started walking back to where his wife was talking to a middle-aged black woman. She was tall and expensively dressed, and wore very little makeup. Besides sporting an attractive hairdo, her fingers and neckline were weighted down with several pounds of jewelry. It was Fletcher Washington's widow, Carmille, who had remarried and was now living in Puerto Rico, the 51st state, with her second husband, Georgi. She was actually Cuban, but had escaped shortly after Castro took over. Stu had once told him that she had come from a very rich and influential family who had presumably bought their way to freedom.

She turned when he approached, her face beaming with delight. "My goodness but you look good for an old white man," she declared, eyes and teeth sparkling. "If you'd been around 30 years ago, I would have latched onto you like a remora onto a shark," she chuckled, as she wrapped her arms around his midriff and gave him a light peck on the cheek.

She was quite attractive, smelled delicious, and had a terrific personality; Matt told himself he probably would have taken her up on the offer if he hadn't already been married.

"I bet you say that to all the guys in uniform," he rejoined good-naturedly. He knew Georgi was in the Navy and was currently at sea, serving a six-month tour in the Mediterranean. The Puerto Rican always accompanied Carmille whenever they came to Vegas to visit.

She just smiled at his quip and gave Barb a wink. "Did you have a good trip down?" she queried in a more serious vein.

"We got here late and had to rush," Matt replied. "I still can't understand why it's so crowded around Christmas time. Flights are always booked solid, and yet you can jump on the lunar shuttle and be on the moon quicker than it takes to unpack your bags. You'd think people would stay home and smell the roses for a change."

"I hear you, honey," she answered sympathetically as they began walking to a black Cadillac parked under a stand of cypress. "You and Barb must come to my place and try my *soupcon of lemon* before goin' back." Carmille lived off base in the Condado area, not too far from there. Matt always seemed to gain five pounds every time he tried one of her Cuban-style delicacies.

"I wish we could, dear," he said apologetically. "But Barb and I have another stop to make on the way home." He gave a quick glance at his watch. "And we have less than an hour to catch the plane." *That's the real reason we were late to the funeral*, he silently admitted. He had to make several calls and make last minute connections to people who owed him favors.

"My goodness. By the tone of your voice, it sounds like you're goin' to another funeral. Okay then. At least let me take you people to the airport. On the way we can talk about some happy times. I get so tired of listenin' to bad news. China's ready to explode, and the stock market's down again. And did you hear that another boat has come up missin' in the Triangle? That makes three this month. Heard about it on this morning's news. A young couple vacationing from Rochester, New York."

"No, I didn't hear," Matt confessed. He hadn't read the local news. "Where were they staying?"

"Chatter's Cay."

Matt's heart skipped a beat. The name of the out-of-the-way diver's resort brought to mind painful memories. Obviously Carmille hadn't heard about the latest happening in another part of that deadly zone, or she would have surely brought it up.

Barb looked at her husband askance, but didn't say anything. She knew what he was thinking.

The San Juan Airport was a bedlam of holiday travelers crisscrossing each other's paths like an army of ants. Matt and Barb said their good-byes to Carmille, promising to e-mail her regularly. It was like an obstacle course as they made their way to the proper gate that was boarding for Washington, D.C. Matt was out of breath and his nerves were stretched to the limit by the time they clambered aboard the jumbo jet. The cramped conditions of coach seating and the temperament of the passengers seemed to have changed little since his first trip down to the islands. It was always a challenge avoiding a swinging elbow by passengers bent on stuffing small overheads with oversized bags. By the time they reached their seats, the detective felt like a punch-drunk fighter who had just survived a 10-round decision. Matt always insisted on sitting as far back in the tail section and as near an exit as possible. His fear of flying had diminished little in 27 years.

I've got to lose more weight, he mentally admonished himself. Now that he was retired, he would have plenty of opportunity to start jogging and getting back in shape. Taking over the business after Tom had disappeared hadn't left him much time to focus on anything else.

As Matt settled into his seat, his thoughts briefly flashed back to the day when he said his last farewell to Tom and his family at their posthumous funeral service.

On that same day he had vowed to get on with his life. To dwell on his partner's loss, or that of the *Proteus,* would have driven him crazy with guilt. He thought he had done a good job of keeping that promise … until today, that is.

The shocking news had come from out of left field. It was like getting sucker-punched in the groin. He started to feel cold icicles retracing a path up and down his spine. He shook it off and reached into his back pocket to pull out a frayed newspaper clipping that he had torn out of the *USA Today* he had picked up earlier that morning. He opened it up and read it again for the umpteenth time.

SCIENTIST'S BOAT FOUND ALONG WITH MISSING SAILOR

Ensign Salvino Bernelli, from Wichita Falls, Kansas, a 21-year-old helicopter pilot aboard the U.S.C.G. Cutter *Proteus,* was found yesterday afternoon after a 27-year hiatus. The missing pilot was part of a boarding party aboard the *Explorer,* a scientific research vessel that reportedly was lost in Hurricane Minerva, also of that same time period. The ship was found drifting near the island of Curacao by Coast Guard units out of Maracaibo Naval Base in Venezula. After much speculation, naval officials would not comment on the officer's condition other than to say the Bermuda Triangle was not responsible for his disappearance. The *Explorer* is being detained at the U.S. Guantanamo Naval Base in Cuba for study while Ensign Bernelli was sent to Bathesda Naval Hospital in Washington, D.C. for further evaluation. After U.S. medical authorities gave a cursory examination of the officer, it was reported by inside sources that Bernelli was in perfect health and hadn't aged a day since he was listed missing. No further details are available at this time.

THE END

ABOUT THE AUTHOR

Ty Jodouin joined the Navy after high school, and spent two years sea duty in the Mediterranean. He has 12 years scuba diving experience, in both fresh and salt water. A retired fire department Lieutenant, he now spends his time in Nokomis, Florida, with his wife Helen.

The author has written newspaper articles and pieces for *Guidepost Magazine*, and a novel, *Rogue Planet*. *Voyage to Oblivion* is his second novel.

Coast guard res 90 +
160 #

Sustained excitement
of tsunami hit 208(?)

Printed in the United States
23756LVS00001B/25-33

9 781420 801293